D0122168

son

something missing

Matthew Dicks

broadway books

new york

Copyright © 2009 by Matthew Dicks

All Rights Reserved

Published in the United States by Broadway Books, an
imprint of The Crown Publishing Group, a division
of Random House, Inc., New York.

BROADWAY BOOKS and its logo, a letter B bisected on the
diagonal, are trademarks of Random House, Inc.

ISBN-13: 978-1-61523-255-0

PRINTED IN THE UNITED STATES OF AMERICA

For Elysha

You saved me first

acknowledgments

In his book *On Writing*, Stephen King wrote, "And whenever I see a first novel dedicated to a wife (or a husband), I smile and think, *There's someone who knows*. Writing is a lonely job. Having someone who believes in you makes a lot of difference. They don't have to make speeches. Just believing is usually enough."

Many people have contributed to this first novel, but none more than my wife and best friend, Elysha, who has believed in me like no other, even allowing me to write while on our honeymoon. She is, in King's words, my "constant reader" and the only one for whom I truly write.

Much appreciation to Mark Campopanio, the high school English teacher who first taught me that words can change minds, and to Patrick Sullivan and Jackie Dailey, Manchester Community College professors who convinced me that I had something to say.

Thanks to the Wolgemuths, Justine and Charles, for the indelible mark that they left on this book. It was Justine's story of the loss of a single earring that first planted the seed of Martin in my head, and three years later, it was Charles who suggested the title that this book, minus one question mark, now bears.

Throughout the writing, I had many Dickens-esque readers who followed along chapter by chapter, and to each one of these people, I cannot express the appreciation that I feel for all of your support. I've always been an instant gratification type of guy, and writing can be anything but instant. Knowing that you were out there, ready to read the next chapter just hours after it was finished made all the difference for me.

A few people of particular note:

Cindy Raynis, who could always be counted on to drop everything in her life (save her children) and read the latest chapter with the greatest of enthusiasm. Her eye for detail allowed the first draft of this book to be cleaner and clearer than I could have ever managed on my own.

Jane Casper, whose constant barrage of questions about the book and its characters helped me to find the heart of Martin. When she began to speak of Martin as a real human being, I knew that I was onto something good.

Kelly Shepard, who probably loved Martin before me. Her instant affection for the character and her sage advice helped me discover aspects of Martin's character that I did not know existed.

Matthew Shepard, the reader who seems to share my brain. I could always depend upon Matt to notice an amusing play on words or a vague and nearly indiscernible reference that other readers might miss. Many a time I would write a sentence, smile, and think, "No one else will notice this, but Shep will love it." Rarely was I wrong. His comments, critique, and suggestions shaped the book into what it has become. The world will be a more interesting place when Matt picks up a pen and begins writing himself.

Melissa Danaczko, my editor, who dispelled all my fears that an editor is a mean and scary person who wants to tear down a writer's work, sentence by sentence. Melissa managed to skillfully guide the work in the right direction while allowing me to retain ownership of the process. Through her keen insight, Martin and his story came into a sharper and deeper focus than I could have ever envisioned on my own.

Taryn Fagerness, known officially as my literary agent, is a person who I think of as my friend in writing. For all her skill and expertise on the business end of publishing, it was Taryn's unwavering support of this book, her love for Martin, and most important, her ability to collaborate with a fledgling author on this book that made this possible. When a manuscript is miraculously plucked from the slush pile, it is a credit to the author for the work that he or she has done, but I believe it is even more a credit to the agent, who was willing to take a chance on a non-credentialed nobody from nowhere and shout "Yes!" when so many others said "No." She has been my hero, my guiding force, and in many ways, my partner on this literary journey.

Martin opened the refrigerator and saw precisely what he had expected. The Pearls were nothing if not consistent. A gallon of milk, long since expired, cold cuts, opened jars of jam, tomato sauce, a carton of eggs, and, in the door, what Martin had predicted: salad dressing. More salad dressing than anyone would ever need. Newman's ranch, blue cheese, Thousand Island, French, Italian, two brands of balsamic vinaigrette, and Martin's favorite, parmesan peppercorn.

In the nine years that the Pearls had been Martin's clients, he had yet to see a head of lettuce or a fresh tomato in their refrigerator, yet there was always an excellent supply of salad dressing. And unlike most of his clients, the Pearls' salad dressings rarely reached their expiration dates, so someone in this house was using the dressing, but to what the dressing was being applied remained a mystery.

Martin took the bottle of parmesan peppercorn and examined it in his gloved hand. Satisfied with its expiration date, he placed it in the burlap sack and scanned the rest of the refrigerator. The sack, which hung off his left shoulder by a length of rope, was more for appearance's sake than anything else, a means of projecting an image of which he was quite proud. In Martin's estimation, he was at the top of his game, a master of his craft. Though any bag or sack would do, and some might serve him better, he had become attached to his burlap, and so on his shoulder it remained.

Martin then checked the butter drawer and found four and a half sticks. Selecting two and placing them in his sack, he closed the refrigerator door and headed for the pantry, reexamining the list that he had tucked carefully into his coat pocket. The list was written in French, so that in the event he was one day caught, it would be indecipherable by most police officers. Realistically, Martin knew that it wouldn't take long for any self-respecting detective to have the list translated, but the cautious nature of the list enhanced the image that Martin attempted to project.

beurre [butter]
sauce salade [salad dressing]
détergent à lessive [laundry detergent]
conserve [canned vegetables]
savon [soap]
diamant [diamond]

Martin found the Pearls' pantry well stocked with vegetables and selected two cans of peas, a can of corn, and two large cans of whole, peeled potatoes. Had the supply of vegetables been low, he would have bypassed this item on his list, adhering strictly to Rule #1:

If the missing item will be noticed, don't acquire it.

Certain items could be taken from a home without anyone ever noticing, particularly if one is familiar enough with the homeowner's inventory to determine how long an item has been in stock. A bottle of Liquid Plumbr, for example, should never be taken during its first month on the shelf, because the homeowner has likely purchased it for a specific reason. A kitchen sink is slow to drain. The bathtub is filling with water during a shower. In these instances, a missing bottle of Liquid Plumbr, which isn't cheap, might be noticed. But after thirty days, it's safe to assume that the homeowner has solved whatever plumbing problem from which he or she might have been suffering, and then the bottle can easily vanish without a trace. Sure, the client might one day think, "I thought I had bought an extra bottle when it was on sale," or "I didn't think I had used it all up," but as long as Martin followed Rule #2, these thoughts would be quickly dismissed.

Always married, without children, maids, or dogs.

Rule #2 was based upon a theory that Martin had proven long ago, and one that he considered to be the keystone of his success: When items go missing in a house, the suspicion of theft occurs only if the possibility of a thief exists.

The secret behind Martin's success was that the possibility of a thief operating in his clients' homes never entered their minds. And as long as the notion of theft didn't occur to a client, he would never be caught. This was achieved by choosing all clients with great care.

Single people, particularly those living alone, made for poor clients. They were simply too incalculable. When a person lives alone, he or she can monitor household inventory rather closely, and often does. Take Martin, for example. He knew that there were two tubes of Crest whitening toothpaste in the small drawer underneath his medicine cabinet. He knew this with certainty because he was the only one doing the shopping for his household, and he alone used the products that he purchased. If a tube suddenly went missing, there was no one in the household to blame for the disappearance but himself, and therefore, someone outside the home must have taken it. If these disappearances happened often enough, the possibility and probability of a thief would eventually enter Martin's mind. And because he lived alone, the identity of the thief would prove to be quite a mystery. Mysteries promote investigation. Investigations inevitably lead to evidence. Singletons were simply too much of a risk to take on as clients.

The couple must always be married as well. Roommates made the worst potential clients, simply because household expenses are often split between roommates using odd and indiscernible formulas that inevitably lead to strife. Roommates, in Martin's estimation, seem to always be fighting over whose bologna is sitting in the meat drawer, who used whose shampoo, and who made the thirty-nine-minute call to Denver on Wednesday afternoon during peak hours. Roommates, no matter how friendly they may be, always live with a certain level of mistrust for one another, and therefore when something goes missing, it is usually assumed that the roommate took it. The possibility of theft easily and immediately comes to mind with the presence of a roommate, and thus it becomes an option to consider.

No maid or children either, because these two types are frequently blamed for theft, no matter how insignificant the loss. Sticky-fingered maids and dishonest children are so common that they have almost become cliché.

And no dogs, because dogs bark at strangers and bite.

Martin did not like being bit.

One might think that the presence of children and maids and even roommates would be good for a man in Martin's line of work, by deflecting blame from himself and placing it upon more likely suspects, but this is where Martin separated himself from the amateurs. Though it might seem initially beneficial to have a theft blamed on a maid or a roommate, their mere presence establishes the likelihood of a theft. Their existence allows for the possibility of theft to enter the client's mind, and once these maids and roommates are cleared of all charges, the suspicion of theft lingers. An investigation begins. Investigations lead to evidence, and evidence leads to discovery. No, the key to Martin's success lay in the fact that his clients never really noticed that anything was missing, and when they did notice that an item was gone, they simply assumed that they had misplaced the item, lost it, or that the item had been moved or used by their spouse.

Of course, there was the occasional married couple who lived more like roommates than husband and wife, maintaining their own checking accounts, splitting expenses, and living separate financial lives, but Martin's careful screening process also eliminated these couples as potential clients. Besides, Martin found this arrangement to be ridiculous and destabilizing to the marriage, and he preferred to work with clients whose marriages were on a sound footing.

Exiting the pantry, making sure that the door was relatched, Martin passed through the kitchen and into the adjacent living room, stopping for a moment to inventory the items in the room in the event that the Pearls had added or deleted something since his last visit. A sectional sofa, brown leather and well worn, occupied the center of the room, facing a large, flat-screen television and an enormous fieldstone fireplace topped with a teakwood mantel, none of which showed any evidence of recent use. In fact, Martin noted that the same four logs were stacked upon the hearth exactly as they had been when Martin first entered this house more than nine years ago.

A Steinway in the northeast corner of the room (Martin took great pride in being able to identify the compass points in every one of his clients' homes) displayed a number of photographs of Sophie and Sherman Pearl at various locations around the world. A tropical beach at sunset, Cinderella's castle in Disney World, the front lawn of the Taj Majal, and atop the Great Wall of China were just a few of the couple's destinations. In each picture, Sherman, a thin, middle-aged man with horn-rimmed glasses and an incongruous shock of curly red hair was always standing to Sophie's left, right hand around her trim waist, their smiles almost always identical. Martin doubted that the couple, who had been married for a dozen years, were aware of the photographic pattern into which they had fallen, but concluded from it that this was a couple who enjoyed the safety and stability of their marriage. Based upon their frequent travel, Martin assumed that the Pearls had postponed children in favor of long hours at the office and exciting trips around the world. Sherman was a dentist who operated his own practice over the mountain in Avon, and Sophie owned an upscale and highly successful salon in Hartford, starting out years ago in a strip mall adjacent to a Stop & Shop but recently relocating into the center of town, doubling her business almost overnight. She looked the part of a successful salon owner. Her nails were always perfectly manicured, her dark hair was short and stylish with a streak of blond running through her bangs, and she looked about ten years younger than her actual age. Both she and her husband worked long hours, earned plenty of money, and enjoyed spending it on themselves.

The Pearls' lifestyle fit perfectly into Martin's third rule of selecting clients:

Never too rich, never too poor, and never, ever through inheritance.

Clients who inherited their wealth were out of the question. Martin believed that when individuals become wealthy by means of a parent or grandparent's prior labor, they often become overly involved with the distribution of this wealth. Sure, they may give a great deal to charity, but they are also able to account for every nickel that leaves their possession, because either they seek to honor their benefactor by using the money wisely or this is the first time the inheritor has had any money and is therefore more aware of its value.

Neither of these client types appealed to Martin very much.

He believed that taking on poor clients was an equally bad idea, as they tended to be keenly aware of everything they owned, since they owned so little.

Martin also believed that wealthy couples made the worst clients, and this is where amateurs often went wrong. He believed with absolute certainty that the wealthier an individual, the more he or she cared about the things that he or she owned. The wealthy had time to enjoy their belongings, to keep track of each item, and since the wealthy often didn't work for a living, they found gratification and self-esteem through the things they owned rather than the things that they did. These people noticed when something went missing, however mundane the item might have been. This, plus their propensity for security systems, maids, and inconsistent schedules, made the wealthy the worst choice of client.

Upper-middle-class couples, comprised of hardworking and successful individuals, were Martin's bread-and-butter clients. The ideal client was a two-income couple who earned enough money to own nice things but simply did not have the time to enjoy them. The Pearls were a perfect example. Sherman and Sophie were able to afford a beautiful home with a fieldstone fireplace, but they never had the time to actually use it. They purchased the Steinway about six years ago but had yet to purchase a music book or take a piano lesson. The Pearls were making excellent money, more than a quarter of a million dollars a year between them, but they were simply too busy with work and travel to monitor or enjoy their *things*, and this made them one of Martin's most reliable couples.

Of course, Martin knew all this and much more because he had screened the Pearls for more than five months prior to signing them on as clients, and he continued to remain as informed as possible about their lives.

Martin did not believe in skimping on research.

Staying as close as possible to the west wall so as to avoid the picture window that faced the street, Martin made his way through the living room to the stairway leading to the second floor. Before ascending, he popped his head into the dining room to his right, doubting that the Pearls had changed this sparsely furnished room in any way (since it appeared that the room went virtually unused), but wanting to be sure nevertheless. An unused dining room was another sign of a couple who had no time to spend enjoying their home. Dinners were often eaten in the kitchen, in a restaurant, or in the car. The dining room, with its black-lacquered, handcrafted Italian table, was as unused as the Pearls' fieldstone fireplace and dusty Steinway.

Satisfied that the dining room was as sterile as ever, Martin climbed the stairs slowly and methodically, authenticating his purchase on each step before ascending.

Years ago, Jim, Martin's only real friend, had been reading from a book of lateral-thinking puzzles over pizza and beer when he offered this puzzle to his friend:

A man calls 911 from a home, saying that he is injured and needs help. The police and ambulance arrive, and he is taken to the hospital, where the man is later arrested. What is the man arrested for?

After more than fifteen minutes of yes-or-no questions, Martin finally solved the puzzle. The man who called 911 had been a burglar who had broken his leg coming down a set of stairs in a house that he was robbing. Trapped in the home, with no hope of escape and in great pain, the burglar was forced to call for help and was later arrested after receiving treatment at the hospital. The author of the lateral-thinking book also noted that this puzzle was based upon a true story.

As the solution to the puzzle had dawned on Martin, his heart quickened and his face flushed. Was his friend of almost thirty years aware of Martin's true career? Was he using this puzzle as a means of broaching the subject, or had this simply been a coincidence?

Martin and Jim had met over a game of Chutes and Ladders a couple weeks into their kindergarten year, when it had become clear to both of them, even at their young age, that no one else was interested in playing with them. Alone in a new world of shiny linoleum, tiny chairs and desks, and inflatable letter people, the two were forced into a friendship that had lasted for almost their entire lives. Though Jim had escaped the isolation of kindergarten and gone on to a more normal life of marriage and children, he had always made room in his life for his friendship with Martin. And for Martin, Jim was one of the only people in the world, perhaps the only person in the world, with whom he was at ease. Therefore, as he solved Jim's puzzle, he worried that he had slipped in some way. It's difficult to bluff someone who has known you longer than you've been able to read. If anyone could uncover his secret, Martin reasoned, it would be Jim.

After hearing Martin's solution to the puzzle, Jim had quickly moved on to another, more difficult one, hoping to stump his friend and leaving Martin to believe that the choice of puzzle had been merely a coincidence. But it had also left Martin with a cautionary tale that he took very seriously. As he climbed the stairs to the second floor landing, he was exceptionally careful of his footing on each stair. Only an amateur would allow himself to get arrested by breaking a leg in the midst of a client visit.

At the top of the stairs, Martin turned left, passing by a bathroom and guest room on his way to the end of the hall, where the master bedroom was located. He had been in this room many times, during each visit to the house in fact, but this time would be different. He wouldn't simply be inventorying

Sophie Pearl's jewelry box as he had done for the last seven months. Today he would finally be taking something.

Exactly seven months ago, Martin had acquired an earring from Sophie Pearl's jewelry box, a 1.3-karat diamond stud, leaving its twin behind. He had chosen this earring after a yearlong inventory of the jewelry box that was based upon time-lapse digital photography. For a year, during each visit to the Pearls' home, Martin would photograph Sophie's jewelry box with his Cannon Sure Shot and download the photos onto his computer at home. After examining the chronological, photographic history of the jewelry box, Martin was able to identify the best item to procure.

First, Martin noted that the diamond earrings were absent from the box only once during the entire year, which included at least one inspection each week. Other than their one disappearance, the earrings were always located in the same spot, the southeast corner of the bottom tray (based upon the jewelry box's customary position on the bureau). This was not the case for many other items in Sophie's box, a clear indication that certain items were being worn and returned quite often but this pair of earrings was not.

There were also some items in Sophie's box that were never missing, but Martin had no intention of touching these. A pair of infrequently worn diamond earrings might go missing without concern, but a family heirloom, put away for a future daughter's wedding day, would probably be noticed immediately.

The earrings in question were also frequently covered by Sophie's string of black pearls, so as to not be visible by their owner. In fact, for a three-month stretch, the pearls had covered the earrings on every visit. This indicated that Sophie was unlikely to notice the disappearance of the earrings, since she rarely saw them for long stretches of time. Martin guessed that

Sophie probably wore these earrings with a specific dress and otherwise forgot about them for the rest of the year.

Two other items in Sophie Pearl's jewelry box fit this criteria for potential targets: a heart-shaped gold locket worth very little and an antique diamond ring, more than three karats of diamonds in all, that was probably worth a lot. Martin chose the earrings because they were of substantial value to make the acquisition worthwhile but not so much as to cause great concern to a successful couple like the Pearls if their disappearance was discovered.

On February 17 of this year, Martin had taken one of the earrings during a visit, and then he waited. When he returned to the home two days after the procurement, he looked for signs that the earring's absence had been noticed. The jewelry box looked nearly identical to the picture taken on procurement day. A similar pair of gold hoops, smaller and slightly oval, had replaced a pair of large, gold hoop earrings, but otherwise there were no noticeable changes. There was no evidence that Sophie Pearl had emptied her jewelry box in search of the missing earring.

The disappearance had gone unnoticed.

An amateur would have taken Sophie's other diamond stud at that point, but Martin knew that this operation would require more finesse. Sophie would eventually notice that the earring was missing. He knew this because she wore this pair on occasion, though infrequently, and if she found both gone, she might, just might, suspect theft. But if a single earring was missing, then Sophie would almost certainly assume that she had misplaced the other, since no conceivable thief would think of acquiring just one earring, and so she would begin a search. On a day in mid-June, Sophie had conducted just such a search.

Martin was sure of this because on the Wednesday of that

week, he had found Sophie's jewelry box in disarray. Items that hadn't been touched in months had been moved to new locations, and it appeared that the bottom tray of the box had actually been removed, probably in order for Sophie to inspect underneath. Martin knew this from the thin piece of tape that he had placed between the bottom tray of the jewelry box and the box itself on the initial day of procurement, a piece so thin that it would go virtually unnoticed if someone were to lift the tray, but quite noticeable to a professional like Martin. On that day, the sliver of tape was gone, and after a few moments of searching, Martin had actually managed to locate it, lying between Sophie's clock radio and a stack of *Real Simple* magazines atop the bureau. This confirmed in his mind that Sophie had conducted her search and had found nothing.

So Martin waited again, knowing that patience and professionalism would eventually win the day. He wanted to be sure that Sophie wasn't taking measures to replace the earring, by taking it to the jewelry store where it was purchased, for example, and matching it up with a new twin. Martin waited three months for a new earring to appear in Sophie Pearl's jewelry box before deciding that today, September 17, would be the day to acquire the second. After removing the earring from the jewelry box and sliding it into a small plastic bag, he placed the bag into a Velcro pouch sewn into the inside seam of his baseball cap. If he were arrested, he did not want to be caught with the earring, and after experimenting for years with false-bottomed shoes and hidden coat pockets, and considering the possibility of placing stolen jewelry in bodily cavities (a concept Martin could never stomach), he had settled on the baseball cap, deeming it the last place a police officer would look and the easiest item of clothing to ditch in the case of police pursuit.

Pleased with his new acquisition, Martin photographed Sophie's jewelry box again, scanned the bedroom for any recent changes, and then backtracked to the second floor bathroom, where he acquired two bars of Dove soap from the neat stack of eight in the cabinet underneath the sink. Martin also took a moment to photograph the inside of this cabinet after noticing a large supply of toilet paper and two new bottles of Scope mouthwash. Although the theft of either or both of these items would probably go unnoticed by the Pearls, and though he knew that his own supply of mouthwash was running low, Martin never acquired items that did not appear on his original shopping list. Instead, he would photograph the items while in the house and later use the digital photos to plan his next visit, calculating the value of the items taken from the home over the past month, as well as the time these items had spent on the shelf, before deciding which items were safe to acquire. After all, Martin had plenty of other clients, so if he wasn't able to stock up on toilet paper at the Pearls' house, there were always others available to meet his needs.

Before the days of digital photography, Martin had used a pencil and notepad to keep track of the inventory in each of his clients' homes, and this system had worked well. When the idea of taking digital photos first occurred to Martin, he immediately rejected it on the grounds that he was a professional, and professionals didn't need fancy gadgets in order to be successful. Martin considered himself an old-school pro, as evidenced by his burlap sack and his cautious nature, and digital photography was anything but old school. However, after thinking about it some more (because Martin believed that professionals constantly reevaluated their decisions), he began to see the tremendous potential of digital photography for his business. And though there was nothing wrong with holding on to old-school beliefs, Martin also came to realize that professionals, old-school or otherwise, also kept abreast of the times, paid attention to new technology, and found ways of making their business better while adhering to traditional values. Digital photography was a way to make his business even better.

By taking digital photos, Martin was able to reduce the overall number of minutes spent in each of his clients' homes, a huge benefit in a profession where stealth and speed were of the utmost importance. Martin also found that digital photos were easier to rid himself of in the event of capture. The camera that Martin owned stored photographs on a memory stick that could be completely erased by pressing a combination of four buttons (a process that he practiced until it could be completed in less than seven seconds), or the memory stick could simply be broken in half, rendering it unreadable. With this new technology, Martin found that he was able to gather more information about his clients in far less time, and in Martin's mind, information was invaluable.

Exiting the bathroom, Martin made his way back down the stairs with equal care (if not more, since the thief in the lateral-thinking puzzle had broken his leg going *down* the stairs) and passed through the Pearls' dining room into the hall that connected the kitchen with the home office, the family room (complete with a second unused fireplace), and another guest bedroom at the western end of the house. Directly in front of him was the first floor bathroom, a large teal-and-peach rectangle complete with a full shower and monogrammed towels. Martin entered, sliding aside the white louvered doors on his left to reveal a matching washer and dryer. He quickly scanned the laundry supplies on the shelf above the appliances, locating a bottle of Tide two-thirds full, and proceeded to pour half of the remaining laundry soap into a clear plastic container that he had stored in his burlap sack.

Closing the bottle of Tide (now a little less than a third full) and returning it to its perch, Martin checked his watch, a black

Seiko that was waterproof and reliable in three atmospheres. The digital display, counting down, read 1 minute and 43 seconds, giving him just enough time to exit the premises. Martin was uncompromising on his time limit. No more than fifteen minutes inside a client's home, no matter what was left on his list. Longer than fifteen minutes and any newly installed silent alarm or nosy neighbor reporting his presence would give the police ample time to arrive.

This, of course, would never happen. First, no homeowner with an ounce of sense would ever install a silent alarm in his or her home. The purpose of an alarm is to frighten off burglars. Silent alarms only served to trap burglars inside homes, oftentimes along with the unwitting homeowners. In these instances, dangerous hostage situations often occurred as the police surrounded the home, entrapping the burglar and the home's occupants inside.

Second, in the event that any alarm was installed, the homeowner would almost certainly place a sticker on the front of their home, alerting thieves to its presence. This was a signal that Martin had grown to adore. While these signs served as effective deterrents, protecting the homeowners who possessed them, they also served to exploit the neighboring homeowners who did not own a sign. After all, if your next-door neighbor's home was protected by ADT, with its blue, octagonal sign posted prominently around the house, why would you install a similar alarm system in your home but keep it secret? Wouldn't this be just inviting disaster? Martin thought so. In fact, in Martin's many years on the job, he had yet to run into a house with an alarm that did not also have a sticker alerting him to its presence, but some of his best clients had been those living adjacent to homes protected by alarm systems.

Nevertheless, Martin remained cautious and always left a

client's home in less than fifteen minutes. No sense in taking chances, as remote as they might be. This time limit was easy to abide with long-term clients like the Pearls, whose homes Martin knew almost better than his own. But in a new client's home, the fifteen-minute restriction often left Martin unable to inventory rooms and complete assigned tasks. *There's always tomorrow,* he would think to himself in these circumstances (because he also avoided speaking aloud while inside a client's home), and he would force himself to leave no matter how much valuable information there might still be to collect. Unlike in many jobs, when Martin made a mistake, it might mean the end of his career.

Though he had hoped to photograph the Pearls' home office today (Martin was in need of printer paper and staples), his watch was telling him to leave, so he made his way to the back door in the mudroom adjacent to the kitchen. In many clients' homes, 1 minute and 43 seconds would still be a world of time, but the Pearls' home posed a special challenge for Martin. Though he considered them one of his best clients, the Pearls' home was closer to the road and to their neighbors' homes than any of his other clients, and this made exiting especially dangerous. Fortunately, the Pearls' backyard, a nice quarter-acre slice of grass and bushes that was frightfully exposed to the neighbors' adjacent backyards, also abutted Mill Pond Park, a large area of grass, trees, playground equipment, and a public swimming pool, spaced around a quaint little duck pond. If Martin could make his way across the backyard unnoticed and pass through the row of hedges that marked the end of the Pearls' land, he could be walking in the park in seconds, free as a bird.

Making it across the backyard always made Martin nervous, principally because it was his only means of exiting the Pearls' home. In every other client's home, Martin had at least three means of egress and would use each on a random basis (rolling a ten-sided die that he kept in his pocket to determine each day's exit, since Martin found that unconsciously falling into patterns was far too easy to do). The only thing that made this risk even remotely acceptable to Martin was his comprehensive knowledge of the Pearls' two adjacent neighbors.

To the east were the Goldmans, a couple very much like the Pearls, who might have made excellent clients had their home not been equipped with three ADT stickers, thank you very much. The Goldmans both worked dependable schedules and late hours. Their home was not equipped with a garage, so Martin could always tell if Mr. or Mrs. Goldman were home sick (which almost never occurred). Therefore, the chances of them witnessing Martin's exit during the middle of the day were infinitesimal.

To the west of the Pearls lived Noah Blake, a convicted sex offender who had been released from Walpole State Prison in Massachusetts more than ten years ago after doing six months on a third-degree sexual assault conviction, a fact to which Martin did not think the Pearls were privy. Martin had been unable to acquire the details of the arrest, but he did know that Noah Blake's mother had passed away shortly after his release, and that her son had inherited the house free and clear, something Martin had done as well when his own mother passed away. Other than his one apparent indiscretion, Noah Blake was a hardworking, reliable mechanic at Mike & Son's Automotive in Plainville, where he had recently become part-owner with Mike's lackadaisical son, Darryl (Mike having retired from the business years ago). And Noah Blake's home also did not come equipped with a garage. Therefore, as long as Martin's visits to the Pearls' home took place between 10:00 a.m. and 4:00 p.m. (avoiding lunchtime in the event someone decided to come home), he felt sure that his exit was a safe one.

Still, it made him nervous.

Securing his burlap sack inside a black backpack that he had left just inside the door upon arriving, and making sure that his house key was still on the chain around his neck (he had acquired a key to the Pearls' home years ago, as he had for many of his clients), Martin removed the rubber moccasins that covered his sneakers (and thereby prevented footprints), placed them in the backpack as well, and exited the house, crossing the back lawn as casually as possible. In less than thirty seconds, he was walking across the expanse of field that led to the bicycle racks on the far side of the park.

By the time Martin began pedaling, his appearance had changed dramatically. The blue baseball cap, emblazoned with its Northeast Utilities symbol, and the hairnet underneath had been replaced with a white and red cap declaring his allegiance to the St. Louis Cardinals. Martin, of course, cared little about the sluggers of St. Louis, and had chosen this cap as randomly as he had chosen his mode of transportation for the day. Patterns, he knew, were dangerous in his line of business, and were easy to fall into without even trying. A man who rode through the park on a mountain bike every Tuesday morning, wearing a St. Louis Cardinals baseball cap, might eventually become a fixture in the memory of one of the park's regular inhabitants. An observant individual might even come to expect to see this mountain bike–riding man each week. Becoming a memorable part of any landscape was exactly what Martin wanted to avoid.

Martin was riding his mountain bike today because of the roll of a 3 that he had made on his ten-sided die over breakfast earlier this morning. Had the die come up a 1 or a 2, Martin would be walking the mile or so to his car. A 3, 4, or 5 placed him on his mountain bike; a 6, 7, or 8 would have had Martin parking his Subaru Outback in the lot adjoining the swimming pool and basketball courts. A 9 or a 0 would've had Martin jogging back to his vehicle. Martin had experimented with other modes of transportation in the past, including Rollerblades, skateboards, and a brief flirtation with the possibility of a motorized wheelchair, but each of these, he'd realized, attracted more attention than necessary, so Martin had decided to stick with the ordinary. Ordinary, at least on the outside, was safest for someone trying to remain inconspicuous.

Had Martin been able to alter his physical stature, he might have shaven an inch off his 5' 11" frame, favoring the 5' 10" of the average American male. He did, however, make a concerted effort to keep his weight around 180 pounds, the average weight for a white American male aged 30–39 years. In addition to his weight, Martin kept himself clean-shaven at all times and wore no jewelry, in hopes of eliminating any distinguishing marks from his person. He was a good-looking man, he knew, but he also knew that he wasn't too good-looking, and this pleased Martin more than it would most. Excess in appearance was to be avoided at all costs.

Martin's greatest concern was his ears. Though they were not excessively large, they were positioned on his head at such an angle to appear so, jutting out like the bolts from Frankenstein's neck. As a child, his classmates had made fun of his ears, referring to Martin as "Dumbo" and "Big Ears," both names failing to impress Martin even back then. Despite the ineffectiveness of his classmates' verbal abuse, Martin had tried to readjust his ears so that they would appear more normal. In sixth grade he used superglue to pin his ears to the side of his head, and although the glue held his ears back for more than three days before losing its potency, it failed to permanently alter the orientation of his ears in any discernible way. He tried this method several more times that year until the jeers of his classmates, who noticed the change in his physiology and accurately deduced the cause, forced Martin to abandon the attempt. Hats, it turned out, were Martin's most effective means of concealing his ears, and therefore he wore them often, as he did on this day.

In addition to the change of hats, Martin had also removed his blue button-down work shirt, stuffing it into his backpack and revealing a yellow and black long-sleeved cycling jersey beneath. A pair of mirrored sunglasses had been added to cover his clear blue eyes, and once he had mounted his bike, an aerodynamic helmet had been planted atop the Cardinals cap to complete the image.

Today Martin's path would take him west around the duck pond, following the paved path onto the bridge by the picturesque Mill Pond Waterfall. Many a couple, dressed in pale gown and tuxedo, had stood on that bridge overlooking the falls, unwittingly beginning their divorce proceedings with the simple phrase "I do." From the bridge, Martin would leave the path, pedaling across a soccer field out to Willard Avenue, where he would double back to his car, parked at the foot of the falls.

This was just one of the many routes that Martin could take to his car, and the parking lot at the foot of the waterfall was just one of many locations to leave the Subaru. Martin could also have parked in the lot on Brookdale Avenue, adjacent to the tennis courts; at the public library on the opposite end of the park; at the Newington Town Hall (across the street from the library); or at the CVS pharmacy, a half mile up Garfield Street. If Martin wanted to bike slightly farther (and he often did), then all of Main Street opened up to him, offering him an almost limitless number of spaces in which to park his vehicle. Today Martin had chosen the parking lot at the base of the waterfall because it was one of the closer places available to him, and the weatherman on Channel Four, a professorial-looking man of at least two chins, had warned of the possibility of rain later that morning. Though Martin often chose his parking spot randomly as well (there was always a die in Martin's pocket), he didn't want to be stuck with a three-mile ride through the center of town during a torrential downpour. To anyone who looked out their shopwindow at the right moment or drove by in their car, this would have been a memorable sight indeed.

Arriving at his car, Martin popped open the hatch and began to unload his newly acquired items into the back of the station wagon. A large cardboard box containing several empty grocery bags from the local Foodmart was sitting beside a Stanley toolbox and a case of bottled water. Martin transferred his newly acquired items from his backpack to the plastic grocery bags, much the same way as a bagger might do in a supermarket (keeping the canned goods together in one bag and items like soap and butter in another), and then neatly packed the three bags that he had filled into the cardboard box. His hope was that if he were ever pulled over by the police for any reason, it would appear that he was returning home after grocery shopping and not from a visit to one of his client's homes.

Martin then took a quick look around to be sure that no one was watching, and after he was certain that he was alone in the parking lot, he reached under the left rear bumper of his car and removed a small magnetic box that had been attached to the metallic underside of the Subaru. Into this box, which was designed to hide an extra key (the lid was actually imprinted with the words "Hide-a-Key"), Martin placed Sophie Pearl's diamond earring, sliding the box shut before returning it to its original position underneath the bumper. If Martin was ever pulled over on suspicion of burglary, the police would find it difficult, if not impossible, to locate the diamond.

Attaching his bike to the rack atop the Outback, Martin tossed his backpack, now nearly empty, into the passenger seat and climbed inside. Once his seat belt was buckled, he extracted the first-aid kit from inside the glove compartment.

Upon opening the first-aid kit, all appeared very normal. Band-Aids, gauze, a cold pack, and a thin tube of antibiotic cream were all assembled in neat order. Beneath the large gauze pads, however, was a plastic flap made from the same white plastic of which the kit was constructed. Martin was quite proud of this piece of handiwork. Lifting the camouflaged flap revealed a grid of small pockets, a total of twelve, all but one containing a key. Martin removed the chain with the Pearls' key from his neck and placed it in the empty pocket. Keeping the key around his neck was something Martin began doing after accidentally leaving a key in the lock of a client's home a number of years ago, one of his worst mistakes while on the job. He had managed to reacquire the key that day, but only after risking a second visit to the home, something Martin almost never did. Leaving the key around his neck guaranteed that he wouldn't make that same mistake again. And concealing the keys in this modified first-aid kit prevented a police officer from questioning him about the inordinate number of keys that he would otherwise need to carry.

Having keys to his clients' homes made Martin's job a whole lot easier. Of his current twenty-three clients, Martin was in possession of keys for sixteen of their homes, and thirteen of those were for side or back doors, Martin's preferred method of entry for a number of reasons, particularly their limited exposure to street traffic.

Keys, it turned out, were not terribly difficult to acquire once you had access to a client's home. Not surprisingly (though Martin was admittedly surprised at first), people are quite careless with their extra house keys if these keys are locked inside the home. After all, if you were able to break into the home in the first place, why steal a key? In addition, most people in Martin's line of work were what Martin referred to as "one-timers" or "smash-and-grabbers." Martin despised these amateurs. One-timers or smash-and-grabbers broke into homes, usually by means of a broken window, acquired a few large-ticket items that would surely be noticed missing when the client returned, and then exited, never to come back again. Because there were so few who maintained a regular clientele (and Martin often wondered if he was the only one), homeowners generally felt safe about leaving their house keys in rather obvious places, and Martin was adept at finding them. The Pearls, for example, had three extra house keys in an I LOVE NY shot glass on Sherman's desk in the home office, mixed with a handful of Kennedy half dollars (of which Martin had acquired two a few years back). Martin's next client of the day, the Gallos, actually kept two complete sets of extra house keys on a hook by their front door. Martin had found house keys in jewelry boxes, underneath flowerpots, and inside toilet tanks (a place used surprisingly often for hiding things). Clients also tended to leave keys out in the open when away on vacation. Four weeks ago, for example, one of Martin's newest clients, the Wilkinsons, had gone to Florida to visit relatives, and Mrs. Wilkinson had left her set of keys (car, house, and presumably work) in a wicker basket on the kitchen counter. Up until that point, Martin had been unable to locate a single spare key in their home, but thanks to the trip to Florida, his access to the Wilkinsons' home had recently gotten a lot easier.

Duplicating the keys, however, required some preparation. Martin rarely entered a home twice in one day, but copying a key required removing the original from the house for at least a day, and oftentimes for a week or more. In order to do this without arousing suspicion, Martin had spent more than a month creating a collection of replacement keys matching every size, shape, and color imaginable. Of course, these temporary replacements were not cut to open the locks on the clients' doors but served only to hold the place of the real spare key until the copy could be made and returned. These substitute keys, thirty-seven in all, were actually cut from a collection of old apartment and house keys that Martin initially had saved for posterity. Gold keys, silver keys, small round keys, large triangular keys, and many, many more filled a tomato jar on the top shelf of his pantry. It was quite uncommon for Martin to run into a spare key for which he did not have a veritable match, and when this happened he would photograph the spare and find a duplicate that matched, adding the new key to his growing collection.

Since homeowners rarely required their spare, Martin felt it safe to assume that a swapped spare key would go unnoticed. And in the unlikely event that the spare key was required while the real one was in Martin's possession, the homeowner would simply assume that the replacement key had been cut poorly or that the locking mechanism in the door had become worn from use. Martin felt certain that no homeowner would ever suspect that someone had stolen their spare key and replaced it with a nearly identical match.

There were more than a dozen hardware stores that Martin used for key duplication, and he purposely avoided the small, individually owned stores because the owner or manager was often the same person responsible for duplicating keys and seemed to always be working. Big-box stores like Home Depot had a different employee duplicating keys each day, allowing Martin to maintain his prized anonymity.

Of course, all this depended upon Martin's ability to gain initial entry to the home.

When he first went into business, he'd thought that this would prove to be his biggest challenge, but without much effort, Martin had found more than a dozen businesses that would sell him lock-picking tools and instructional manuals with virtually no questions asked. For example, the website where Martin had recently purchased his newest set of tools, lockpickpro.com, listed this disclaimer: "It is the responsibility of the buyer, and not Lock Pick Pro, to ascertain and obey all applicable local, state, and federal laws in regard to possession and use of any item ordered. Consult your local and state laws before ordering if you are in doubt."

Other lock-picking sites declared that their instruction manuals were for "academic study only" and "were not intended for any use other than magical or escape artist purposes."

Martin didn't consider his purposes purely academic, and he wasn't a professional magician or escape artist at the time (nor did he ever expect to be). And although he was fully aware of the local and state laws regarding his possession and use of lock picks, Martin purchased that first set anyway, making the payment with a Stop & Shop money order and having the lock picks shipped via UPS to the home of Mr. and Mrs. Timothy Marino, future clients of Martin's who were vacationing in Tahiti for two weeks. Ordering over the phone had made Martin nervous enough, but to have the equipment shipped to his own home seemed ludicrous. It was just the type of information that the police might one day use to incriminate him. Instead, Maureen Marino had been the answer.

Mrs. Marino was a regular customer in the Starbucks where Martin worked part-time, and she was quite friendly with Martin's manager, an earthy-crunchy, tree-hugging twenty-something named Nadia who referred to everyone as "honey" except for Martin. Over the obscene screaming of the milk steamer, Martin had overheard the two ladies chatting about Mrs. Marino's upcoming and *absolutely fabulous* vacation to the South Pacific. Later on, a check of the phone books of the surrounding towns found Mrs. Maureen Marino living at 13 Cranberry Circle in Martin's hometown of West Hartford, a mere twelve minutes from his own house. A visual inspection of the home told Martin that the Marinos would suit him just fine. Set back away from the road, with plenty of distance between their house and the neighbors', the Marino's home was equipped with a wide front porch, capable of hiding any packages left by delivery persons.

Martin timed the placement of his order so that his package would arrive in the middle of the Marinos' vacation, leaving plenty of room on either end for error. Prior to delivery, he also noted the time that the UPS truck typically made its rounds through the Marinos' neighborhood, so that he could be prepared to receive his order upon delivery. By shipping through United Parcel Service, Martin had also managed to bypass the hold that the Marinos had presumably placed on their mail through the U.S. Postal Service. Martin simply watched the Marinos' home from across the street for three days until the brown UPS truck stopped in front of their house, then watched as a man dressed to match his truck stepped onto the Marinos' porch, knocked, and waited. After determining that no one was home, the driver, a middle-aged man who appeared to be going through the motions of life with little zeal, placed the package on the Marinos' porch swing and left. Martin removed the package later that evening after the sun had gone down and the neighbors had gone to bed.

Thus, for an initial investment of just under $1,000, Martin had managed to purchase a top-of-the-line lock-pick kit, complete with instruction manuals in three different languages, half a dozen tension wrenches, two standard sets of lock picks, and two pick guns, including an electric model. Another $500 in locks of various types, purchased at the same impersonal hardware stores where he had his keys cut, and Martin was ready to begin his training, which was surprisingly simple. He installed more than thirty standard door locks, dead bolts, and the like along a set of two-by-fours in his basement, and for more than three hours each day he studied, practiced, and perfected his craft. After years of training, Martin could now pick all but the most complicated tubular locks. And since most dead bolts operate with cylinder locks (the simplest and quickest to pick), Martin's continued attempts with tubular locks were more of a hobby than a genuine professional interest. In fact, all of Martin's lock-picking skills, honed through years of study and practice, were largely irrelevant thanks to the advent of the pick gun.

Developed to allow law enforcement officers who were unskilled in the art of lock-picking to open locks with speed and minimal instruction, the pick gun had become one of Martin's most important occupational tools (he still considered his ten-sided die the most important). Rather than opening locks by the picking and raking techniques of a standard pick, a pick gun relies on the transfer of energy to compromise locks. A pick gun basically consists of one or more vibrating pick-shaped pieces of metal. These long pieces are inserted into the lock, just as one would insert a key. As the metal pieces vibrate, they push up the pins inside the lock. By turning the gun as the picks vibrate, the pins are caught at the shear line, allowing the lock to open. With very little practice, Martin was able to open more than half the locks he encountered in a matter of seconds, oftentimes faster than a homeowner would take to locate the correct key and use it to open the lock normally. After years of practice, it was rare for Martin to run into a lock that he could not pick in less than thirty seconds, and he had increased the effectiveness of his pick gun to more than 80 percent.

It also helped that homeowners often put so little thought into the locks used in their houses. While front doors were often equipped with complex tubular locks that resisted most of Martin's efforts, the side, back, and garage doors of most houses (the doors that Martin preferred to use for entry anyway) were often safeguarded by simple dead bolts or cylinder locks built into the doorknob.

Martin's lock-pick kit was at home this day, hidden in a space behind the paneling in his partially finished basement, covered by a Mondrian print in primary colors. Because of its incriminating nature, Martin carried his kit around as little as possible, limiting his visits to the eight clients whose locks still required picking on the same days as his visits to potential new clients. When traveling with the kit, Martin kept it stowed in the back of his wagon, hidden in a space beneath the spare tire. When in use, his picking tools were inside his backpack or within the inner pockets of the coat that he might be wearing, though all of the locks that still required picking could be opened quite easily with the pick gun with the exception of two, where old-fashioned lock picks were still needed.

For the next three visits of the day, however, no picking would be required.

Martin pulled out of the parking lot, heading toward Route 9 at three miles over the posted speed limit, the speed at which Martin always drove. Martin believed that driving the speed limit made a person look suspicious, so he hoped that his three-miles-over-the-limit policy made him look like an average Connecticut driver. About fifteen minutes south was the town of Kensington, the home of two more of Martin's clients.

At the Gallos', a pair of plump professional chefs who owned an upscale and successful breakfast-and-lunch café in Wethersfield, Martin acquired three boxes of long-grain rice, a bottle of pinot noir from their extensive wine collection, two rolls of toilet paper (in Martin's estimation, the Gallos had excellent taste in toilet paper), three cups of olive oil (stored in a water bottle that attached to the frame of Martin's bike), and three cotton bath towels embroidered with small, smiling goldfish. The Gallos happened to own bath towels identical to those owned by another of his clients, the Archambauts of Middletown, and upon noticing the similarity (with the help of some digital photos), Martin had slowly begun to assemble a matching set for himself by culling from the two clients' supplies. With each couple owning more than a dozen of these towels, Martin guessed that if three went missing from each home, they would not be noticed, and half a dozen would make him a decent set. He had already acquired a set of matching face cloths with the same design, and next month he would begin collecting hand towels to complete his set. This was Martin's first foray into the realm of bath towels and he was very pleased by his success. By the end of next month, he would own a completely new set of towels to replace the threadbare robin's-egg-blue set his mother had left him when she died.

From the Gallos', Martin drove west for ten minutes before arriving at the home of the Grants, two middle-aged high school teachers who also owned and operated a successful travel agency from their home. From the photographs that Martin had seen throughout their house, it was apparent that Lucy Grant had married her husband, Maurice, for reasons unrelated to physical appearance. Even in portraits, the man appeared less than appealing, with an amoeba-like bald spot atop his head that seemed to mysteriously change shape and size from photo to photo and a single brow stretching across two beady eyes. A short, pudgy man, he appeared to have difficulty smiling even in his wedding photos. In contrast, Lucy Grant was a trim, sophisticated woman who was probably coloring her hair but otherwise appeared a dozen years younger than her fifty-three years. The impetus behind her attraction to Maurice had managed to escape even Martin's keen detective skills.

Maurice and Lucy Grant's children, Maurice Jr. and Susan, were both married thirtysomethings who had left the nest a long time ago, making the Grants ideal clients. Not only could Martin be fairly certain that neither Maurice Sr. nor Lucy would ever return home during the school day, but he was also able to remain keenly in tune with their vacation schedule just by logging on to their school's website and checking the calendar that was posted.

The Grants' home was also nearly adjacent to the town's large, oval-shaped reservoir, allowing Martin unlimited parking options. Unlike at the Gallos' home, which was more than three miles away from any public parking, Martin could park less than a mile from the Grants' home and walk, jog, or bike there while blending in with the multitude of stay-at-home moms, lunchtime power walkers, and retirees who lapped the reservoir each day. In keeping with his cycling persona from earlier in the day, Martin had chosen to take his bike to the Grants' home, laying it down on the side of the road under the cover of several bushes about five hundred feet from the Grants' driveway before proceeding the rest of the way on foot.

Despite the advantages of maintaining the Grants as clients, things had not started out very smoothly. His first visit had almost ended in disaster. Every initial visit to a client was stressful for Martin, for a number of reasons. Though he didn't see any sticker advertising an alarm system, he could never be sure that the house was unprotected until he first cracked the door. It was also impossible to predict what he might encounter upon first entering the home. Though his surveillance of the Grants' home hadn't indicated the presence of a dog, it was always possible that he had missed something. The first few moments in a new client's home were the most trying of Martin's career.

Martin began his initial entry to the Grants' home, as he did with all visits to his clients' homes, with a ringing of the doorbell. If someone was unexpectedly home, he or she would open the door and Martin would offer a look of surprise, indicating that he must have the wrong home. "My uncle Bill asked me to stop by to pick up a mattress. Do I have the wrong house?" he would ask, followed by a heartfelt apology and a quick exit. Ringing the doorbell would also help him to determine if a dog was present inside the house, and though no one had ever answered the door following the ringing of a doorbell, Martin had managed to identify the presence of a dog more than once by this maneuver. While it was easy to determine a client's schedule through careful surveillance, the presence of a dog was sometimes difficult to ascertain from a distance.

And Martin hated dogs.

Using his pick gun, Martin had disabled the relatively simple lock on the Grants' back door and swung it open slowly. As he placed his moccasined foot onto the welcome mat, he was greeted by a voice from somewhere within the home.

"Welcome home, sweetie pie!"

The greeting had startled Martin so badly that he had fallen backward down the steps, landing in a puddle of slush, his pick gun clattering to the cement patio. His first instinct had been to run. Execute the escape route that he had planned for each of his clients' homes in case of emergency. In the Grants' case, this route would take him across their backyard (an approach Martin wouldn't normally consider with fresh snow on the ground at the time), over the chain-link fence that backed onto a grove of scrub pine, and through the trees for about seven hundred feet before emerging onto Chamberland Avenue. Cross Chamberland and Martin could be on any of the reservoir's many footpaths in seconds, safely mixing in with the crowd until he reached his car.

But as this thought flashed in his mind, the unexpected voice repeated itself from the house. "Welcome home, sweetie pie! Welcome!" and it was this second greeting that had caused Martin to realize that the speaker was not human. Unnerved but feeling slightly more at ease (and frightfully exposed at the bottom of the Grants' back steps), Martin quickly retrieved his pick gun, made sure that his hairnet and rubber moccasins were still in place, climbed the back steps again, and entered the home, bypassing standard procedures in favor of locating the source of the voice as quickly as possible.

Normally Martin would begin his first visit to a client's home by mapping the entire house on a sheet of the graph paper that he carried in bulk on a clipboard. Beginning at the point of entry, he would work his way forward, step by step, room by room. Dimensions would be roughly estimated at first, rooms labeled, and large furniture drawn in as best he could, strictly observing his fifteen-minute time limit. A search for spare keys in the usual locations would also be conducted, and if time permitted (and it usually did, thanks to Martin's efficiency), photographs of the refrigerator, pantry, and shelf contents would be taken. In subsequent visits Martin would catalog the contents of each room, begin a photographic study of the couple's household supplies, and search for information that would eventually prove invaluable to his business. This would include inspecting checkbook registers, the contents of file cabinets, and files on the couple's computer, if these files weren't protected by passwords. More than three quarters of his clients' computers were not password protected, and the information stored on these machines had helped Martin more than any shred of paper that he had ever found, particularly when the client kept financial information on the computer as well. With this information, Martin could often determine a client's net worth, recent purchasing history, and occupation, if that had not yet been determined.

Eventually Martin would spend time examining photo albums, searching through boxes of old letters and greeting cards, and reading diaries (though sadly most of his clients kept no such written record of their lives). He watched his clients as they aged, celebrated holidays and anniversaries together, and suffered through hardships. On one occasion he followed a client through her diary entries as she discovered a lump in her breast, was diagnosed with cancer, and battled her way to recovery, losing a breast in the process. There were mornings when he was in tears as he read through her words while sitting at the woman's desk. Through this detailed and thorough analysis, Martin began to understand the course of his clients' lives. All of this information would be considered when deciding which items were safe to acquire and when the acquisitions would take place. Without this information, he would be flying blind.

But standard procedures were put aside that first day at the Grants' home as Martin made his way toward the source of the unexpected greeting. In those few moments of unplanned movement through the house, thirty-four spontaneous steps in all, Martin felt more alive and more terrified than at any other time in his career. With warning bells sounding off in his head, urging him to leave immediately, he pressed on, through a frightfully unmapped living room and into a foreign kitchen of black-and-white tile and suspended pots and pans. To the east (though he didn't know it was east at the time, forgoing the use of his compass in favor of speed) was a wide hallway lined with several closed wooden doors, and to the west were four stone steps that descended into a paneled den. At the far end of the den, perched atop a wooden post that resembled a coat rack, was a bird more than a foot tall. Covered in shades of gray feathers with a bright red tail and a solid black beak, it turned its head in Martin's direction as he came into view, made eye contact, and squawked, "Gimme kiss."

Martin froze for a moment, unsure what to do. The bird wasn't confined in a cage, and it didn't appear to be tethered to the post. For all he knew, it could attack at any moment. The warning bells began sounding again in his head, insisting that he leave at once.

But Martin maintained his ground, staring the bird down for more than a minute before slowly descending the stairs into the dimly lit den. The bird followed his progress, ruffled its feathers once, causing Martin to pause, and then repeated, "Gimme kiss."

With no intention of obeying the bird's command, Martin began surveying the room, automatically returning to familiar routines. About fifteen feet long and ten feet wide, the room was carpeted in olive green shag and dominated by a gas fireplace centered on the south wall. A small, well-stocked bar was positioned at the foot of the stairs, and a couch and several plush chairs were situated around the room. Without a conscious thought, but keeping the bird in his periphery, Martin removed the fine-point pen from his right ear, lifted the clipboard into a writing position on his hip, and began diagramming the room, noting smaller details as his eyes scanned the space. Photos of the couple lined the fireplace mantel, as well as a son and daughter at various ages and wedding photos for both. Built-in bookshelves filled the entire east wall, crammed with leather-bound novels and a complete Funk & Wagnalls encyclopedia, all of which appeared more decorative than utilitarian. The room was wallpapered in a simple floral pattern, and the curtains in the two large windows along the north wall were dusty (a confirmation of no maid service) but stylish. A teardrop-shaped coffee table with a glass top was positioned in front of the couch, covered by a round, wide vase of silk daisies (also dusty) and a neat stack of magazines, topped by Martha Stewart's *Living*. As his eyes took in these details and many more (the texture of the ceiling, the wattage of the bulbs in the overhead lamp, the temperature at which the thermostat was set), he returned his attention to the bird and noticed a small souvenir license plate nailed to the post just below the perch, the kind you find revolving in racks at shops in the airport or along the boardwalk, seemingly filled with every name but your own. The state represented was Connecticut; a blue background with raised white lettering that read "Alfredo."

"Hello, Alfredo," Martin whispered, unconsciously breaking his rule of silence when inside a client's home. The sound of his own voice startled him, shocked him really, but not nearly as much as what followed from the bird.

"Hello chickadee! What's cooking?"

At this outburst Martin gasped and found himself holding his breath, though he wasn't sure why. This was a bird, after all, and he had dealt with pets before. Never dogs, of course, but cats were common to many of his clients' homes, and he was once in a house where a ferret had been on the loose. Birds were also nothing new to Martin, though the birds he had seen thus far had been tiny little things jammed into iron cages. This bird was large, free, and talking. Worse still, it was responding to Martin's words and actions.

"Scotch and soda, please, neat," Alfredo squawked, ruffling his wings again. "Thanks mate! What's cooking? Gimme kiss! Gimme kiss! Gimme kiss!" With each word, the bird grew louder and more agitated until it appeared as if it would leap off its perch at any moment.

At this, Martin's warning bells became a cacophony of screaming sirens. He could feel himself beginning to sweat and felt a tremor in his hands. At last he succumbed to instinct. Moving quickly, unaware of his dramatic shift in speed, Martin backed up the four stairs to the kitchen, through the living room, and out the door, barely remembering to relock it as he left. Walking more quickly than he should, Martin backtracked halfway down the Grants' quarter-mile driveway before cutting into and through the woods and emerging back on Sidle Road, a side street adjacent to the reservoir, where he had parked his car in the small dirt parking lot. He drove for more than two miles before realizing that he was still wearing surgical gloves and rubber moccasins and that his lock-pick gun was lying out in the open on the passenger seat. Turning into the parking lot of a family grocer, Martin took several long breaths before restoring his Subaru and himself to proper traveling order.

Martin's initial reaction was to cancel the Grants as clients immediately, and for three days he operated under this assumption, planning no further visits to their home, though he did not delete any of the files on the Grants from his computer. Prior to his visit, Martin had conducted surveillance of the Grants' home on fourteen separate occasions, at varying times of the day, in order to identify patterns in their life. Sitting in his car, armed with his laptop, or walking the block several times with a digital voice recorder in hand, Martin would gather the information required before entering a client's home. It was during these sessions that he would look for signs of dogs and maid service, determine departure and arrival times to and from work, and identify clients' shopping patterns. Were the Grants the type of couple that stopped at the market each day, or did they do all of their shopping on Sunday? Information of this type was invaluable to Martin, and by the end of his fourteenth day, he had gathered a great deal of it on the Grants. Though he had told himself that the correct move was to cancel them as clients and delete his computer files, something inside him was still holding out hope.

Oddly enough, the reason was Alfredo.

Something about the parrot had caused Martin's mind to stir for days. Unaccustomed to daydreaming, he was surprised to find himself thinking about the bird at the oddest possible moments: while cracking hard-boiled eggs in the kitchen, while photographing a client's pantry, and while flossing for the fifth and final time that day before going to bed. He tried to dismiss his musing as ridiculous, but still his thoughts returned to the bird that had caused him to break several of his most important rules and flee recklessly from a client's home. Eventually Martin began considering a return to the Grants', for reasons he could not imagine. He didn't need the business. He had plenty of clients and plenty of new referrals worth investigating. Still, something inside him continued to tug, and so by the fourth afternoon, Martin found himself at his computer, researching parrots online. In no time he had identified Alfredo as an African gray parrot, had seen pictures of birds nearly identical to Alfredo, and had learned a great deal.

With a lifespan of up to eighty years, the African grays' claim to fame is their incredible intelligence. With vocabularies of more than a hundred words (with some birds mastering more than two thousand) and the ability to understand and use these words properly, African grays are the most verbal of all birds able to reproduce speech. Grays can also mimic just about any sound that they hear and can perform many tasks on the same level as a four-year-old child, including distinguishing colors, shapes, and numbers of objects.

But Alfredo's mental acuity wasn't the only thing that had interested him. Martin's career demanded that he work alone, and for the most part he enjoyed this element of his profession. He was his own boss, never saddled by inefficient or incompetent coworkers, yet there were times when he craved a little human contact. To combat this need, Martin maintained an almost continuous running monologue in his head, a mixture of play-by-play and commentary on his ongoing actions and decisions that filled the silence of his day. He was constantly analyzing, debating, and reconsidering his choices, and he actually found it difficult at times to turn this internal conversation off.

But there were occasions, such as when Jim told stories about interesting or unique coworkers, or spoke of receiving recognition for a job well done, that Martin lamented the solitary nature of his profession. Martin believed that he was the best there was at his work, but sadly there was never anyone with whom to share his success or celebrate his achievements.

It was also impossible for Martin to meet new people or make new friends, save at Starbucks, where Nadia and his three usual coworkers seemed to have plenty of time to chat with customers but not enough time for anything but pleasantries for their barista. Though he often said that he didn't need anyone other than Jim (and almost always believed this to be true), Martin found people to be entertaining and enjoyed getting to know them better. More precisely, he enjoyed figuring people out, uncovering their predilections, understanding their nuances, and determining what made them tick. Without coworkers, these opportunities were unavailable to him.

Recently, Martin had found himself particularly envious upon learning about Jim's new colleague, Peter. Peter was a vegan in the strictest of senses, refusing to eat even food that contained whey, a by-product of the making of cheese that manufacturers use in the production of crackers and cookies because it is both nutritious and illegal to dump into rivers and oceans (two reasons that always seemed to collide in Martin's mind). Vegetarians of Peter's ilk, as Jim had explained, do not eat whey because they do not eat cheese and eggs, and this was because of the impact that dairy consumption had on the nondairy producing animals such as bulls and roosters. Because they could not produce milk or eggs, bulls and roosters were instead killed for meat, and therefore dairy consumption indirectly contributed to the deaths of these animals.

This alone made Peter interesting to Martin. Then Peter's marriage had recently ended when his wife of a dozen years realized that she was a lesbian and had fallen in love with another woman. Though the divorce had been relatively amicable, the couple underwent a complex negotiation over the four dozen animals that they had cared for as part of their animal rescue shelter in Milford. Peter's vegan beliefs, the negotiated settlement of sheep, cats, dogs, chickens, piglets, and a goat, as well as the soap opera–type breakup, made him an interesting character in Martin's mind, but one he would probably never have the opportunity to meet because of his own career choice.

Though Alfredo was hardly a militant vegan with a lesbian for an ex-wife, he was a creature capable of communication and seemed to possess some degree of self-awareness and intelligence. To someone deprived of human contact during work hours, this appealed in ways Martin had never expected.

So, three days after his research on the African gray parrot was complete, Martin made his second visit to the Grants' home, this time planning to follow the rules that had made him so successful. Choosing a lot by the reservoir at random, Martin parked his Subaru and approached the house the same way as he had on his first visit, by cutting through the woods on Sidle Road until he emerged more than halfway up the Grants' long crushed-stone driveway.

Using his pick gun to quickly unlock the back door, Martin set his watch to count down fifteen minutes and entered the house. Though he was braced for Alfredo's greeting, he still jumped at the sound of the bird's voice.

"Welcome home, Mommy dearest!" the bird squawked.

Ignoring the greeting this time, Martin moved out of the foyer and into the living room, beginning the process of mapping that should have taken place on his first visit. Completing the outline of the room in less than three minutes, Martin crossed into the front hallway, mapping its dimensions and features, including the staircase to the second floor that he did not plan to explore on this visit. Backtracking, he turned, moving down the same hall that he had passed through on his first visit and into the kitchen, where he stopped and began mapping again.

"G'day, governor!" the bird called as Martin came into view. Stifling a smile and giving Alfredo a cursory glance to determine if the bird was on his perch (he was), Martin refocused on the kitchen and all its details. After sketching the approximate dimensions of the room, the major appliances, and the furniture, Martin turned his attention to the refrigerator doors. Refrigerators held particular interest for Martin, because they often contained revealing information about his clients. Among the assortment of photographs and recipes that decorated the Grants' Frigidaire were two items of particular interest.

The first was an appointment card from the Grants' dentist, Dr. Alfred Adams, for a date in mid-April, probably during the teachers' spring vacation. It appeared that Mr. and Mrs. Grant had scheduled their appointments back to back for convenience's sake, the first at 9:00 a.m. and the second at 9:45. This told Martin two things. First, the Grants were probably not going away on vacation in April, as many teachers did; and second, that the home would be empty from 9:00 to 10:00 a.m. on April 22, an ideal time for a visit.

The second item of interest was a wedding invitation for a weekend in late June on the Cape. Though Martin couldn't be sure that the Grants would be attending this wedding, it was something he could probably determine as the date drew near, and if they were attending, Martin could safely schedule a rare weekend visit to their home. Processing this information quickly, Martin took two pictures of the items stuck to the refrigerator before checking his watch (9:03 left) and turning east down the hallway that he had failed to explore on his first visit. The hall was flanked by two wooden doors on each side and came to a stop twenty-five feet away at a fifth door. In a home as large as this one, Martin's goal was to complete a rough sketch of every room on the first floor, locate a spare set of keys if possible, and, if time permitted, photograph the clients' food stock. Because more than 90 percent of Martin's acquisitions were made from the first floors of clients' homes, he would save the mapping of the second floor for the next visit.

Investigating each of the unlocked rooms, Martin found a spare bedroom and a bath to the north, a walk-in pantry and some type of sitting room to the south, and a home office at the end of the hall, directly east. He took six photographs of the pantry's contents, checked the usual locations for keys in the home office (finding none), and made his way back to the kitchen, photographing the interior of the refrigerator and freezer, and a shelf of cereal boxes over the sink.

He then checked his watch. Just over four minutes left. Normally Martin would use this last bit of time to make a more thorough search for spare keys, looking for hooks inside closets and behind the doors to the basement and garage, searching desk drawers and any bowls and mugs that might be spread decoratively around the house (particularly on fireplace mantels, a most common location for spare keys), and inspecting the insides of the toilet tanks. Martin knew that keys were often hidden outside as well, under flower pots and garden stones, but searching the exterior of the house was something Martin never did for fear of being seen. Even passing in front of an exposed window was something he avoided.

But Martin had come back to the Grants' house for a specific reason, for Alfredo, and so he chose to spend his last moments with the bird, though he wasn't exactly sure what he'd do. Descending the steps into the den (Martin had labeled it as such during his first visit), he approached the bird slowly. From his research, he had learned that African grays were extremely social birds and rarely aggressive, but still, he wanted to be careful.

Five steps away, the bird began speaking to Martin, more rapidly than he could have ever expected. "Hey, stupid! What's your problem? Hey! I'm talking to you! Gimme kiss! Gimme kiss! Kissy kissy!"

Though Martin was armed with his research and excitement over the bird's ability to communicate, this outburst still managed to startle him and cause his heart to race. He immediately wondered if this were a mistake after all, if he was taking too great a chance.

As doubts began to creep into Martin's mind, Alfredo began again. "G'day! G'day! G'day mate!" A brief pause, and then again. "G'day! G'day! G'day!" The bird continued this pattern, ruffling its feathers and becoming more agitated with each series of greetings. Martin found himself with an all-consuming urge to respond to the parrot, and was certain that if he did respond, the greetings would stop. But responding was dangerous, because Alfredo seemed capable of repeating anything that he heard. If his owners came home and found that the bird had acquired a new vocabulary word, they would begin to wonder from where the bird's newfound knowledge had come.

Then it occurred to him.

Although he couldn't introduce any new vocabulary to the bird, he could certainly respond using words that the bird already knew. And though he also knew that many of these birds can actually mimic the voice of an individual as well, Martin thought that if he spoke in a voice that approximated that of the bird, he would probably be safe. He considered this for a few more moments, looking for potential flaws in his logic and finding none. He would be forced to break his rule of silence while in a client's home, but found himself surprisingly willing to take the risk. Martin had established the rule in the event that there was ever a recording device running in a client's home (intentionally or accidentally), and he had adhered to it religiously until the day he'd first spoken to Alfredo. Nothing had come of that indiscretion, and though Martin despised violating any of his rules, his desire to communicate with the bird had become overwhelming. So after considering all his possibilities, Martin responded to the bird's sixth iteration of "G'day" with his own, slightly squawked "G'day, mate."

Alfredo immediately calmed at the sound of Martin's voice, settled back down on his perch, and stared with as much intensity as a bird can muster. Martin quickly removed the pen from his ear and began to make a list adjacent to the sketch of the Grants' home.

G'day
Mate
Scotch and soda please
Kissy
Gimme kiss
Hey stupid

Martin knew that the bird had said more, but he couldn't remember the words for sure and it was nearly time to go. With just over a minute left, he took one last look at Alfredo and turned in the direction of the kitchen.

"Hey stupid," the bird squawked. "Gimme kiss."

"Hey!" Martin answered, oddly hurt by the comment but stopping before saying more than his limited vocabulary would allow.

"Hey!" the bird repeated. "Hey! Hey! Hey stupid! Kissy! Kissy!"

Martin speculated as to what might constitute a kiss for a bird but had no intention of finding out. He turned again, needing to move faster this time.

"Hey dumb-ass! Scotch and soda! Neat! Neat! Neat!"

Martin wondered if Alfredo had timed his comment to match the moment that he passed by the Grants' well-stocked bar. Either way, he had to move now, ignoring his desire to turn around and scold the bird, with the dozen or so words currently available. Despite his initial affection for Alfredo, the insults were starting to wear on him.

Martin made his way back into the kitchen, taking one last peek at the bird before moving on. As he turned the corner and moved into the living room, he heard Alfredo squawk, "Arrivederci!"

"Arrivederci!" Martin squawked back, quickly adding the word to his list.

"Dumb-ass!" the bird squawked one final time, causing Martin to doubt the future of their relationship.

Since that day more than four years ago, Martin had added more than seventy words and phrases to his list and had committed most of them to memory. Today Martin spent more than five minutes with Alfredo, listening to the bird speak, responding in turn, and kissing the bird whenever Alfredo demanded. It turned out that a kiss was merely the rubbing of Martin's nose to the bird's beak, an action that had frightened Martin at first but had become second nature by now. In fact, in the time that he had gotten to know the bird, Alfredo had become very familiar with Martin, often leaping from his perch onto Martin's shoulder, as he had done today as Martin approached.

Martin was particularly amused today by a routine that he had seen only once before. Alfredo began by pretending to kiss his own foot, cooing and imitating the sound of large, wet kisses, and then suddenly, without provocation, the bird would bite his foot, screeching "Ow! You jerk! No biting!" He would then hold his foot in front of his face, staring it down like a child in a no-blinking contest. After a moment, his expression would soften and he would begin cooing again, squawking "Gimme kiss! Gimme kiss Mommy dearest!"

Martin did not believe that Alfredo had come up with this routine on his own, but he found the flair with which the bird performed the bit to be astounding. Though Martin often wore a smile of satisfaction during the workday, the smile that Alfredo brought to his face was quite different.

It was the smile of pure joy.

Following Alfredo's routine, Martin began the business that had brought him to the Grants' home in the first place. With the bird still perched on his shoulder, Martin moved to the kitchen and pantry, filling his burlap with half a bag of flour, two handfuls of artificial sweetener packets, five potatoes, a pound of lean hamburger, three boxes of frozen vegetables, and a bottle of barbeque sauce that had been in the pantry for six months without being opened. He took photographs of the usual locations, inspected the desk in the office, sorting through the mail and examining the Grants' checkbook register, looking for anything new (he would inspect the Grants' computer files the following week, as scheduled), and quickly made his way to the dining room, on the west side of the living room, the site of Martin's latest project.

Martin called large-scale acquisitions like Sophie Pearl's diamond earrings "projects" because they required more time and research than the acquisition of a few potatoes or a bottle of barbeque sauce. He had made large-scale acquisitions at the Grants' before, a string of pearls in 2005 and another in 2006, but it was the Grants' crystal and silver that had been garnering large profits for Martin most recently.

An enormous oaken hutch along the south wall of the dining room contained the Grants' collection of silver, china, and crystal. Wine and champagne glasses were hung from racks across the upper half of the hutch, and drawers of silver and a cabinet filled with china and crystal comprised the lower half. Inside the cabinet, plates, saucers, and bowls were neatly stacked in front of a large assortment of crystal that was wrapped in thick sheets of bubble wrap. When he inspected the hutch during the Grants' first month as clients, Martin had dismissed these items as unlikely future acquisitions. They seemed like the type of items that homeowners would use quite often. Still, in keeping with his thorough nature, Martin took photographs of the hutch's interior and placed a thin sliver of tape across the drawers and cabinets, just in case. When he re-inspected the hutch six weeks later, he was surprised to find the tape still in place, indicating that the cabinets and drawers hadn't been so much as touched.

His interest renewed, Martin began a more careful, two-week study of the hutch, removing each item, placing it on the dining room table to photograph and catalog, and then returning it to its original location. Crystal candlesticks and bowls were removed from their bubble wrap, silver was sorted for inventory purposes, and china was meticulously photographed for its distinctive markings. At home, he began his research, starting with a study of crystal, and he found the market to be surprisingly healthy. On eBay for example, Martin found Lalique crystal bowls selling for as much as $5,300, and Waterford decanters eliciting bids of $2,000 and more. Though the Grants did not appear to own any crystal of this value, they did own several pieces worth at least $1,000 each. And he found silver to be almost as promising.

Martin continued to survey the hutch for more than a year before planning his first acquisition, continuing his research in the meantime. In casual conversations, Martin would question Jim and his Starbucks coworkers about their silver and crystal, feigning interest by claiming that his mother had left him some when she died. In general, he found that people fell into one of two categories when it came to crystal and silver (Martin lost interest in the Grants' china since it seemed to be used more often than the other pieces).

The first category was comprised of homeowners who prized their silver and crystal and used it regularly. These people, like Jim's wife, Karen, seemed to schedule dinner parties with the express purpose of displaying their finery. Their silver was always polished, and their china and crystal pieces could be found on museum-like exhibit in glass cabinets and handmade cupboards throughout the house. These were the type of people who would likely notice if even a single piece went missing.

The second category, fortunately for Martin, were folks like the Grants, who probably received their crystal, silver, and china as wedding presents, registering for it out of obligation rather than desire. These were the homeowners whose silver was polished only on the rare days on which it was put into use and who kept their crystal stored away in cabinets and closets, still wrapped in the bubble wrap in which it was originally packaged, waiting to be passed on to some unfortunate offspring.

In the year that Martin waited and prepared, the Grants had opened their hutch cabinet twice and had opened the silver drawer three times. Each time it appeared that the only items removed from the hutch were flatware and plates, and these items were always returned by the time of Martin's next visit. Assuming that the flatware and china were probably being used for formal dinners, Martin identified a Waterford crystal bowl, wrapped in bubble wrap and stored in the rear of the cabinet, as his first target.

Martin timed this acquisition to take place immediately after the holidays. If the bowl would be used at all, he thought, it would probably be used sometime between November and January, when the Grants expected a great deal of family to visit for Thanksgiving and New Year's Day (e-mails on the Grants' computer had informed Martin of these plans). But observing no apparent use during the holiday season, Martin acquired the crystal bowl in mid-January, the first of three acquisitions from the hutch thus far. The bowl netted Martin a profit of $889, and his other acquisitions, a silver pie server and a crystal decanter, had netted a total profit of just under $3,000, minus the cost of silver polish.

The most recent project that Martin was working on was the acquisition of a silver serving tray worth more than $3,500. The tray was stored on the bottom shelf of the cabinet with a number of items atop it. Covered in a thick layer of dust, Martin was certain that the tray hadn't been touched in years, but as it was a very large item, acquiring it made him nervous. He had continued monitoring the hutch, taking photos of the contents as he normally would, but was also going so far as to apply a thin slice of tape across the cabinet doors whenever the previous seal had been broken. Martin reasoned that if the Grants weren't opening their hutch very often, it would be unlikely that they would notice the missing tray.

Martin had scheduled this next acquisition for later on in the month if everything continued on its present course, and so as he made his way across the living room and into the dining room, Alfredo still resting on his shoulder, he hoped that the hutch would show no signs of recent use. To his delight, the tape across the cabinet was still in place, indicating that the Grants had not touched it in almost six weeks.

"Hubba-bubba," Martin whispered, an expression that he had picked up from Alfredo a while ago, and one that he had begun using with Jim, much to Jim's chagrin.

"I can't hear you," Alfredo sang out. This was one of Alfredo's favorite phrases.

"Pretty bird," Martin replied apologetically, knowing that this would please his friend. Checking his watch, Martin saw that he had just over a minute before time expired, and so he moved quickly, returning Alfredo to his perch and handing the bird a walnut (making sure that it was completely eaten before turning to leave). As he exited the back door, locking it behind him with keys that he had copied long ago after finding a spare set hanging on a hook in the basement stairs, he heard Alfredo's familiar "Arrivederci!" ring out through the house.

"G'day mate!" Martin replied, stuffing the burlap into the large black backpack that he had left by the door, heading south-west through the trees toward his car, with a surprising spring in his step.

Twelve miles southeast, in Middletown, was the home of doctors Max and Emma Reed. The Reeds, a couple not yet in their forties, were among Martin's best clients for a number of reasons. Financially, they fit his criteria perfectly. Highly successful but rarely home, the Reeds' kitchen was well stocked with items that often gathered dust, passed their expiration dates, and generally went unused. The Reeds did their grocery shopping through Peapod, a delivery service operated by a local supermarket chain that allowed homeowners to place their grocery orders online and have the products delivered for a minimal charge. As busy as they were, the Reeds had a standard order that they placed each week with little variation. This meant that the same two pounds of tomatoes were delivered to their home every Tuesday, regardless of their current supply. Upon receiving the new order, the Reeds would simply rotate the week-old tomatoes into the trash bin, since it was unlikely that they would find a need for four pounds of tomatoes in any given week. For the Reeds, the money wasted in discarded perishables was offset by the time it would take to inventory their stock and alter their order.

This worked out beautifully for Martin. Having become familiar with their standard order (after accessing the Reed's personal computer), and by timing his visits just prior to a Peapod delivery, he was able to acquire items, particularly perishables such as meat and produce, with little concern over the Reeds becoming aware of his acquisitions. In fact, he felt that he was doing the Reeds a favor, since these items would normally be discarded anyway. He was simply reducing their wastefulness.

The Reeds also spent many weekends at their home in Vermont or their studio in Manhattan, allowing Martin the unusual opportunity of a weekend visit to a client. And determining whether or not the Reeds were home was simple thanks to Emma Reed's enormous collection of flags, the type that homeowners typically hang vertically off the side of a house or a garage. In all, the Reeds owned more than seventy different flags, each folded in 6" x 6" squares and stored along the north wall of the garage. There were decorative flags, American flags marking different periods in history, flags representing the seasons, holidays, sports, and even a Confederate flag, though Martin had never seen that one displayed. There were eight flags for Hanukkah, each one showing a menorah with an additional candle lit. There were flags for Arbor Day, Election Day (BE AMERICAN! VOTE!), and there were even flags for each of the Reeds' birthdays. Emma's flag was a green patchwork emblazoned with the phrase HAPPY BIRTHDAY EMMY! and Max's was a square of red fabric dominated by a birthday cake that was currently adorned with thirty-eight candles. Each year, someone (Emma, likely) squeezed another candle onto the already crowded cake with a needle and thread, adding to the patchwork of fiery reds and yellows.

But what appealed most to Martin about the flags was that each day, without fail, Emma Reed would change the flag that was displayed off the side of her garage, unless, of course, she was away. So although Martin was often able to identify the weekends that the Reeds were away by keeping track of the calendar hanging in their kitchen, the flags served as a fail-safe way of guaranteeing the couple's absence. If the same flag that had been displayed on Friday was still up by Saturday afternoon, the house was most certainly empty.

Thirteen minutes after arriving at the Reeds' house, Martin was locking the back door, backpack weighed down with a bottle of caffeine-free Diet Coke, a pound of boneless chicken breast, an avocado, half a dozen carrots, a green pepper, several cherry tomatoes, half a head of lettuce, and a book of stamps. In addition to the fresh produce and meat that Martin was often able to acquire, the Reeds unaccountably maintained a large supply of postage stamps on hand, at least five books at a time, so Martin was often able to acquire enough stamps to handle his own postage needs.

Loading the last of his groceries into the Outback, which was parked in Lot C on the campus of Wesleyan University, Martin turned back onto Route 9, heading north, heading home.

Some people can point to a specific day in their lives when everything changed. For Martin, that day was a Wednesday in October.

It was three-fifteen on an overcast afternoon and Martin was visiting his final clients for the day, Cindy and Alan Clayton of Cromwell. Cindy was a schoolteacher in Wethersfield (second grade, the last time Martin checked) and Alan owned a construction company that bought large tracts of unused woodlands and converted them into mortgage payments. When evaluating them as clients, Martin had been initially concerned about Alan's line of work, envisioning a man with the freedom to come and go as he pleased, stopping at home for lunch or taking an occasional afternoon off, but after more than a month of surveillance, he was comforted by the discovery that Alan was a workaholic, never arriving home before seven in the evening. The Claytons also kept a meticulous schedule posted on a bulletin board in their kitchen, detailing every job site and meeting where Alan would be each week, presumably so that his wife would know his whereabouts at all times. Of course, this allowed Martin to know where he was as well.

With four minutes left in his visit, Martin was in the second-floor bathroom, inventorying the contents of their medicine cabinet in preparation for a future acquisition. The Claytons' shelves were always well stocked with over-the-counter medications, more than two people could ever need. Pain pills, cold and flu treatments, skin ointments, and allergy remedies littered the shelves, and acquiring these medications had always been a fairly simple procedure. Though he would never think to acquire an entire bottle of Advil, for example, Martin considered it safe to remove a small number of pills from the bottle without anyone ever noticing. Sometime next week, after he had compared the Claytons' inventory to his own, Martin would visit again, this time equipped with a supply of plastic containers that once held rolls of camera film, each marked with the name of a medication that he planned on acquiring that day. In addition to sorting pills by type, Martin would also mark each container with an expiration date since he wouldn't have access to the original bottle at home.

Completing his inventory, Martin reached out to shut the medicine cabinet, simultaneously glancing at his watch (3 minutes, 27 seconds remaining), when the sleeve on his left arm brushed up against Cindy Clayton's electric toothbrush, standing upright at the edge of the sink, nesting in its charger. Cindy Clayton's to be sure, for the ancient plastic toothbrush, nearly devoid of bristles, that was kept in a drawer below the sink was surely her husband's. The toothbrush tottered for a moment, clinging to its perch, and then succumbed to gravity and toppled over, falling toward the open toilet bowl beside the sink.

Martin saw all this happen, as if the events were occurring in slow motion, but did nothing, his left arm frozen over the empty charger and his right affixed by his side like a slab of beef. He watched in a mixture of awe and terror as the toothbrush completed two and a half turns before slicing through the water in the bowl as smoothly as an Olympic diver. A baritone *plop*, followed the toothbrush's contact with the water, caused him to start out of his trance. Had he been more alert, there was a good chance that Martin could have caught the toothbrush on its way down, or perhaps stopped it from leaving the charger entirely, but the incident was beyond his initial comprehension.

It was something for which he was completely unprepared.

Contingency plans were Martin's bread and butter, the secret to his success, the reason he was able to work with very little anxiety or fear. He had designed plans for every conceivable emergency and genuinely loved preparing and rehearsing them. He had fire-escape plans drawn up for each of his clients' homes and rehearsed these plans yearly, as children are instructed to do when firefighters visit their schools in September with coloring books and blankets used to simulate smoke. He knew what to do in case of an earthquake and had identified the best place to stand in each of his clients' homes, even though the last earthquake of any magnitude to strike Connecticut took place on May 16, 1791 (a date Martin had committed to memory). He even had a plan of action in the event that he encountered a genuine burglar while visiting a client's home (drop to the ground, cry and beg for mercy while pretending to be a visiting cousin from Pennsylvania with little familiarity of the home). Even this he rehearsed yearly in each home (practicing the actual crying and begging from the confines of his own home), because one can never be too prepared.

But this situation was anything but conceivable. "The toilet lid should've been down to begin with!" he thought as he watched the toothbrush bob up and down in the bowl. "Why can't people put the lid down? *Why can't people put the lid down?*"

But now what?

With time running out (2 minutes, 40 seconds and counting), Martin had to make a decision. His choice seemed simple and yet impossibly difficult. He could remove the toothbrush from the bowl (thankfully he was wearing gloves, though the thought of reaching into the bowl still made him cringe), run it under hot water, dry it off and return it to the charger. No harm, no foul.

Only there would be a foul, the foulest of fouls, because this would mean that despite any amount of washing, Cindy Clayton would be brushing her teeth this evening with bristles that had been bobbing in her toilet like a buoy. And though Martin had never come face-to-face with Cindy Clayton, he felt as if he knew her intimately, and in many ways he did. Short, blond, and freckled, her photographs bespoke a woman with an easy smile and a casual style. Little makeup, even less jewelry, and a willingness to wear a wrinkled T-shirt, a pair of jeans, and a baseball cap to many a family gathering.

Martin couldn't help but like her.

In addition to knowing her eating habits, her musical preferences, and the ways in which she spent her money, he also knew the color of her panties (almost exclusively black, with a couple of jungle prints and a lacy little thong probably bought by her husband in order to spice things up), her bra size (34B), and the time of the month she menstruated (thirteen days ago). He knew that she was on the pill, kept a journal that was probably a secret from her husband, and had a vibrator in the bedside table that he suspected was not. With this knowledge, he felt as if Cindy Clayton was not only his client but was also his friend, and as such, he also felt that he had an obligation to her. He simply couldn't allow her to use a toothbrush that was, in all likelihood, permanently contaminated with fecal matter.

So his options were limited. He could remove the toothbrush from the home, but this would mean violating Rule #1:

If the missing item will be noticed, don't acquire it.

Surely Cindy Clayton would notice that her toothbrush had disappeared, and though this might prevent her from brushing her teeth with the contaminated device, it all but assured that

Martin would also be forced to discontinue the Claytons as clients.

Discontinuing a client was nothing new to Martin. He had done it many times, but never as a result of a mistake on his part. Most often, a client would become pregnant, and with the prospect of children on the way and a less predictable schedule, Martin would be forced to end the relationship. This was never easy, for he typically invested an enormous amount of time getting to know his clients, so the loss was a great one. Not only did he feel as if he was losing a business partner, but he often felt as if he were losing a friend. It was never a happy time for him, despite the couple's likely joy over the news. Typically, Martin found out about the pregnancy shortly after the client, and oftentimes on the same day. Early on in his career, he had made a point of searching the bathroom waste cans for evidence of a used home pregnancy test, and six times had found the remnants of such tests. Each time he could clearly see that the client was pregnant. Discontinuation would follow shortly thereafter.

But to discontinue the Claytons at this juncture was not something that Martin wanted to do. He liked the Claytons immensely. He found them to be a neat, orderly, and extremely reliable couple that could always be counted on in terms of schedule and acquisition potential. The Claytons did not like change. They stocked their refrigerator and cupboards with the same items each week and always placed them in the same spot. They rarely switched brands, vacationed at the same Caribbean resorts each winter, and showed no signs of planning for a new family member. Losing the Claytons would mean losing one of his most reliable clients.

It would mean losing a friend.

This left Martin with only one option: replace the toothbrush. He would have to switch Cindy Clayton's toothbrush for a new one. This meant that he would need to exit the house, acquire an identical toothbrush, and return before Cindy arrived home from work around 4:30. He knew from the calendar hanging in the kitchen that Alan was expected home at 5:00 that day for a dinner date with his wife at Chowder Pot, a Hartford-area restaurant, so as long as he was out of the house before 4:30, he would be safe. He quickly glanced at his watch again: 1 minute, 27 seconds remaining in his visit, and in the top right hand corner of the display, the actual time: 3:19. He was surprised to see that only a minute had passed since the toothbrush had taken its fateful dive. It felt like hours had passed as he had stood there, staring into the bowl. He would have just over an hour to acquire a new toothbrush.

He thought it could be done.

One more decision would need to be made before he could begin. Should he remove the toothbrush from the house in order to find its match, or should he instead commit to memory the type and model number, and perhaps take a photograph of it? Though memorizing the brand and model number initially seemed to be less dangerous than removing the entire toothbrush, Martin was worried that if he failed to return in time, Cindy Clayton would unknowingly use the contaminated toothbrush this evening, and there would be nothing that Martin could do to stop her.

On the other hand, if he removed the toothbrush and did not make it back in time, he would have no choice but to discontinue the Claytons as clients. A missing toothbrush would likely be more obvious to a client than a missing china plate or pearl necklace. Therefore, the decision was clear. He would take the toothbrush with him. As much as he valued the Claytons as clients, he could not take a chance on Cindy Clayton placing this contaminated device in her mouth.

With less than fifty seconds remaining, Martin went into action. Moving quickly, he scooped the toothbrush from the bowl, shaking it over the sink briefly in order to prevent dripping, and then slid it into his pants pocket.

As he exited the bathroom, he made a mental note to burn these pants later that day.

He then turned and headed for the rear door adjacent to the Clayton's kitchen, scooping up his backpack along the way, removing his rubber moccasins, and relocking the door with the key that he had made seven years ago after locating the spare set in the Claytons' empty sugar bowl. He was crossing the patio and squeezing between a space in the high hedgerow that bordered the rear of the Claytons' property when the alarm on his watch began vibrating, indicating his time in the Clayton home was up.

The Claytons lived in a relatively new housing development off Route 3 in Cromwell. A total of eight large homes lined the short street that ended in a cul-de-sac, and these were spaced sufficiently apart to allow Martin to exit the property without being seen. The Claytons' backyard, which included a swimming pool and bocce court, was also enclosed by a high row of hedges, allowing Martin complete concealment when gaining entry through the back door. Best of all, the Clayton home, on the eastern side of the cul-de-sac, backed onto six acres of state-owned wetlands, complete with several walking trails. In less than ten minutes, Martin could safely cross through this forested area and make his way into a retirement village with plenty of visitor parking.

As Martin crossed through the forest, picking up a trail that headed directly east toward his car, he began unconsciously thumbing the ten-sided die in his coat pocket. There were four other trails that he could have chosen, and on a typical day he would have rolled the die before leaving in order to determine his route, but time was suddenly of the essence, and so he chose the shortest and most direct means of returning to his car, even though he recognized that this was breaking another of his important rules.

He wondered how many more rules he would need to break in order to correct his mistake, and, more important, what consequences it might bring.

With this thought in mind, he broke into a run.

As he climbed the short hill leading out of the forest and into the parking lot, Martin began plotting his next move. He would need to locate a match for Cindy Clayton's toothbrush as quickly as possible, and he had several alternatives. About two miles down the road, at the junction of Route 3 and Route 9, was a Stop & Shop, a CVS pharmacy, and a little farther down the road, a Walgreens, any of which could potentially carry the toothbrush that he needed. With about an hour before Cindy Clayton arrived home, it was imperative that Martin choose the correct store.

After slamming his car door, tossing the incomplete sack of acquisitions into the backseat (another serious violation of routine), and starting the engine, Martin removed the toothbrush from his pants pocket (while keeping his latex gloves firmly affixed to his hand) and examined it more closely. About six inches in length, the toothbrush was primarily white, with green stripes stretching down opposite sides and a green on/off button in its center. The brand was Braun. Alongside one of the stripes were the words "Plak control ultra." The upper portion of the toothbrush, containing the bristle attachment, was also white and marked by the phrase "Oral-B." Other than these few distinguishing features, there were no other marks on the brush. No model or serial numbers. Martin was pleased with his decision to take the brush with him. Finding a match with this limited information would have proven difficult.

He also recognized how fortunate it was that the toothbrush, bristle attachment included, appeared to be fairly new. Had Cindy Clayton not been so vigilant about changing the bristle attachment, switching it for a new one would have been impossible. Still, Martin would need to compare the new bristles to these contaminated ones before he made the switch, to ensure that they were similar enough to pass for the old ones. He was suddenly appalled to realize that he had failed to factor this in while standing inside the Claytons' bathroom. *This is what happens when rules are broken and work is rushed*, he thought to himself as he shifted into drive and made his way out onto Route 3.

Eliminating Walgreens because of its distance from the Clayton home, Martin refrained from finalizing his decision between Stop & Shop and CVS until the last possible moment, hoping to receive divine inspiration during the eight minutes it took to enter the plaza's crowded parking lot.

None came.

In the end, Martin chose CVS because he knew the store carried electric toothbrushes of some kind, and armed with this bit of information, he made the decision. But in choosing a parking spot, he chose to hedge his bet, landing a spot seven rows deep between the two stores. Throwing the car into park and checking his watch (3:41), Martin uncharacteristically raced toward the pharmacy's automatic doors.

Upon entering the store, Martin headed for the back, knowing well that toothpaste, dental floss, and mouthwash were found in one of the back rows of his own local store. As he walked quickly through the magazine aisle, an elderly man pushing one of CVS's miniaturized shopping carts gave him an odd stare and continued to stare until Martin turned the corner and entered the "Oral Hygiene" aisle.

"Bingo," he whispered to himself, standing in front of a large display of electric toothbrushes. Reaching into his pocket,

Martin removed Cindy Clayton's toothbrush for a second time, suddenly realizing that he was still wearing the latex gloves that he had put on before entering the Clayton home. This triggered another realization. He was also still wearing the hairnet that he had put on as well, and because he had apparently lost his hat somewhere between the Clayton home and the pharmacy (*Did I take it off in the car?* he wondered), he must have looked fairly odd to anyone who had seen him, including the old man in aisle 4.

Martin quickly removed the hairnet and stuffed it into his coat pocket but kept the gloves on, still loath to make contact with the contaminated toothbrush. Holding it up in front of him, he began slowly moving it from left to right, comparing it with the wide variety of electrics on display. In less than a minute, he had located the brand and type for which he was searching, but much to his horror, could not locate the green color that he required. Navy blue and maroon were present in great numbers, but no green.

He considered asking a clerk to check the supplies in back, then looked again at his watch (3:45) and determined that trying Stop & Shop would likely be quicker. In less than two minutes, he was once again facing a display of electric toothbrushes, this time in the wider and better-lit aisles of the grocery store, and to his relief, saw the required toothbrush in the required brand and color almost immediately. Grabbing it, he ran toward the register, fearful of the attention that he was drawing with his dead sprint but finding exhilaration in it as well. This type of reckless abandon was something new for Martin, and he could feel every nerve in his body tingle like never before. He was equally pleased to see that while the regular checkout lines were long, the express line (ten items or less) was empty.

It was as he was placing the toothbrush on the unmoving conveyor belt that he realized he did not have his wallet. He never carried his wallet while visiting clients, considering its presence unnecessary and a potential danger. His general rule was to carry only those things that were required for the job, and he adhered to this rule save one sentimental item that he kept tucked away in his back pocket whenever he worked. Anything extra posed a hazard, and a wallet, capable of identifying him beyond a shadow of a doubt, posed the greatest hazard of all. Instead, he kept his wallet in a small compartment in the Subaru, just below the radio. It was sitting there as the cashier reached to scan the toothbrush.

"Wait!" he stammered, reaching his latexed hand out and snatching the toothbrush from the cashier's grasp. "I forgot my wallet."

Martin turned and ran for the exit when the cashier's voice brought him to a stop in front of the automatic doors. "Sir! You can't take that with you. You haven't paid for it."

The cashier's voice was loud enough for all around them to hear, and Martin felt a hundred eyes suddenly fall upon him, including those of a bullet-shaped man wearing a striped tie and a gold Stop & Shop name badge identifying him as a manager. The man took two slow steps in Martin's direction, apparently waiting for Martin's next move.

"Sorry . . . ," Martin said with a smile, suddenly understanding how the situation must appear. A man wearing latex gloves is seen running for the doors as a cashier shouts for him to stop. His haste was causing him to act erratically. *This can't be good,* he thought.

With as much calm as he could muster, Martin sidled his way back to the cashier and handed the toothbrush back to the boy, a teenager of pimples and piercings, and asked that he hold on to it for a moment. "I'll be right back."

Martin then walked out of the store as casually as possible while the eyes around him slowly returned to their prior business. Once in the relative anonymity of the parking lot, he burst into a sprint again while simultaneously fumbling for his keys in his jacket pocket.

Martin did not see the Nissan bread truck pulling away from the curb as he ran directly into its path, causing the truck to come to a screeching halt less than a foot from Martin's now frozen position. He could see the driver, a man who looked more tough and weathered than Martin could ever hope to be, glaring down at him, the middle finger on his right hand extended in Martin's direction. Martin bowed awkwardly toward the man in an act of panicked contrition and then resumed his flight to the car. Less than a minute later he was reentering the store, transitioning his sprint to a trot as he made a hard right through the produce section back toward the checkout lines.

He was pleased to see that since he had been gone, only one person had gotten in line in front of him, a middle-aged lady wearing a ridiculous combination of paisley skirt, fuzzy pink socks, and black patent-leather shoes. She had a purse large enough to house a family of rabbits and was in fact piling celery, carrots, parsley, and oatmeal onto the short conveyor belt, as if planning for the family's next feast.

Martin took up his position behind the woman and watched as she scrutinized each item as it was scanned with the concentration of a cellular biologist, eyes buried in a microscope. Twelve items in all, Martin noticed, two over the express-line limit, but since the cashier had scanned the first item (oatmeal, a brand that the Reeds were fond of as well), Martin decided that it would be quicker if he just allowed her to pay and leave.

The problem was that the woman appeared to have no inclination to pay. While Martin stood ready with two twenty-dollar bills in hand, the woman's hands were white-knuckled around the handle of her purse, squeezing it shut as if the rabbits inside were attempting a jailbreak. Frozen in place, her eyes shifting from the product being scanned to the computer monitor that illuminated its price, she made no effort to speed up the process.

Martin glanced at his watch, and as he did, his mind filled with numbers. 3:51. 7 items to go. 4 miles back to the Claytons' house. 10 minutes through the forest, maybe 5 if he sprinted. 4:30 deadline. 5 items to go. $3.14 for the celery.

And still the woman hadn't moved.

Finally the last item was scanned and bagged, and the cashier announced the total in a voice that sounded as if the boy was battling puberty and losing. "Your total's $23.58." Martin watched in shock as the woman still refused to move, standing there for a moment as if she was deciding if the total was acceptable. After an interminable pause, she placed her bag down, opened it up, and began fishing through its contents (Martin imagined a pair of withered hands pushing baby rabbits aside), at last removing a thick red wallet. Wallet retrieved, she placed it down, opened it, removed a checkbook (*She's paying by check!* he screamed to whoever might be listening inside his head), and requested a pen from the cashier. The boy paused for a moment, looked across his work area, and then found the pen resting atop his keyboard. Slowly, the woman began to write.

"Is it all right if I make it out for twenty extra?" she asked as she finished filling in the date.

"Yeah," the cashier replied. "As long as you have a Stop & Shop card."

"Well, I showed you my card before you checked me out, so you know I have it," the woman shot back, causing her to pause once again.

"Yes, I know . . . I just meant . . . that that's why I . . . I mean . . . you can do it."

"What was my total again?" she asked, irritation still lingering in her voice.

"If I don't make it back in time," Martin thought, "it will be because of this ridiculous conversation."

Two minutes later the check was finally written. The woman had received her twenty dollars ("Could you please give me three fives and five ones?"). She then began reversing the process. Without surrendering her position in front of the cashier, she recorded the check amount in the check register, closed the checkbook, and returned it to the wallet. She then closed the wallet and returned it to the purse. Finally, she closed the purse and gathered her bags.

Martin was afraid to look at his watch.

Toothbrush in hand and $38.14 lighter, Martin started his car and headed for the parking lot exit, only then daring to look at the time: 4:02. This meant that Cindy Clayton was already on her way home.

When Martin had initially researched the Claytons as potential clients, he found that the final bell at Cindy Clayton's school rang at 3:50 each day. Children spilled out of the classroom doors, buses pulled away from the building, and about ten minutes later Cindy Clayton would walk across the playground to her car and begin the thirty-minute drive home. In the three weeks that Martin followed her, Cindy Clayton never arrived home before 4:30 and would oftentimes stop to pick up groceries at a small market down the street before coming home, putting her arrival time closer to 5:00.

Martin desperately prayed that this would be one of those days.

There were a total of four traffic lights between the store and the Clayton home, and on the way to the store Martin had gotten very lucky, catching them all green. His return trip was not so fortunate. Three of the lights were red, including the light at the intersection before Route 9, which had a line of cars so long that it took Martin nearly four full minutes to get through. As he sat in the car, waiting for it to turn green a second time, staring at the clock in the dashboard (which was synchronized to his watch), he tried to visualize what he would need to do next. By visualizing future actions, Martin had found, he was able to reduce his anxiety and act with confidence. Acting with confidence might mean the difference between success and failure.

He pictured himself pulling into the nursing home, parking illegally in one of the numbered spots closest to the path, and running as fast as possible to the Clayton home, using the most direct route he knew. Crossing through the hedgerow and across the yard, he would open the back door, leaving the key inside the lock in order to save time. A few precious seconds might end up meaning a great deal, and once inside the house, his only method of egress would be through the rear door, so leaving the key wouldn't pose a problem as long as he remembered to take it as he left. He made a quick mental note in his head, connecting the key to the Claytons' bocce ball court. By linking the two in his mind, imagining one literally atop the other, he would automatically remember the key as he passed by the bocce court if he hadn't already. This was a strategy that Martin had used for most of his life with great success.

Inside the house, he would make his way to the upstairs bathroom, slowing only to ascend the steps. Once in the bathroom, he would place the new toothbrush in the charger, removing the batteries from the old brush and placing them in the new one. Though part of him was loath to place the contaminated batteries in Cindy Clayton's new toothbrush, this was a sacrifice that he was willing to make. On a future visit, he would switch the batteries for clean ones, hopefully before Cindy Clayton found the need to change them herself.

With the toothbrush in place, he would make his exit as quickly as possible, once again slowing only to descend the stairs.

Once outside with key in hand, he would cross the backyard, pass through the hedgerow, and step into the relative safety of the woods behind the Clayton home, where he would resume his normal routine. He visualized each moment in his mind, imagining himself carrying out his plan with every possible detail. If things went well, he estimated that he could make it to the Clayton home and be in and out in less than twenty minutes. If he could arrive at the nursing home in the next eight minutes, he might have a chance.

At 4:13, three minutes behind schedule, Martin's Outback roared into the Shady Glen parking lot and screeched to a halt in the space marked 73. He was out of his car and running through the forest in less than a minute.

The first flaw in his plan became evident as he reached the hedgerow guarding the rear of the Clayton property. His watch read 4:22, meaning there was a chance, however slight, that Cindy Clayton was already home. If he reentered the house without knowing for certain that it was empty, he would be placing himself in great jeopardy.

Without pausing for more than a moment to consider the problem, Martin began moving east along the hedgerow, far enough along to bring the driveway, which was thankfully adjacent to the east side of the house, into view.

No car.

Standing behind the hedgerow, trying to force his body to conform to its prickly contours, Martin thought back upon his month of surveillance, trying to recall if Cindy Clayton typically parked her Toyota Corolla in their three-car garage. He couldn't remember for certain. Considering that the garage doors were on the side of the house and not facing the street, anyone who parked in the driveway would have to walk through the garage or around the house to the front door in order to gain entry.

Quickly scanning the many windows that faced the backyard and not seeing anyone moving within the house, Martin passed through the hedgerow and maneuvered around the pool toward the garage, keeping low and moving quickly. He came to a stop at a small window that offered a view to the inside of the garage. Flattening his body as close to the vinyl siding as possible, he peeked in and was relieved to see that it was empty.

Cindy Clayton was not yet home.

Moving with more freedom now, Martin made his way across the back lawn, stopping to pick up the cap that had fallen off during his hasty exit from the home. He had completely forgotten about the hat while inside Stop & Shop and had never bothered to check the Subaru for it on the way over to the nursing home. This uncharacteristic carelessness ground away at the confidence that he was so desperately trying to muster. Martin moved to the rear door and opened it, leaving the key in the door as he had planned and taking a moment to replace his hairnet and cap. This was a step that he had forgotten in his visualization exercise, and his near neglect frightened him.

What else might he have forgotten?

Crossing the threshold and closing the door behind him, Martin made his way through the kitchen, past the living room, and toward the stairs, taking a moment to look outside at the street to see if any cars were visible in the cul-de-sac.

None.

As he reached the stairs, he risked a glance at his watch.

4:26.

He had wasted more than two minutes determining if Cindy Clayton was home, and it suddenly occurred to him that he could have called the Claytons on his way through the forest to ascertain this information. Another missed opportunity, and because of it, he had even less time to spare. Moving as quickly as he dared up the stairs, Martin arrived back in the bathroom with a sigh of relief. Almost over. He was about to pull off the most daring stunt that he had ever attempted.

But Martin's problems were just beginning.

As he removed the new toothbrush from his jacket pocket, he realized with unmitigated horror that the toothbrush was still encased in its plastic container, the type of plastic designed by the communist architects who built maximum security prisons for the North Koreans.

For the first time that Martin could remember, his hands began to shake inside a client's home.

Examining the plastic that encased the toothbrush, Martin saw a thin dotted line completely encircling the perimeter of the two pieces of plastic that had been fused together around it. Though part of his mind screamed that this dotted line was only a mocking attempt at perforation, Martin nevertheless gripped the plastic with all his might and began pulling, listening for the satisfying sound of popping plastic but hearing nothing. Sweat began to soak his skin like never before. After about thirty seconds of effort, he surrendered, realizing his only choice was to find a pair of scissors and cut the toothbrush free.

Martin paused for a moment, placing the toothbrush on the sink, forcing himself to calm down and think. He had searched the Clayton home many times and should know where they kept their scissors. Unfortunately, however, scissors had never appeared on any of Martin's acquisition lists (his mother had left him several excellent pairs), so the whereabouts of the Claytons' scissors had never made an impression in his mind. Martin also knew that scissors were an item that people kept in the most random places possible—sewing baskets, desk drawers, kitchen drawers, junk drawers, tool benches—and that their location often changed following each use.

And then it hit him. Cindy Clayton owned an impressive set

of Wüsthof knives that likely included a pair of poultry shears. Though Martin's mother had forbidden him from ever using cooking shears for anything but food (once reprimanding him for using them to cut paper), he felt that this was an emergency.

Moving at what Martin would have considered an unsafe speed on any other day, he bounded down the stairs two at a time and skidded to a stop in the kitchen, finding the shears in the butcher-block knife rack, exactly where he expected them to be.

Unfortunately, he had failed to bring the toothbrush with him, and his watch now read 4:31. Cindy Clayton could be home at any minute.

Grabbing the shears, Martin turned and headed back upstairs for the third time today, faster than he had ever ascended stairs before, which was especially dangerous considering the kitchen shears in his left hand. Once inside the bathroom, he tried to remain calm and cut along the plastic in a spot that seemed most logical, but he quickly found himself tearing haphazardly at the plastic with the shears. He could feel the panic building yet could do nothing about it. Blind action had taken the place of reason, and he was acting on adrenaline and instinct. In a little more than a minute, the toothbrush had been extracted from its plastic shell and he was opening the battery compartment at the bottom of the brush in order to load the batteries.

It was at that moment that Martin heard a car door slam.

Cindy Clayton was in her garage.

Martin had hoped to hear the automatic garage door issue a final warning to flee the premises in the event that Cindy arrived home before he could complete the job, but the noise of the kitchen shears battling the herculean plastic shell had apparently masked the expected sound. His hands began shaking uncontrollably at the double beep of a car alarm being activated.

He looked up in the mirror of the medicine cabinet and saw a man about to fall apart.

Despite the sweat that streaked his hair and face, his skin was frighteningly pale. His eyes were huge and seemed to be erupting from their sockets. His breathing was rapid and shallow. His heart raced. His feet felt rooted to the bathroom tile. He wondered if he would be able to move again before the police arrived.

With the new toothbrush poised in his right hand, battery compartment now open, Martin paused in the upstairs bathroom of Cindy Clayton's home, with the homeowner in the garage and just seconds from entering the house. He stopped all action, lowered his shoulders, unclenched his teeth, and relaxed the tight fists that he had unconsciously formed. He stared into Cindy Clayton's bathroom mirror for more than thirty precious seconds, slowing and deepening his breathing, attempting to relax his body. He knew that he had one chance. If he could regain his wits and begin to think logically, he might have a chance to escape.

Martin heard the connecting door between the garage and the house open, and listened to Cindy Clayton's first step into the mudroom. Still he remained fixed in place, empty battery compartment anxiously awaiting its new arrivals. He waited fifteen seconds more until he was sure that he was calm enough to proceed, until the man in the mirror was ready for action. His breathing had returned to normal. The color was returning to his cheeks. The quaking of his hands was finally subsiding. As he listened to Cindy Clayton drop her keys onto the marble countertop of her kitchen, Martin began to move like the methodical Martin of old.

As quickly and carefully as possible (for he couldn't risk dropping something on the floor now), he removed the batteries from the old toothbrush and placed them into the new one, making sure that they were facing the correct way, positive side up.

Cindy Clayton closed a door downstairs, and a moment later Martin heard a toilet lid connect with the toilet tank. He smiled. Even though she was home alone, Cindy Clayton was one of those people who always closed the door when using the bathroom.

He wasn't surprised.

Martin placed the new toothbrush on its charger and quickly compared the old to the new. Though the bristles were not an exact match, they were close. Martin felt sure that Cindy Clayton would never notice the swap.

Downstairs, a toilet flushed.

Martin quickly scanned the bathroom, retrieving the four pieces of plastic that had been discarded in the sink during the extraction process. He placed the plastic shards, as well as the shears, into his right coat pocket and exited the bathroom, moving as silently and slowly as possible into the upstairs hall.

Downstairs, Cindy Clayton was washing her hands. Martin was happy to discover that Cindy washed her hands after using the bathroom, even when no one was around to notice. He knew that only one in six Americans washed their hands after using the bathroom. He also knew that someone as predictable and neat as Cindy would be one of them.

To Martin's right was a six-foot stretch of hall that ended with the entrance to the master bedroom. To his left were two guest bedrooms and an office. He moved into the guest bedroom closest to the stairs, careful not to make a sound, and pressed himself against the wall adjoining the door. There he listened and waited.

Downstairs Martin heard a refrigerator open and close, heard liquid being poured, and heard the refrigerator door open and close again. This also pleased Martin. He knew that Cindy

Clayton was not the type to leave the refrigerator door wide open while pouring a drink. Everything that he might have guessed about the woman was so far correct.

Confidence began to replace fear.

Martin then heard steps and listened as Cindy Clayton moved through the kitchen, across the living room, and began ascending the stairs toward him. Again he was relieved. Had she spent too much time in the kitchen, she might have noticed the missing shears. Had she gone into the backyard, she would've seen his key sticking in the lock. Martin had left a great deal of evidence behind, but so far his luck had held out.

At the top of the stairs, Cindy turned left toward her master bedroom.

This would be Martin's opportunity to make it down the stairs undetected. Only six feet of hallway to cross before the first stair. But the problem was that Cindy Clayton's master bedroom was at the very end of the hallway. If she were standing in the center of the room, she would be able to see into the hall as Martin made his move.

Quickly, he brought to mind the layout of the bedroom, a room he had been in dozens of times. Closets to the far left of the room, well out of sight of the hallway. The bed in the center of the room, facing the hall, with bureaus flanking it along the back wall. A hope chest and rolltop desk on the far right wall. The television just to the right of the door, positioned for ideal viewing while lying in bed. A treadmill off to the right, also far out of view.

If Cindy decided to watch television, he would be trapped. She would probably be sitting or lying on the bed in order to do so. If she changed her clothing and opened one of the sliding closet doors, Martin would likely hear the door move on its track and could move then. He waited, listened, and hoped.

A muffled thump. Probably a bureau drawer. A period of

silence. Another thump. An exhale. And then the television. Oprah Winfrey's voice. She was talking about some kid in West Virginia who had saved his dog's life, or maybe the other way around. Martin's shoulders sagged.

He was trapped.

As he began considering the possibility of hiding under the bed overnight and waiting until Cindy and Alan left for work the next morning, a loud humming emerged from the bedroom, followed by the rhythmic thumping of feet. Cindy Clayton had stepped onto her treadmill. Oprah was keeping her company on her walk to nowhere.

Without wasting a second, Martin moved into the hallway with confidence, knowing that as long as he heard the thumping of feet, he would be clear of Cindy's view. He moved to the stairway, staying as far left as possible, worried that Cindy might be able to see the edge of the stair from her treadmill if she was leaning over at all. He paused for a moment at the top of the stairs, took a deep breath, and began walking down, slowly and silently, his feet registering no sound on the carpeted surface. Though he felt the irresistible urge to run, a feeling similar to the one that he had experienced as a child when ascending the stairs from a basement that frightened him badly, he fought the urge and remained calm.

As he reached the bottom of the stairs and began turning right into the living room, feeling home-free, he heard a toilet flush in the downstairs bathroom, just feet from where he was now standing.

Alan Clayton was also home.

Unlike his wife, Alan Clayton did not believe in closing the bathroom door while urinating, nor did he feel that washing his hands was terribly important. On the sound of the flush, a streak of fear, electric and tangible, shot through Martin's body, and he began to involuntarily back up in the direction of the staircase that he had descended just seconds before. As he stepped back into the recess of the living room, he caught a momentary glimpse of the bald-headed homeowner as he emerged from the bathroom, turning right toward the kitchen. The button-down shirt that he was wearing was untucked and open, exposing a once-white undershirt underneath. Though shorter than Martin, the man was huge in bulk, his biceps and shoulders stretching the fabric of the undershirt. His hands also looked large, no doubt muscled from hours at a construction site.

Had he not been fumbling to refasten the button on his jeans (completely dressing oneself before exiting the bathroom was apparently not a priority for Alan Clayton either), he might have seen Martin moving backward, just beyond his field of vision. A second later, the man appeared in full view, turning into the kitchen, his back to Martin.

Martin stood less than fifteen feet from the man, a bulky thirtysomething, exactly one room away, the only demarcation between the two rooms being a changeover from beige carpet to kitchen tile. The two men were standing close enough for Martin to hear Alan Clayton's breathing, and for this reason, he was holding his own breath.

Martin knew that he had little time to make a decision. There were only three exits from the living room. The first was through the kitchen and out the patio door that still held his key. This exit was inaccessible as long as Alan Clayton occupied the kitchen.

The second was through the front door of the house, located at the foot of the stairs, but Martin did not dare open that door and create the sounds surely associated with its opening.

The third was back up the stairs to the second floor, where Cindy Clayton could still be heard thumping away on her treadmill. Though this was clearly the safest option, Martin wasn't sure if he could make it back up the stairs quickly and quietly enough to remain undetected, and moving further into the house and away from his only method of egress was not at all appealing.

In most homes, Martin would have been able to walk past the stairs into another room, customarily a dining room or den, but since the Claytons had designed the home themselves, a coat closet stood where an entrance to another room was usually positioned. Though this might also make a decent hiding place, the door to the closet was also closed, and Martin couldn't risk the sound of it swinging open and shut.

Still frozen in the southeast corner of the living room, Martin watched as Alan Clayton strode across the kitchen, opened the refrigerator door, and stuck his reflective head inside. He sensed that there were only seconds in which to act. If Alan Clayton turned even slightly, Martin's frame would fill his line of sight.

With beer in hand, Alan Clayton closed the refrigerator door, popped the tab on the can, and turned directly toward the living room. "Hey!" he shouted loud enough to send a second streak of fear through Martin's body as he lay crouched behind the sofa along the south wall of the room. There was just enough space for a person to navigate between the sofa and the south wall, and Martin had ducked into the space with just seconds to spare, stomach pressed to the ground, shoulder jammed against a gold-plated lamp, willing himself to be small and compact as possible.

This was actually a very good hiding spot. If Alan Clayton's intention was to visit his wife upstairs, he would likely walk right past Martin without noticing him. Only by taking a severe turn to the right or looking over his shoulder while passing the sofa would he discover Martin's location.

"How's it going?" Cindy Clayton responded breathlessly to her husband's call, the first time Martin had ever heard the woman's surprisingly soprano voice.

"Good!" Alan replied from somewhere in the living room, probably less than ten feet from the intruder hiding behind his sofa. The voice was so loud and so close that Martin couldn't believe that he hadn't been seen yet and then began to wonder if he had been spotted and was now being stalked by the home-owner.

"When are we leaving?" the man shouted.

"In an hour or so," his wife replied. "I'm going to run for another twenty-five minutes and then get ready, okay?"

"Fine," Alan replied in a cheery voice but then growled so that only Martin could hear, "Then why the hell did I need to be home by five?"

"Did you need to shower?"

Even without a wife, Martin recognized this statement for what it was. Cindy Clayton was telling her husband to shower, framing the command as a question.

"Yeah, I'll shower," Alan Clayton replied without much enthusiasm, and Martin breathed an infinitesimal sigh of relief.

With one homeowner on the treadmill and another soon to be in the shower, his opportunity to escape was likely near.

The sound of the television, the voice of two men arguing about the state of American tennis, followed by the billowing of the fabric covering the rear of the sofa, caused Martin to quickly rethink this assumption. Though there might be a shower in his near future, Alan Clayton was settling in for some television, less than three feet away from Martin's prone position. In fact, in turning his head and looking up, Martin could see the back of Alan Clayton's bald head, almost within arm's reach. The two men were literally inches apart.

Martin's situation had suddenly become even more dangerous. Though his hiding spot had made it difficult for anyone ascending the stairs to see him without looking back, someone coming down the stairs and turning into the living room would undoubtedly spot the strange man crouching behind the sofa. If Cindy Clayton came down the stairs to check up on her husband before Martin was able to move, he would almost surely be spotted.

Violence was the first, albeit uncharacteristic, solution that entered Martin's mind. With the element of surprise on his side and a relatively large, metallic lamp within reach, Martin felt that he could probably knock the considerably larger man unconscious and escape before Alan Clayton ever knew what hit him. The more he thought about it, the more he became convinced that it was possible. He envisioned himself reaching over and silently unplugging the lamp from its socket (thankfully it was off), rising to his knees, head down, gripping the lamp's thin stalk with both hands, and then swinging in one swift, violent motion. If his aim were true, the base of the lamp would connect with Alan Clayton's skull and, if not render him unconscious, certainly stun the man long enough for Martin to effect his escape.

Martin was not an aggressive man and had only once in his life committed any act that might be considered violent, and so his decision to spare Alan Clayton's skull was likely the result of his natural aversion to violence. But what finalized this decision was twofold.

First, despite his precarious position and potential for discovery, Martin continued to think of Alan Clayton as a client rather than an adversary, and so harming him in any way was unacceptable. After all, the client had done nothing wrong. Though it was probably his fault that the upstairs toilet lid had been left open that day, Alan Clayton was acting like any client should. Martin knew that the man was expected home by five o'clock that day, and so he had simply complied with his kitchen calendar. His actions were both scheduled and predictable, so if anyone was to blame for Martin's current predicament, it was himself alone. Martin knew that it had been a mistake to reenter the house in the first place. He had violated one of his most important rules. There was no reason for Alan Clayton, a loyal and dependable client for years, to suffer as a result of Martin's failure. Though a bit of a slob and not the kind of guy Martin would normally befriend, Alan Clayton was also the man who wrote to his mother in Nevada at least once a week and always included a $100 check with a message on the memo line reading *Have some fun on me, Mom!*

He might be disgusting by Martin's standards, but he wasn't a bad guy.

But it was the lack of hair atop Alan Clayton's head that truly sealed his decision. As Martin visualized the attack, he also visualized the result of the blow, and on a bald-headed man, this vision was not pretty. Had Alan Clayton been blessed with a full head of hair, Martin's imagination might have been able to ignore the deep gash and spurting blood that would surely result from the head wound that he intended to deliver. But with a skull shaved perfectly bald, the result of the blow would have been impossible to ignore. Though he doubted that he would permanently harm or kill Alan Clayton, the exposed damage that would be left behind was too much for Martin to contemplate.

With a violent solution cast aside, Martin began pondering other possibilities and accepting the notion that he might soon be found. Only once before had he been discovered by a client, and that incident had occurred long before Martin had turned professional.

In many ways, the event had propelled him forward on his career path.

Martin had been nineteen years old at the time. He had been on his own for about four months, living with Jim in a two-bedroom apartment in Vernon, Connecticut. Working part-time at the Dunkin' Donuts on Talcottville Road, he had had almost no disposable income and was often forced to eat elbow macaroni and Campbell's soup for breakfast, lunch, and dinner. Jim was attending the University of Connecticut, and his parents were paying his tuition. But other than the check that they sent to the college twice a year, Jim was also supporting himself. And with a full class schedule, he was under even worse financial constraints than Martin. Between the two of them, they could barely afford rent and electricity and had spent their first winter together without heat except on the coldest of nights.

Things became desperate in January when Dunkin' Donuts began cutting back on Martin's hours as business slowed following the holidays. Working less than twenty hours a week, he had been looking for other employment when the alternator on his 1978 Chevy Malibu failed, Jim came up short with his share of the rent, and their toilet became hopelessly clogged. Though he managed to repair his car and cover Jim's rent that month (an act of kindness that Jim had never forgotten), he was left with absolutely no money for groceries, including the Liquid Plumbr that he would need in order to clear the pipes in his toilet. With no other options, Martin turned in the only direction he could.

His parents.

Martin's mother had remarried when he was seven years old, and so the stepfather that he would grow to hate more and more through the years was the only father that Martin had ever truly known. Martin remembered his biological father as a brave and strong man who had failed to act as such when thrown out of his house by a wife who had fallen in love with another man. He had left with his proverbial tail between his legs, and Martin was left with a stepfather whom he despised.

By the time he was a junior in high school, his stepfather (aided by his mother's compliance) had managed to convey the message that upon graduation, Martin would be moving out, releasing his parents from any financial responsibility. Avoiding words, his parents had initiated their plan with a series of gifts designed to convey this message for them: a microwave oven for his sixteenth birthday, a set of towels at Christmas of the same year, and a vacuum cleaner and set of dishes on his eighteenth birthday. All of these gifts sent a clear message to Martin: You will need these things because you will be leaving us soon.

Despite his solid academic background, "college" was a word never mentioned in Martin's home, and somehow he had managed to escape high school without a guidance counselor ever discussing the prospect with him. Perhaps Mr. Malloy had called Martin's parents early on and received word about their unspectacular vision of Martin's future. Or, more likely, Mr. Malloy, who also served as the school's track and field coach, had spent all his time on athletes and student government members and had forgotten about the quirky little kid with good grades but little personality.

So in January, with the heat set at forty-five degrees and the cupboard literally bare, Martin went home for help. His initial plan had been to explain the recent string of bad luck to his parents and ask for assistance until he found more work. It was a Tuesday evening in February when he arrived at the front door of his parents' house and found the windows completely dark. His parents were uncharacteristically out for the evening, and Martin couldn't imagine where they might have gone. If anyone had a predictable schedule, it was his parents.

Martin turned and headed back toward his car when he realized that he still had a house key, and with a belly grumbling from a day's worth of missed meals (apart from the doughnuts he devoured at work), Martin decided that it was time to eat.

It was odd to think of himself as a stranger in his childhood home, but as he fried eggs on a stove that his mother had used to cook his meals for more than eighteen years, the sense that he was an intruder intensified. Though it hadn't occurred to him when he cracked his first egg, by the time the toast was brown and the eggs were well scrambled, he had begun to suspect that his parents, particularly his stepfather (though his mother would surely be standing beside her husband, silent and compliant), would not approve of his unsanctioned use of the kitchen and his consumption of their food. By the time Martin was buttering the last piece of toast, he had convinced himself of the severe reprimand that he would receive from his parents for the intrusion, and had decided to make every effort to escape before being noticed.

Not knowing where his parents were or when they would return made this process a stressful one for Martin. He began by rinsing off the dishes, initially forgoing the time it would take to apply soap but quickly realizing that if he did not take the time to wash the dishes thoroughly, his parents would determine on their own that someone had been in the house. Suspicion would then naturally fall upon the only other person with a key. This stress-filled balance between washing quickly and washing meticulously served as the basis for many of Martin's future business decisions.

He never wanted to be in a similar situation again.

With the dishes washed, dried, and replaced in the cupboards as close to their original positions as he could remember (another problem Martin would later rectify, through the use of digital photography), he turned his attention to the kitchen surfaces: the stove, the sink, and the small round table upon which he had eaten. Wiping these surfaces with paper towels that he then stuffed into his pants pockets, he had the entire kitchen cleaned and returned to what he hoped was its original condition in less than ten minutes. He was pleased with himself. He thought that the chances were good that his presence would go undetected.

Martin felt less confident about the food that he had eaten. Four slices of bread for toast, three eggs, and nearly a half stick of butter were impossible to replace without more time. He felt that the missing bread would likely go unnoticed, but he was less certain about the eggs and especially the butter. His mother loved to bake, and if she had recently cooked up something that required butter, she was likely to remember exactly how much was left. In addition, butter was not a product whose loss was easily attributed to someone else in the home. It would be difficult for his mother to imagine that her husband had gone through half a stick of butter on his own. After all, there's only so much a person who doesn't bake can do with butter.

In order to deal with this problem, Martin removed a whole stick of butter from the box in the refrigerator (leaving three sticks behind), and lopped off slightly less than a third of it before placing the rest on the butter dish. He stuffed the remaining butter in his pocket, reasoning that it was more likely that his mother knew how much butter was on the butter dish than how many sticks were left in the box.

As for the eggs, there was nothing Martin could do except move three of them forward to the front row of the egg drawer, hoping that their loss would go unnoticed. Despite the missing food items, Martin felt that his chances were good that his visit would remain undiscovered.

He was exiting the house, wishing he hadn't parked in the driveway, when the need to urinate reminded him that his toilet at home was still clogged and in desperate need of Liquid Plumbr. This was a product that his parents always kept on hand (his mother had always been a practitioner of the lots-of-toilet-paper single-flush method), and Martin felt with certainty that he could remove a bottle without it ever being missed. He raced to the upstairs linen closet, found two bottles in their accustomed spot on the closet floor, and took the one already open. This, unlike the butter, was a product whose disappearance could easily be attributed to another person in the house, as its use was probably not advertised.

With Liquid Plumbr now in hand, Martin had made it halfway down the brick walkway to the driveway when the lights of his parents' Oldsmobile blinded him. Not expecting another car in the driveway, his stepfather skidded to a halt just inches from the Malibu's rear bumper. He was out of the car in seconds, shouting at Martin as he closed the gap between them.

"What the hell do you think you're doing parking in the middle of the drive like that? Jesus Christ, I almost hit you! This driveway's got plenty of room for two cars if you don't park dead center . . . and hello? What the hell is that in your hand? Huh?"

Martin stared up at the man, just over six feet tall with the hint of a middle-aged gut beginning to show, and quickly sought out an excuse, a lie, to extract himself from this situation. But knowing that there was little he could say other than the truth, and feeling completely defeated over his current financial situation, he mumbled, "My toilet's blocked and I couldn't afford any groceries this week. I needed a little help."

"Help? Is that what you call this?" his stepfather shot back as if this response had been preplanned. Martin had always despised this about his stepfather. No matter the situation, he always seemed to have the perfect retort. "Help is when you ask someone for something and they give it to you. This isn't help. This is stealing."

Martin's mother was now out of the car and approaching the two men. "What's going on, Martin?" she asked, the tone indicating that she knew precisely what was going on but was feigning ignorance. This was one of his mother's favorite ploys. She would allow her husband to come down hard on Martin and then sweep in, ignoring the remarks that had already been made and adding her own, gentler rebuke on top. Martin knew that this time would be no different.

"I'm sorry, Mom. I ran out of cash this month and I needed some Liquid Plumbr. It's expensive and my toilet's blocked. I'll pay you back."

"I understand, Martin. It would be nice if you had asked, though. That's the difference between borrowing and taking. All you have to do is ask."

"Yeah, I know. It's just that you weren't here and I really needed to . . ."

"We all need things," she interrupted. "But we don't just walk into people's houses and take them."

"Yeah, I know," he replied, unable to look her in the eye. "I'm sorry."

"Well," his mother said, leading up to a phrase he had heard all too often growing up. "I'm going inside. It's freezing out here. Will you be right along, Bill?"

"Right along" were two words that Martin's mother adored.

They meant that her husband now had a window of opportunity, not too long, in which to issue a final reprimand. And because his mother would not be present, she would not be implicated in whatever might be said.

"Right along, Jeannie," he replied, not taking his eyes off Martin. He waited until his wife had entered the house before leaning in and adding, "Keep the stuff. I would've given it to you if you'd asked. I'd hate to think what you might do if I don't let you have that bottle." He then leaned in even closer, lowering his voice, and whispered, "Never thought I'd be worried about you turning into a thief. And a bad one at that. Don't try to fool me again, mister. You can't and you won't. You hear me?"

Those few words began Martin's career. Though not officially a challenge from his stepfather, Martin had taken it as one. He saw this as his first opportunity to best the man who had been besting him all his life.

It was the last time that Martin had ever been caught.

Three weeks later, while his parents were spending the day in New York, Martin entered his childhood home wearing surgical gloves that he'd purchased at a local pharmacy. With his car parked more than two miles away in the lot of a local high school, Martin made his way through the neighborhood on foot, crossing the tree line that bordered the rear of the property, and entered through the back door. In the course of an hour, he acquired two boxes of macaroni and cheese (leftovers from a time when he still lived at home), a bar of soap, two pounds of hamburger (his mother kept at least ten pounds in the freezer at all times), one stick of butter, three apples, and the Mike Greenwell rookie card that was displayed in protective glass on the mantel above the living room fireplace.

The card, one of his stepfather's most treasured possessions, had been signed by the Red Sox outfielder after an August game in 1988 during which he had smashed two home runs and driven in five on the way to a Sox win over the hapless Tigers. Greenwell would have his best year in 1988, hitting .325 with twenty-two home runs and 119 RBI and finishing second to Jose Canseco in the MVP race. At the time, the wiry left fielder was quickly winning over the Red Sox faithful, reminding fans of their beloved Fred Lynn from a decade before with his gritty attitude and aggressiveness at the plate. Sadly for the city of Boston, the Gator (as he was affectionately known) would never hit more than fourteen home runs and never drive in more than 100 RBI for the rest of his career. But on that hot summer day in 1988, Mike Greenwell was at the top of his game and fans like Martin's stepfather thought that they had found their next great Red Sox hero.

He had been waiting outside the players' clubhouse for more than an hour after the game, in the hopes of getting an autograph from his favorite ballplayer, when Greenwell stepped out from the door marked PLAYERS ONLY and into the blinding sunshine. With desperation in his voice, his stepfather had finally managed to acquire his hero's attention just before the team boarded a bus that would take them to Logan Airport to begin a lengthy road trip. Much to his delight, Greenwell signed the card and shook his stepfather's hand before disappearing behind tinted windows.

Martin knew how much his stepfather loved this card, had heard the story of how he had acquired the autograph many times, and also knew how easy it would be to acquire another one. Though Greenwell was a lifetime .300 hitter, his lack of power from the outfield position, and the numerous injuries that had kept him off the field for much of his career, had transformed the once promising star into little more than a scrappy, average ballplayer by the time he had played his last game. The card, released by Topps, was valued at more than twenty-five dollars in 1988, and was probably worth much more with the autograph, but on the day that Martin entered his parents' home intent on acquiring it, the card was worth less than five dollars. It was the autograph, and the memory attached to it, that made the card so valuable to his stepfather.

Martin was in possession of three of these cards that day, having acquired them a week earlier at a baseball card convention in Lowell, Massachusetts. None of these cards was signed, of course, but this was what Martin had wanted. Standing in his parents' living room, he removed the cards and a black pen from his coat pocket and placed them on a table beside the television. He then removed his stepfather's prized card from its glass protector and, using it as a model, proceeded to replicate Greenwell's signature on the new, unmarked cards. His second attempt was so well done that Martin didn't bother marking the third, returning it to his pocket with the first (a rather clumsy effort) along with his stepfather's original card. He then took the forged card and carefully placed it into the glass protector and returned it to the mantel.

"Can't fool you, huh?" Martin said as he admired his handiwork.

Martin's parents would remain his first and only clients for a long time after that day. Almost a year later, a series of house- and pet-sitting jobs arranged for him by his mother would allow Martin to pick up new clients and expand his business (though these clients had been discontinued long ago). Despite his rising success, Martin found no greater pleasure in those early years than visiting his childhood home and listening to his stepfather retell the story of the day he met Mike Greenwell and had his baseball card autographed. The thought always made him smile.

Martin was still in possession of the original card. He kept it in his back pocket whenever he worked, serving as a constant reminder of the day he was caught by his parents exiting their house, so that he might never find himself in that situation again.

Despite Mike Greenwell's presence in his back pocket, Martin now found himself trapped behind a client's sofa, just inches from a man almost twice his size, and in danger of being caught once again. Time was rapidly ticking away and he knew that if he did not find a solution to his predicament soon, Cindy Clayton would finish her exercise regime and make her way downstairs to see if her husband was in the downstairs shower. At that point, he would surely be caught.

Alan Clayton belched, the kind of belch that men release when they are alone or drunk, causing Martin to flinch in surprise. This was followed by the crunching of aluminum and a slight shifting of the sofa, indicating to Martin that his client might be on the move. He listened intently, hoping for a clue as to Alan Clayton's next destination. The two sportscasters on television, who had finished with tennis and moved on to steroid use in baseball for the last five minutes, had been temporarily replaced by a commercial for underarm deodorant. Martin watched from his crouched position between the sofa and wall as Alan Clayton rose from his seated position and walked out of view, presumably toward the kitchen. He surmised that the man was either heading for the bathroom to begin his shower or getting another beer. Either way, Martin thought this might be his only chance. Moving slowly, he rose from his hiding spot and saw that his client was halfway across the kitchen, heading for the refrigerator, thankfully turned away (the underarm commercial apparently not captivating enough to hold the man's attention). Now standing in full view, heart thumping, hands balled unconsciously into fists, Martin took two steps toward the stairway when the rhythmic pounding of Cindy Clayton on her treadmill suddenly stopped and Cindy called, "Alan!" Frozen in place by a combination of uncertainty and terror, Martin watched as Alan Clayton paused with one hand on the refrigerator door, turned his head slightly and replied, "Yeah?"

Just three feet from the foot of the stairs but still in plain view, Martin tried to remain as still as possible, afraid that any movement might be picked up by Alan Clayton's peripheral vision. He listened as Cindy Clayton stepped off her treadmill and began walking around her bedroom, the creaking of a floorboard and her soft footsteps on the carpeted surface sounding like thunder in Martin's ears.

Should he be spotted by either homeowner at that point, his plan was to exit through the front door (hoping the dead bolt was not engaged) and run as fast as he could down the street, eventually cutting back into the woods once out of sight. He thought this plan might work. It was unlikely that Alan Clayton would pursue a potentially dangerous intruder, though the look of the man, tough and weathered and no-nonsense, made Martin wonder.

"Are you planning to shower soon?" his wife asked, her orders once again expertly phrased as a question.

"Yes," Alan Clayton replied, a hint of irritation sneaking into his voice as he turned his attention back to the refrigerator and opened the door. On the television, Martin could see a Ford pickup bouncing over unreasonably rough terrain while a voice-over announcer proclaimed the vehicle fit for any challenge that nature might have to offer. He watched the light in the refrigerator switch on as his client stuck his bald head back in, searching for his next beer. He heard the refrigerator's compressor turn on and noticed that the crushed can was now sitting on the kitchen table, even though the trash can was less than five feet away. He heard Cindy Clayton sigh upstairs, drop something on the floor (perhaps a shoe), and shout, "I'm going to shower now, okay?"

"All right," Alan Clayton replied, head still in the refrigerator.

Holding his breath, Martin began moving again, arriving at the coat closet at the foot of the stairs in less than three steps. As quietly as possible, he swung the door open, turned, and backed in, allowing his body to push the coats and jackets aside to make room. He then slowly pulled the door closed, catching a final glimpse of Alan Clayton's head as it emerged from the refrigerator just before the closet door carved out all incoming light.

Martin pulled the door almost entirely shut, stopping just short of allowing the latch to click, and breathed an enormous (though silent) sigh of relief. He felt his rapidly beating heart begin to slow, felt the adrenaline that had filled his body begin to recede, and began to relax the muscles of his shoulders and hands. Stepping as far back into the closet as he dared without risking sound, Martin stood completely still and waited. He listened to the water begin to flow in the upstairs shower and the humming of Cindy Clayton, her thin frame presumably standing beneath the warm water. He heard the channel change on the television, from sports talk to the local news. He listened to Alan Clayton belch twice more, laugh once at a remark from a local politician (the kind of sarcastic "Yeah, right" laugh that bespeaks distrust and contempt), and shout a "Goddamn it!" at the news that there was rain in the forecast for the next two days. Martin waited in the darkness, hoping that the man would use his downstairs shower soon, affording Martin an opportunity for escape.

Luck was not on Martin's side. Shortly after listening to the rain-filled weather forecast, Martin heard the squeak of a faucet turning and heard the sound of running water cease upstairs. Cindy Clayton's shower was finished. He could picture her standing in the bathroom, towel wrapped around her torso in such a way as to conceal the portion of her body from her breasts to her knees, a maneuver that seemed to magically extend the fabric of the towel beyond its physical dimensions. She was probably standing in front of the steam-covered mirror, another towel wrapped around her long blond hair, preparing to do whatever it was that women did to ready themselves for the world.

Martin waited, debating whether to attempt an escape if and when both clients were upstairs, or if it would be safer to just wait in the closet until they exited the home. He began calculating the odds that either homeowner might open the closet door before they left, and wondered how much room there might be on the floor of the closet for him to hide if necessary.

Cindy Clayton called down to her husband again, inquiring for a third time whether he planned on showering soon. "Just give me a minute, okay?" he replied, and Martin heard the hiss of a beer can opening. It was followed a minute later by the whine of a hair dryer from upstairs.

Martin continued to listen and wait, seeking clues that would give him an idea of his clients' movements and positions. Minutes later, with the hair dryer still blowing, he heard the sound of rushing water in the pipes once again. The downstairs shower was running this time. Alan Clayton had finally decided to obey his wife ("Has he finished his beer or taken it to the shower with him?" Martin wondered), and now there was a decision to be made. He felt it safe to assume that Alan Clayton was no longer obstructing his escape out the patio door, but Martin now had to worry about Cindy Clayton standing in the upstairs bathroom, drying her hair. The bathroom's door was almost perfectly aligned with the staircase, so if she had left it open before showering, there was a good chance that it would still be open now, and she would be able to see down the stairs as Martin attempted his escape.

On the other hand, if the bathroom door was closed, then

Martin would be able to escape without risking detection at all, and this might be his last chance. He listened more intently to the whine of the hair dryer, attempting to discern from the quality of the sound whether or not it was muffled by an obstruction of some kind (preferably a wooden door). He couldn't be sure. What Martin did know was that when Cindy Clayton used the bathroom for urinating, she shut the door, even when she thought she was home alone. He wondered if this same rule would logically apply to showering and hair drying. Again, he couldn't be sure. He couldn't remember hearing the bathroom door shut, and he felt that urinating and showering were two entirely different procedures, so to make a guess about one based upon the other would be foolish and dangerous.

He continued to ponder the situation when the decision was taken from his hands. The hair dryer stopped its whining and shortly thereafter the shower stopped as well, making it impossible for him to mentally place either homeowner anywhere within the house. Realizing that his only chance to escape might have passed, Martin squatted down and began feeling around the rear of the closet for room to hide. The closet was less than four feet deep and only about five feet wide, making it difficult for a man, even one with his thin frame, to disappear in the shadows. Fortunately, however, Martin had two things working for him. First, the closet had no light, so if he pressed his body against the baseboard along the rear wall, he might be able to conceal himself in the darkness.

The closet was also packed full with coats, jackets, several garment bags, and a collection of items from the dry cleaner, still preserved within their long, thin plastic bags. These bags and several of the coats reached nearly to the floor and would afford Martin some degree of concealment if need be.

Not seeing a reason to delay this move any further, Martin

moved from his crouching position to a completely prone one, pressing his back into the corner created by the junction of the wall and floor. In the dark, it was impossible for him to tell which parts of his body were concealed by the hanging garments and bags and which were not, but there was little else he could do. In the event that the closet door was opened, he planned to close his eyes to prevent the reflection of light off his irises, but otherwise he could only lie there and wait, hoping that luck would carry the day.

He did continue to listen, however, tracking the movements of the Claytons as best as possible in the event that an unlikely window of opportunity might open, allowing him to escape. He listened as Alan Clayton ascended the stairs, presumably in order to change his clothes. He listened to the couple discuss their weekend plans, but because he wasn't certain if Cindy Clayton was still in the bathroom, he remained in his prone position. He heard the hair dryer again, for less than thirty seconds this time, and also heard the whine of an electric toothbrush, the cause of all his trouble. Even so, he felt a great deal of satisfaction knowing that the replacement toothbrush had apparently gone undetected.

He began to worry about the key that was still stuck in the back door. If either client was vigilant about checking doors before leaving home, they would find their patio door unlocked and, if they inspected further, would discover his key. This might lead to a search of the house and his discovery.

This train of thought led him to consider what he might do if discovered. Oddly enough, it was the awkwardness of the potential situation that caused him the greatest concern. What does one say to a homeowner who finds a stranger hiding in their coat closet? He hoped that if they discovered him, Cindy and Alan Clayton would run, retreat to a bedroom or to the garage so he could avoid an explanation entirely. In that case, he would simply exit the house and run himself, hoping to outpace any police cruiser that might soon arrive in the neighborhood. But to have to face them, explain himself, and perhaps ask for mercy was a situation that Martin dreaded. He remembered how embarrassed and completely impotent he had felt that day in his parents' driveway, facing his stepfather red-handed. He would do just about anything to avoid that same situation again.

Martin listened as Cindy Clayton descended the stairs, identifiable by the resumption of her soft humming. He listened to the clink of dishware in the kitchen (she was probably emptying the dishwasher, he thought) and had a momentary fit of panic as he heard the woman declare, "Hello? Are you there?" before realizing that she had placed a phone call, probably to someone on a cell phone with a poor connection. He listened intently to the conversation between his client and one of her friends, though not much was being said by Cindy Clayton. She was apparently an excellent listener, and her friend was obviously not.

Still on the phone, she called up to her husband, inquiring if he would be ready soon. He responded in the affirmative and she resumed her telephone conversation, a discussion on the merits of a local Indian restaurant. He heard the television switch off, heard the sound of running water (probably the kitchen sink), and continued to listen in as best he could to the telephone conversation. Cindy Clayton's friend was named Jeannette. She was married to a man named Larry. He wasn't sure what Larry did for a living, but it sounded as if he worked in some kind of medical facility. Jeannette appeared to be the type of person who turned small problems into big ones, and it sounded as if Cindy Clayton was adept at diffusing them for her friend.

Martin wasn't surprised. Cindy Clayton seemed like the kind of woman with all the answers.

"I'll be ready in two minutes," Alan Clayton called from up-stairs, probably from the bathroom this time. "The forecast says rain tonight, so you might want to bring a jacket."

Martin didn't initially connect Alan Clayton's comment with his current location. He had become so absorbed in Cindy Clay-ton's phone conversation that he had dropped his defenses. It was only when she responded with a "Thanks, honey," her voice much closer to the closet now, that Martin realized that the jacket she was seeking was likely hanging somewhere above him.

"Did he really?" Cindy Clayton sighed as she opened the closet door, flooding the small space with light. Martin closed his eyes, pressed himself as far against the wall as possible, and held his breath. He could feel the garments around his body shift as Cindy Clayton moved jackets and coats aside, presumably look-ing for the right one. He dared to open one eye just enough to glimpse her bare toes, painted red, less than a foot from his shoulders. He felt his body begin to tremble but tightened his muscles in an effort to remain still.

The shifting of the coats suddenly stopped and Cindy Clay-ton sighed again, this time a sigh that caused Martin to momen-tarily forget his fright. It was a sigh that bespoke a longing and a need that Martin could have never imagined. It was a long, windy release of emotion, followed by an interminable pause that both saddened and stilled Martin completely.

"God, I wish Alan would send me flowers," Cindy Clayton whispered into the telephone, though Martin felt as if she were speaking directly to him. "Just a single rose would do . . . one sin-gle rose for no reason at all. Like he used to when we just started dating." Her voice had softened now, sounding almost childlike in Martin's ears. It was as if she was daring to whisper a secret that had been residing within her for centuries, finally allowing the painful truth to pass through her lips. Just inches away from her, Martin felt as if Cindy Clayton's words were meant solely for him.

"But not every guy is like your Larry, right?" And just like that, the moment had passed. Her voice had suddenly, almost miraculously regained its confident, upbeat tone. A moment later, she pulled a coat from her closet and backed away, the topic having already transitioned to Jeannette's plans to visit family in Arizona later in the month. The closet door closed, clicking shut this time, and darkness returned to Martin's hiding space. But the words of Cindy Clayton, and especially her sigh, lingered with Martin as he listened to her conclude her phone conversation. The words had mattered, but it had been her sigh and the pause that followed that had said it all.

Seconds later, he heard Alan Clayton descend the stairs, gather his keys, and ask his wife if she had directions to their intended destination. Cindy Clayton replied in the affirmative and Martin listened as the couple switched off the lights and exited the house through the garage door. Moments later he heard the roar of a car's engine followed by the mechanical hum of a closing garage door.

The Claytons were at last gone.

Martin waited another twenty minutes before moving from the closet, wanting to be certain that the couple would not return. Despite the discomfort, he remained perfectly still at the bottom of the closet, thinking about Cindy Clayton's phone conversation, recalling that interminable sigh, and plotting his next move.

Once he felt it was safe, Martin exited the closet and returned the kitchen shears to their proper position in the knife rack. He then made his way out the patio door, collecting his key, but not before stopping in the kitchen to acquire one of Alan Clayton's business cards from the box beside the calendar. He would need the man's business address for what he had already planned.

As he made his way through the forest and back to his car, choosing a path at random this time, Martin began to mentally organize the specifics of his plan.

He couldn't remember the last time he had felt this excited about anything.

chapter

5

It had already started to rain by the time Martin finally turned
onto his street. The ride home had been mentally chaotic, a
flurry of shocked recollections, potential solutions, and repeated
attempts to quell his growing anxiety. He had just done the impossible, the unthinkable, and he found himself careening from
elation to disgust to disbelief.

He had heard characters in movies wonder aloud whether a
traumatic or surprising incident had really just happened, and
had found the sentiment to be trite and ridiculous. But now he
knew better. He knew precisely how those fictional characters
had felt.

Pulling into the garage and clicking the remote control to
close the large, windowless door, Martin turned off his car and
stepped out, inhaling the sweet smell of pine that infused the
large space.

Finally something familiar. Back to his routine.

More than two dozen pine-scented air fresheners hung from
the three beams that crisscrossed the garage's ceiling, and Martin
replaced these monthly in order to ensure a clean, fresh scent.
He loved his garage, and without it he believed that his career
might never have taken off. He thought of a garage, particularly
one attached to a house like his, as an insulating cocoon, a protective shell surrounding activities in which many families must

engage in the nakedness of their driveways. Without the garage, Martin would have been forced to unload his groceries and other acquisitions in the driveway for all the neighbors to see, an act that he could not understand why others performed so freely. For example, thanks to her lack of a garage, Martin was aware that Mrs. Waggoner, the widowed retiree three houses west of him, was now suffering from incontinence, apparent from the large supply of adult-sized diapers that she purchased each week. He also knew that the Swales, who lived directly across the street, did all of their shopping at Wild Oats, the organic grocery store in town. (Therefore, he was able to categorize them as "health nuts" and knew to avoid them at all costs.) This was the type of information that Martin was able to conceal from his neighbors thanks to the warm, aromatic confines of his garage.

But Martin hadn't always been so fortunate. Immediately following high school and up until his mother's death a dozen years ago, he had lived in a series of apartments and rooms for rent, and these locales had posed serious problems for one who valued discretion as much as he. His last apartment, a second-floor, two-bedroom place on Willard Avenue in the neighboring town of Newington, had been extremely troublesome, especially since his client list had begun to expand during that time. Lacking an attached garage, he had already been doing all of his grocery shopping on Tuesday mornings at 3:00 a.m. at the twenty-four-hour Stop & Shop on Fenn Road, in an effort to ensure that his shopping habits wouldn't become his neighbors' latest topic of conversation. But after building a lengthy client list (about half its current size) and increasing his acquisitions each week, Martin had been forced to dramatically adjust his schedule to accommodate the success of his new business. After completing his morning and afternoon visits to clients, he would eat dinner, clean up, and go to bed around seven, waking up each morning at three in order to transport his acquisitions from his car into the apartment under the cover of dark. These logistical problems also prevented Martin from acquiring most refrigerated and frozen foods in the warmer months, as these acquisitions would often sit inside his car for hours before it was safe to relocate them. The move to his mother's home, with its gloriously insulating garage, had been an enormous boon to his already thriving business.

Taking a moment to breathe in the pine-scented air that he enjoyed so much, Martin turned in a slow, 360-degree arc, admiring the space that he had created for himself and relishing the safety it afforded. Just being inside the garage had allowed him to relax a bit, to slow his breathing and return his body to a state of equilibrium. Routine and regularity were proving to be his mental salvation, beginning with the garage.

The walls were covered with orderly rows of tools used in lawn maintenance: clippers, shovels, rakes, hoes, and many of the smaller, handheld tools used for gardening. Each tool looked as if it had hardly been used, but Martin in fact used his tools quite often and was meticulous in his cleaning of each one after use. Following an afternoon of yard work, for example, a soiled shovel would be hosed down, wiped clean, and dried before being returned to its assigned location, a process that Jim considered odd but one that Martin thought made perfect sense. The process took very little time and yielded excellent results. It eliminated the opportunity for rust to form and kept dirt from entering his otherwise pristine garage. The hooks suspending the tools stretched across the walls in rows that were perfectly straight and parallel with the ground, a fact to which Martin's laser-guided level could readily attest. When he first moved back into the home following his mother's heart attack, one of his first chores was to remove the nails that his former stepfather had pounded willy-nilly into the wall years ago, and replace them with polished silver hooks, straightening out each row as he did.

Below the hooks stood the snowblower and lawn mower that Martin had also inherited with the house, and each of these also looked new, though they had required considerably more time to clean, repair, and repaint than the tools and hooks had. As he did with his tools, Martin would clean and dry these machines after each use, and even went so far as to remove the blade of the lawn mower monthly in order to sharpen it, though the manufacturer's recommendation was to sharpen seasonally. Again, this was not something that Martin considered odd or out of the ordinary, but simply something that made sense. The sharper the blade, the better the cut.

With his moment of admiration over, Martin began the process of unloading the day's acquisitions, trying to put the incident in the Claytons' home out of his mind while he took care of business. But there was so much to ignore.

The danger that he had just faced.

The inconceivable lack of regard for the rules that had kept him safe for so long.

And Cindy Clayton's voice, seeming to speak directly to him, as if he were meant to be in that closet at that particular moment. Only with great effort was he able to put these things out of his mind and concentrate on his work.

Lining the east wall of the garage were three rectangular banquet tables, empty except for a laptop and external hard drive positioned atop the table closest to the door to the house. Martin had set his computer up before exiting the garage earlier in the morning, and now with the touch of a button and the entry of a sixteen-digit password, the computer's fan began to whir and the operating system began to boot.

While the computer readied itself, Martin unloaded the

items from the back of his Subaru, sorting them by where they would eventually be stored within the home. Frozen goods and refrigerated items were placed closest to the laptop for rapid processing, with dry goods, cleaning supplies, and toiletries positioned further down the tables.

Before he could process any of his acquisitions, however, several important tasks needed to be completed. Using a paper shredder that was set up beneath the center table of his staging area, Martin destroyed the four acquisition lists that he had used in each home that day, allowing the machine to devour the flourish of French that he had so meticulously typed less than twenty-four hours ago. Later he would burn these paper shreds in his fireplace along with other potentially incriminating evidence, including the hairnet that he had worn, the four pairs of latex gloves and rubber moccasins—one pair per house—that he had donned before entering, and of course, his pants.

Just the thought that he was still wearing them made his skin crawl, but he knew that, as much as it pained him, processing his acquisitions would have to come before disinfecting his body. Unprocessed acquisitions posed a danger to Martin and his career, and his jeans did not. They would have to wait. But he would most assuredly take great pleasure in watching the contaminated denim burn along with the other essential parts of his work attire.

Thankfully, the items that Martin wore when visiting clients were simple to procure. Hairnets were easy to find in a variety of stores, including pharmacies and supermarkets, and Martin considered them very important, particularly in light of the proliferation of DNA evidence that law enforcement officers were using today. A single stray hair left inside a client's home might be enough to convict him, so although Martin's hair wasn't very long (and he had actually considered shaving his head for a long time but thought that an average head of hair would attract less attention), a hairnet was an essential element of his uniform, and explaining its presence if caught would be simple enough. Though Martin did not suffer from dandruff, the large supply of dandruff treatments in his bathroom (courtesy of Maurice Grant) provided enough evidence of his affliction, so if questioned, he would justify his hairnet as a means of keeping his flaking scalp to himself.

Acquiring latex gloves had also been fairly easy; there were several local medical supply stores that sold the gloves in bulk. But devising a cover story as to why he required so many gloves proved to be quite another matter. The last thing he wanted was to have to explain the presence of five thousand latex gloves in his kitchen cabinet to a law enforcement officer.

After some research, however, Martin found that many homeowners, particularly gardeners, kept latex gloves on hand in order to safely remove poison ivy and other irritating plants from their backyards. Martin didn't keep a garden, but the rear of his property was bordered by a constantly encroaching copse of trees and shrubs, and although poison ivy had never been a problem before, he was certain that he could make it a problem.

That, however, turned out to be more difficult than he had imagined.

After more than two weeks of searching, Martin was unable to locate any gardening store, nationally or abroad, that stocked poison ivy seed or seedlings. Most of his inquiries were met with perplexed and skeptical responses from shopkeepers who thought they were being made the punch line of some ridiculous practical joke. When he realized that purchasing the seed would be impossible, Martin decided to transplant existing poison ivy plants onto his property. Armed with a botanical field guide, Martin made his way on a Sunday afternoon to a forested section of land between a local elementary school and a park, and quickly found the plant in abundance. Despite poison ivy's invasive and persistent nature, transplanting proved to be a challenge. Martin's first three attempts ended in failure, and it wasn't until his fourth try that the plant finally took hold and began to thrive. Several years later, Martin doubted that he could remove the poison ivy even if he wanted to. Consistent watering and the seasonal application of fertilizer had helped his initial three transplants spread and grow into a veritable jungle of the three-leafed irritant.

Disposing of the gloves had also been a concern for Martin, and he had never arrived at a method that he considered satisfactory. He desperately wanted to rid himself of each pair of gloves immediately after use, so that if he were ever pulled over by the police, there would be no used gloves in the car to explain. But this would mean leaving evidence behind, out there in the world for anyone to find, and though this is just what Martin had done for a long time, a scare eight years back had forced him to adopt a new policy.

Following a visit to the Pearls' home on an early April morning, Martin had made his way to a trash can on the south end of the tennis courts in order to dispose of his gloves. As he dropped them into the can, he happened to glance in and notice another pair of gloves still sitting at the bottom of the trash, barely covered by a candy bar wrapper and an empty tennis ball container. Without pause, he plucked both sets of gloves from the can and hurried back to the Subaru, where he sat in the front seat, breathing heavily and waiting for his rapid pulse to return to normal. Though he hadn't used the trash can in more than two weeks, the gloves from a previous visit were still sitting there, covered with his fingerprints and the microscopic bits that they had acquired from the Pearls' home. His pulse began to race even faster as he thought about the thousands of latex gloves he had left about the world over the last several years, in random trash cans and dumpsters around his clients' homes, each one loaded with microscopic evidence of him and his visit.

Though he realized that the chance of someone locating one of these gloves and using the evidence that it contained against him was slight, police officers seemed to canvass crime scenes quite thoroughly on television, and it wouldn't take an exceptionally bright cop to connect the presence of latex gloves in a nearby trash can to one of his visits. So, following his scare, Martin began bringing his gloves home and burning them daily. Latex, he found, burned quite well and left no proof that the gloves had ever existed. And though he concealed his used gloves in a well-hidden space underneath his dashboard (created by the removal of some unnecessary plastic and the repositioning of several bundles of wires), he was always relieved to watch them go up in flames in his fireplace each evening.

Martin now removed the gloves from their hiding spot, placed them atop the shredder, and then moved to the rear of the car and detached the Hide-a-Key from the inside bumper. Earlier that day, he had acquired a diamond and silver pendant from the home of Ron and Donna Gardner, a middle-aged couple whose three children had flown the coop years ago for exciting and exotic careers. As he'd done with Sophie Pearl's earring, Martin had secured the pendant in the Hide-a-Key box for transport to his home. As he removed the pendant from the box, he made sure that the black ignition key to a Subaru Legacy that he had owned more than five years ago remained behind. Though he would never be foolish enough to hide a key to his car *on* his car, he wanted to maintain proper appearances, and if ever questioned about the hidden key he would explain that he had moved the Hide-a-Key from his old car to the new, forgetting to exchange the actual keys in the process. The pendant was placed on the laptop's mouse pad for immediate processing. This would be the most damaging item if law enforcement suddenly arrived, so Martin wanted to process it first.

Lastly, Martin removed Cindy Clayton's toothbrush from the floor of his car (vowing to purchase new floor mats as soon as possible) and placed it into the garbage bin in the rear of the garage. Fortunately, the trash was scheduled for pickup the next day. Had it been a longer wait, Martin might have been forced to dispose of the toothbrush on his own. Just the thought of it lying at the bottom of his garbage bin for more than a day might have been too much of a reminder of what had just happened in the Claytons' home.

Once his car had been completely emptied, Martin removed a large spray bottle containing rubbing alcohol and several clean rags from a cabinet over his worktable and began lightly spraying and wiping down each item on the table, removing all fingerprint evidence. This was a process that he had begun following the latex scare and his horrifying realization about the mountain of physical evidence that he was carrying into his home each week. Every item that he acquired had at one point been handled by its previous owner, and it likely contained dozens of incriminating fingerprints. In putting together a case against Martin, the police could seize items from his home and test them for fingerprints. Finding the print of a different homeowner on items within his cupboards could provide enough evidence for a conviction.

Initially, Martin's attempts at removing fingerprints had been amateurish. Using a bucket of soapy water, he would wash the cereal boxes, milk containers, cans of soup, and jars of spaghetti sauce much the same way one might wash a dog or a car, by scrubbing and rinsing. But this process was time consuming and often left cardboard containers moist and labels peeling. After several attempts at altering this method, the spray-bottle technique finally came to mind after driving his car through an automated car wash one day. As the large rollers scrubbed the pollen and bird excrement from his hood, the blueprint of a fingerprint removal device suddenly entered his mind, complete with a moving conveyor belt, spray nozzles, and drying fans, very much resembling the machinery in the automatic car wash, only reduced in scale. By the time his Subaru was rolling back onto the street, the entire sketch of his machine was complete in his mind, and he was certain that if it were given to an engineer and built to his specifications, he would never have to worry about a fingerprint again. In a way, Martin felt like he understood the plight of Leonardo da Vinci, a man who could envision the plans for the first helicopter but lacked the tools, materials, and technology to fabricate one. He felt a great deal of frustration and pride in this realization.

While the machine would be impossible to build (and even more impossible to explain to anyone who asked what it was for), the idea of a spray bottle quickly replaced that of the complex machinery, and within a week he had cut the time it took to remove fingerprints by more than half. A liberal spray of rubbing alcohol (more effective at removing fingerprints than water), followed by a vigorous wipe-down, would remove all evidence that the item had been handled by anyone. He tested his method early on using a fingerprint kit, which he purchased with a Stop & Shop money order and had shipped to clients who were staying with their daughter in Iowa during the birth of their first grandchild. After a month of testing on random acquisitions, Martin found that with a diligent cleaning, the spray-bottle method was 100 percent effective in removing fingerprints. In all, it took Martin seventeen minutes to cleanse his latest acquisitions of evidence, produce included, and with this finally accomplished, the actual processing could begin.

Thankfully, he hadn't thought of the Claytons once during the cleaning.

Martin's laptop was attached to an external hard drive, in which all his business data was stored. This hard drive, which no one knew existed, was stored in a concealed section of his basement wall behind the sump pump when not in use, leaving his laptop free of all incriminating evidence. Using Excel, Martin opened the spreadsheet in which he tracked his large acquisitions and logged in Donna Gardner's pendant, indicating the date of acquisition but leaving the "Profit" column empty. Once entered, Martin proceeded to hide the pendant in the location he had predetermined earlier that day.

Hiding small items like jewelry had always been easy for Martin, and he could never quite fathom why someone would use a safe, lockbox, or safety deposit box when so many secure locations could be found around the average home. The insides of large household appliances were some of Martin's favorite locations, because they were easily accessible, plentiful, and extremely secure. The back panel of a refrigerator, for example, could quickly be removed with a screwdriver, and a pendant, earring, or even necklace could be well concealed among the various wires or nonmoving parts therein. In Martin's mind, the chances of anyone, including law enforcement officials, looking inside the compressor of his refrigerator for a recently acquired diamond earring were nil. In fact, a safe or lockbox almost implied guilt, or at the very least acknowledged the presence of valuables to anyone searching his home. His refrigerator, on the other hand, only acknowledged the likely presence of bologna, lettuce, and milk, making it much less conspicuous and therefore much more secure. In the past, Martin had hidden his small but valuable acquisitions inside his refrigerator, dishwasher, television, VCR, electric can opener, air conditioner, and stereo, to name just a few places, and once they were hidden, he never gave a second thought to their safety.

Martin had predetermined that he would hide the pendant

within the metallic casing that protected the snowblower's motor, and in less than five minutes it was concealed between several braids of cord within the machine.

With the pendant hidden, Martin started logging in the other items that he had positioned in his staging area, beginning with the frozen and refrigerated goods. In a database specifically designed for groceries, Martin entered the name of each item, indicating where it was acquired, how much of it was acquired, and what it was worth. Thanks to the same Peapod website that Emma and Max Reed used to purchase their groceries each week, Martin had access to an online database that contained the current market price of almost every grocery item that he had ever acquired, so it was easy to calculate his daily profit. Martin also assigned each item a code that indicated from which "grocery family" the item came (meat, produce, dry goods, etc.), and he would later use this information to analyze the history of his acquisitions from each client. His goal was to ensure that he was acquiring a proportionate number of goods from each client and that the average profit from a single household did not change significantly from week to week or month to month. Consistency was the key, for if a client suddenly noticed that their grocery bill was increasing without reason, suspicion might be aroused.

As he was processing, Martin also conducted a visual inspection of each item, looking for distinguishing marks that might indicate the location, date, or time at which the item was originally purchased. Deli meat, for example, often had a tag that indicated the store's name, time, and date of purchase, and smaller, noncorporate grocery stores often used price tags that could be easily identified by a store employee. Occasionally, Martin would also find that a client had marked a product with a particular identifying characteristic. For example, he once acquired a box of cereal from a client who had completed the crossword puzzle on the back, and another time someone had turned the image of Aunt Jemima on a bottle of maple syrup into a devil, complete with horns and a forked tail. These identifying tags and marks would either be removed from the item, or the item would be transferred into a new container before being brought into the house.

Martin peeled the price tags from a pound of hamburger and a chicken breast, each indicating the date and store of purchase, and stuck both tags to a blank sheet of computer paper stored on a shelf over the workbench. With the tags firmly attached, he ran the sheet of paper through the shredder, destroying the tags in the process. In all it took Martin a little over thirty minutes to enter the data on all of his newly acquired items, and looking at the total at the bottom of the screen, saw that he had earned a total profit of $156.36 from his day's work, a slightly below-average day considering the number of clients he had visited.

Of course, the incident at the Claytons' house (he had already begun to think of it as *the incident*) had prevented Martin from finishing his work. There had been several items in the Claytons' linen closet scheduled for acquisition, but these would have to wait for another day. The more he thought about Cindy Clayton's voice and her desperate plea for attention, the more he began to believe that fate had intervened. His less-than-expected profit was no surprise.

What did surprise Martin was the thought that, less than three hours ago, he had been contemplating bashing in a client's skull with a lamp. Had he not been so nimble-minded, he might right now be hiding in the wooded area between the Claytons' house and the nursing home, trying to evade a platoon of policemen carrying flashlights, batons, and Taser guns.

Maybe even dogs.

Had Martin been exceptionally unlucky, it was entirely possible that he could have found himself sitting behind bars at this very minute instead of relishing the orderliness of his garage. With a life built upon predictability and routine, Martin marveled at how quickly his circumstances had changed in the span of a couple hours.

Refocusing on the task at hand, Martin saved his work, shut down his computer, and entered the six-digit combination (randomly generated with dice) that deactivated the state-of-the-art alarm system protecting his home. He had purchased this system within a week after moving back into the house, never understanding why his parents hadn't made the investment themselves but pleased that they had not.

He might have ended up in a very different career had his parents been more cautious.

Martin returned the hard drive to its hiding place in the basement, first enclosing it in a watertight bag and then placing that bag in a large sack of fertilizer for additional concealment, and then began moving the newly acquired items inside the house to their assigned locations. As he moved through the rooms, he was careful to avoid allowing his pants to touch furniture, walls, or any other part of his body. He was almost counting the seconds until they could be removed.

Martin's house was a large, two-story Colonial centered on just under a half acre of land in a suburban neighborhood of West Hartford, Connecticut. The downstairs was a large, almost entirely open space consisting of a modern stainless-steel kitchen that opened into a spacious, window-filled family room, with a mudroom connecting the kitchen to the garage. On the west side of the house, beyond a stairway and dividing hallway, was a combined living room and dining room, complete with fireplace and sliding glass doors that opened onto a raised deck.

Upstairs, a total of five rooms wrapped around the staircase, including a full bath off the master bedroom. As a child, Martin had inhabited one of the smaller rooms tucked into the northern corner of the house, but now this room served as his business office, the door always locked when not in use. Upon inheriting the home, he had moved into the master bedroom and kept the other two rooms as guest rooms, leaving them furnished just as they had been the day he moved back in. In fact, one of the guest rooms had yet to be occupied since the day Martin had inherited the home, and so he had yet to change the sheets that his mother had put on the bed sometime before she died.

The garage wasn't the only place where Martin had made changes to his parents' original design. Almost immediately upon inheriting the house, Martin re-tiled the kitchen floor and countertops, replacing a hunter green, which his mother had installed just a year before her death, with pristine white surfaces. Martin despised the color green and had found it amusing how often his mother would emphasize the word "hunter" when describing the color of her newly decorated kitchen, as if one word apologized for the other.

More significant than just despising the color, Martin also did not approve of dark colors in the kitchen or bathroom, as they served as effective agents in the hiding of dirt and germs. He believed that if there was a germ festering in the kitchen, it was better to be able to deal with it rather than allowing it to hide in the grout between green tiles.

Though much of the furniture throughout the house remained primarily the same, Martin had removed a great deal, emptying shelves of bric-a-brac, throwing away ornamental chairs that decorated corners of rooms but served no real purpose, and tearing up the carpeting in the family room and master bedroom. An empty shelf was a thing of beauty in Martin's mind, with its clean, straight lines and absence of useless objects.

Carpeting was another household furnishing that Martin deplored because it was impossible to keep clean. Dirt on a hardwood floor or on tile could be seen and removed easily, but carpeting allowed dirt to linger and hide no matter how powerful one's vacuum cleaner might be. Though it had cost him a considerable sum, one of Martin's first projects was to hire someone to restore the hardwood floors that his parents had covered with carpeting long ago.

With his newly acquired items stored in their predetermined locations throughout the house, Martin went to the upstairs bathroom to shower, placing his contaminated jeans into a brown paper bag before rolling it closed. Once in the shower, he began scrubbing vigorously, removing any microscopic evidence that he had potentially collected from his clients' homes, as well as any of the fetid remnants of the toilet water that had once covered Cindy Clayton's toothbrush. Even in the presence of these germs, Martin smiled when he considered the contrast between this shower and the showers that the Claytons had taken earlier that day. Standing under the nearly scalding water, Martin's muscles finally began to relax. But just a short time ago, he had been straining to hear the sound of a shower from a nearly unimaginable position.

An incredibly foolish position too, Martin reminded himself. With his years of experience, he wondered how he could've been stupid enough to break so many rules in order to help a client.

All that danger over a toothbrush. It was almost impossible to believe.

As he washed his hair for the second time (as prescribed on the bottle of shampoo that had once belonged to Tracy and Bob Michaud of Kensington), Martin began inventorying the litany of errors that he had made in the course of the Clayton incident, his sense of disappointment and disgust growing with each item on the list. But at the same time, that feeling of excitement had returned with the possibility that he might be able to help the Claytons once more without having to break another rule.

The more he thought about it, the more his idea seemed foolproof.

Once cleaned and dressed, Martin went to the front porch to collect his mail. In addition to the usual bills, magazines, and circulars, he found a total of three cardboard boxes and one large, cushioned mailing envelope. Placing the rest of the mail on the kitchen counter for later processing, Martin brought the boxes and envelope to his upstairs office, unlocking the door with a key from a ring that he kept in his pocket at all times while within the house. On this ring were the keys to Martin's home, his car, his storage unit in Groton, and assorted bike locks, padlocks, etc. No matter where he was or what he was doing, Martin kept his keys with him at all times in case of emergency. If he needed to exit his home quickly, the last thing he wanted to hold him up was searching for keys that he had flung into some conspicuous location in a home full of conspicuous locations.

Though Martin's business was highly profitable, this hadn't always been the case. Before venturing into the realm of large-scale acquisitions, the business had for a long time provided him with groceries and common household necessities, but not with the cash required to pay rent, make car payments, and pay utility bills. So for the first ten years that Martin had been on his own, he had held down a variety of jobs in order to generate the funds needed to survive. Working as a part-time barista at Starbucks had been and remained his primary job (its early morning hours fitting in well with his afternoon client visits), with stints as a pizza deliveryman, a McDonald's cashier, a telemarketer, and an ice-cream vendor filling in the gaps. He hated all these jobs; particularly Starbucks with its corporate brainwashing, pretentiously named coffee sizes, and tattooed-pierced-vegetarian coworkers. But despite the noticeable loathing that he exuded behind the counter each day, Martin's excessively logical and methodical mind, and his affinity for sequence and order, had allowed him to produce the overpriced lattes and espressos for which Starbucks was famous more quickly and efficiently than anyone else in town. Though his manager, Nadia, was clearly an idiot and did not like Martin, she was at least smart enough to recognize his skills, and was willing to put up with his sour face in exchange for quick service for her customers, all of whom she presumed to know intimately each time they came in. As a result of his business's profitability, he had been able to reduce the number of hours that he worked at Starbucks considerably, keeping the job only to maintain the excellent health insurance that the company provided its employees.

Martin had his mother to thank for eventually ridding him of the other low-paying jobs that plagued his existence. Though the possibility of large-scale acquisitions had always been in the forefront of Martin's mind, it was the converting of these items to cash that had always posed the biggest challenge. He had heard the term "fence" before, and understood that in the larger cities thieves could find someone who would exchange cash for stolen goods, but he doubted that Hartford, Connecticut, was teeming with these individuals, nor did he have any desire to associate with such a criminal element. Years went by while Martin missed many, many opportunities for large paydays, until an afternoon in his dead mother's closet changed everything.

Having inherited everything that his mother owned, Martin had begun packing her clothes in order to send them over to the Salvation Army shortly after moving back home. One afternoon Jim was visiting with his wife, Karen, when she noticed a pile of handbags in a cardboard box by the front door.

"Martin, what are you doing with all of these?"

"Sending them to Goodwill," he replied with a smile. "You don't expect me to carry them around myself, do you?" He had been pleased by this witty response.

"Martin," Karen said, fishing through the box, "you can't just give these away. Some of these are worth a lot of money. You could probably get a bundle for these."

"For a bunch of pocketbooks?"

"A bunch of pocketbooks? This one alone is probably worth a couple hundred at least." She was holding up a Dooney & Bourke bag of yellow leather and brass clasps. "Hell, I'd give you fifty bucks for it right now."

"Well, besides you, who am I going to sell them to? A consignment store?"

"eBay, you idiot."

Though he had heard of the online auction house before, it had only been a few years old at the time, and Martin had assumed that it was a marketplace primarily for collectibles. While this was certainly the case during its infancy, eBay had exploded by the time Karen mentioned it, developing into an auction house for almost any item one could think of, including handbags. In fact, an online search of Dooney & Bourke handbags that day had yielded over fifty current auctions, with bids as high as $350. Martin quickly realized that not only was he sitting on a gold mine in terms of his mother's hoard of designer bags, but he might have found a means of moving large-scale acquisitions with relative anonymity.

So began Martin's four-week study of eBay. For at least three hours a day, he explored the site, noting the types of items being auctioned, the means by which people listed their goods, and the many features offered by the online auction house. He quickly discovered that people who dealt in the merchandise that Martin would also be selling (jewelry, crystal, silver, and perhaps even handbags) were primarily women, and so he decided to establish a female identity for himself in order to sell on the site.

Registering under the name Emptynester, Martin assumed the online persona of an upper-class, middle-aged woman from Connecticut named Barbara Teal whose two daughters had recently gone off to college, leaving her behind with an absent-minded husband and a house full of luxuries that she no longer desired (or wanted to trade in for even more luxurious ones). As part of the registration process, Martin was required to provide an address, telephone number, and e-mail address, all of which were easily supplied without sacrificing his prized anonymity. A new address was purchased eight miles away in Simsbury at Mail Boxes Etc. using cash and without having to present identification of any kind. Explaining that he was leasing the mailbox for a mother who was hoping to start an eBay business, he filled out the forms using the alias of Barbara Teal. The e-mail address was a Google account also registered under Barbara Teal's name, and the phone number was a fake, though he doubted that eBay, Mail Boxes Etc., or Google would ever be calling. Actually, the phone number was assigned to a fax machine at a local Office Depot, so that if they ever did call, they would receive the whining screams of a fax machine answering rather than confirmation of a wrong number.

Within a week of establishing his new persona, Martin was ready to list his first item, an Il Bisonte black leather handbag that he had never seen his mother carry and hardly looked used. His listing read:

Nice MESSENGER bag from IL BISONTE. BLACK LEATHER bag in very excellent condition. Another bag that I just had to have, much to my husband Gerry's chagrin—and I did use it for a while—but not for very long and the bag is in very excellent condition. I haven't used it for a long time, and it is time for it to move on to someone who will use it and enjoy it. A bag like this will never go out of style and IL BISONTE just continues to make beautiful and practical handbags, as I'm sure you already know. It opens with a zipper across at the top of the bag and there is a nice zipper compartment inside. The bag was MADE IN ITALY and designed by WANNY DI FILIPPO. My oldest daughter, Emily, thinks I'm crazy to sell it, but I think she's just making a play for the bag herself! Clever girls I have!

The bag is in excellent condition—no marks, scratches, or any sign of wear at all. Bags like this just get better and better as they get older. A bag like this will give someone a lifetime of pleasure, unlike me who just has to have every new bag in sight. 14" high x 14" wide x 6" deep, 20" with shoulder strap up—plenty of room to wear over your shoulder.

Of course, Martin researched handbags extensively before posting his listing, and much of the language was lifted directly from other listings for bags of similar design. He had learned to capitalize keywords like designer names and country of origin after studying some of the more successful sellers on eBay. In all, Martin found the process remarkably simple and in less than two weeks had a money order in his hand in the amount of $167.00. Even more interesting, Martin had received an email a couple of days into the auction from a woman asking about the bag, and his ensuing response (carefully crafted over a two-hour period) had launched a string of e-mails between the two in which he learned a great deal about the woman, a shopkeeper in Rhinebeck, New York, by the name of Jane. In fact, within a week he had acquired Jane's address, the name of her business (The Cozy Chair), the ages and occupations of her three children, and many of the sordid details relating to her recent divorce. In return for this torrent of information, Martin provided similar, though fictional, details about Barbara, and eventually the two had struck up an online friendship. *How remarkable,* he had thought. With relative ease, he had managed to pass himself off as a middle-aged suburban housewife, and this game of false identities thrilled him beyond belief.

Over the next six months, Martin continued to sell off his mother's collection of handbags, designer dresses and coats, jewelry, and even her shoes. Through his listings, he wove the tale of a middle-aged woman who was learning to enjoy the freedom that her empty nest had suddenly provided. He wrote of Barbara's travels to Barcelona, Greece, and the Caribbean, all places that Martin had never been but had studied extensively through travel brochures and online research. He waxed lyrical about the romance that was returning to her marriage after years of busy parenthood. He wrote of her love for fashion, a topic about which Martin knew nothing when he began, but one in which he became quite fluent in a short time. Each listing was more personal than the last, a blend of capitalism and personal blogging before blogging had hit the mainstream, and each revealed another nugget about Barbara Teal and her life, friends, and family. He even bid on several auctions himself and won a few in order to reinforce Barbara's identity, while at the same time acquiring items that he thought he could resell at a higher price later on.

In June, a woman by the name of Rosemary, who had already bought several items from Martin, contacted him about selling some of her own things; handbags and sweaters to start. He had learned early on in his research that some of the sellers on eBay made a business out of selling items for others, collecting as much as 25 percent of the sale as a commission, and so without much consideration, he agreed. Thanks to Barbara Teal's unique and personalized listings, the sweaters and bags sold quickly and were followed by Rosemary's unwanted jewelry, shoes, and a collection of Rookwood pottery, all of which fetched Martin a handsome profit for serving as the middleman. Before long, he had more than a dozen women for whom he was selling goods, and in some cases Martin was bypassing eBay entirely, simply selling one item to another of his regular clients without the hassle of an online auction. By the time he was ready to make his first large-scale acquisition, a Marc Jacobs bag from Emma Reed's extensive collection, Martin had firmly established himself on eBay and had business relationships with almost a dozen women. He couldn't have asked for a better cover under which to move his acquisitions.

Martin also appreciated—adored, really—the way his eBay business fit within his overall business plan. He began to think of the items that he was auctioning for his clients as acquisitions, no different than the tomatoes he routinely acquired from the Reeds' home each week. He was acquiring items that did not initially belong to him, acquiring them under false pretenses (in the guise of Barbara Teal), and was profiting from their acquisition, just as he had been doing for years on a smaller scale.

This is what economist Jim Collins referred to in his book *Good to Great* (which Martin had read a dozen times) as a Hedgehog Concept. In his essay "The Hedgehog and the Fox," Collins explains how the philosopher Isaiah Berlin divided the world into hedgehogs and foxes, based upon an ancient Greek parable: "The fox knows many things, but the hedgehog knows one big thing (how to defend itself by rolling up into a ball, presenting its attacker with a nearly impenetrable sphere of spines)." Collins argued that profitable companies have an understanding of the one thing that they can do best, and are therefore like the hedgehog, an animal with one simple but effective defense strategy. Companies like the fox have a diversified approach to business, but this often leaves them diffused and inconsistent. Martin's Hedgehog Concept was simple: Acquire goods without payment in order to garner profit. This, he knew, was what he did best.

His old bedroom served as an office for his eBay business, and this is why the room remained locked at all times. He had no desire to make anyone aware of his hidden identity or his prosperous business. The room was filled with shipping and receiving supplies: packing tape, box cutters, cushioned envelopes in a variety of sizes, a Pitney Bowes postage machine, scissors, and a desktop computer that he used for all of his eBay transactions.

That afternoon, Martin listed a DKNY sweater, a Louis Vuitton Damier canvas leather wallet (which required some research), an Ernest Borel watch, and a Burberry scarf, which he listed thusly:

Hello friends! I'm back from shopping at a wonderful new corner of our world called the Shops at Evergreen Walk in South Windsor, Connecticut. A delightful little place where you can pick up a latte and a Juicy Couture bag and catch a movie all in one stop! It's the best! My favorite shop is Anthropologie. Don't you just love this place, ladies? My hubby says they've just thrown a bunch of mismatched, expensive items together in one store (knobs and sweaters, furniture and books), and he's right! And that's why we love it!

Speaking of Gerry, my wonderful husband gave me this CASHMERE BURBERRY scarf for my birthday last October. I have tried to wear it, but it's really not my style. As you know, I am more of a Coach girl. And with the leaves on the trees changing color in Connecticut, it's time to make

*room for my annual fall shopping fling! This scarf was pur-
chased from SAKS, but I do not have the tags because I never
really intended to sell it.*

*It's very lovely and brand new . . . I have used it maybe five
times. Though I would never ask him, I'm sure that Gerry
paid over $300 for it at the time, so I'll start the bidding at
$100. Enjoy ladies!*

In a month, Martin would remove Sophie Pearl's earrings
and Donna Gardner's pendant from hiding, photograph them,
and include them among the many other auctions that he listed
that week. By the end of the second month, his profit would be
safely in his hands, the acquisitions gone for good.

Finished with his work, Martin poured himself a glass of
water and sat down on the couch, reviewing his plan for Cindy
and Alan Clayton, searching for potential flaws as he watched
the hairnet, gloves, rubber moccasins, and pants disappear in
flame and smoke. He had escaped that day thanks to his training, quick thinking, levelheadedness, and a bit of luck, but he
vowed never to veer off his prescribed course again. His plan for
Alan Clayton would have to be carefully designed and perfectly
executed, leaving no room for error, and, once finished, he promised himself to never take such perilous chances again.

That promise lasted less than a week.

chapter

6

As promised on Alan Clayton's television screen, the next day
was also filled with scattered rain showers, but Martin's mood
was still so good that he didn't mind a bit. It was Housekeeping
Day, a day on which Martin didn't visit a single client, devoting
his time to tasks that were critical to his business. He normally
dreaded these days, but he left his home that morning with a
surprising spring in his step.

A to-do list (also written in French) was stuffed into his coat
pocket, listing the tasks that he had scheduled for the day. In addition to his customary early morning visit with Jillian, he had
listed lunch, a trip to the dry cleaners, and a client referral
follow-up. But it was the last item on the list that had buoyed
Martin's spirits, an item that had been handwritten (the others
were typed) and was oddly nondescript. The word "Alan" sat at
the bottom of the page, appearing almost as an afterthought, a
late addition to an already carefully constructed agenda. Yet it
was this errand, which Martin would save until the end of the
day, that had him so excited.

The Quaker Diner, Martin's usual breakfast stop, was an old-
fashioned diner in every sense of the word. Set on the corner of
Quaker Avenue and Park Street, the diner was built like a boxcar
and cast the smell of fried eggs and bacon into the neighborhood
streets for more than a block around. Music from the 1940s filled

the greasy air, and an ancient pay phone stood beside the rear door, occasionally ringing as if to remind the customers of a time now past. Martin entered through the front door and made his way down the counter toward his favorite stool, directly across from the grill, where he could watch his meal being prepared without obstruction. Though eating at the counter meant he often had to sit nearly shoulder to shoulder with a stranger, Martin had found that he was able to spend more time with Jillian if he took up a position on one of the stools. It was a sacrifice he made for his girl, and it made him feel good to know that he was going out of his way for her.

Jillian spotted him immediately and shouted out a friendly "Good morning, Martin!" She tossed a lock of her curly blond hair from her eyes as she waved.

"Good morning, Jillian!" he replied as cheerfully as possible. It was an excellent response, he thought, for a couple of reasons. First, it indicated that he was listening intently. A person not paying attention to Jillian's greeting might have just mumbled an arbitrary and disingenuous "Hey!" or "How's it going?" By repeating the "Good morning!" that he had just received, Martin was demonstrating that he listened to and cared about what Jillian said.

Just as important, his response also indicated to Jillian that he approved of her choice of words. Out of all the possible greeting options available to him, he had chosen to use the same one that she had used. If this didn't send her a clear message, Martin didn't know what would.

Martin's favorite stool was occupied by Bob, a middle-aged man who came to the diner quite often. Though Martin had refrained from ever conversing with the man, he knew that Bob enjoyed pancakes a great deal and had once worked for NASA, though in what capacity Martin couldn't be sure. It seemed as if

Bob enjoyed dropping the name of the nation's space agency whenever he could, but didn't like to get into great detail on the subject. For this reason, Martin didn't trust the man.

Martin took up position on a stool two away from his favorite (still providing a decent view of the grilling surface if Freddy didn't cook his eggs on the far left side) and waited for Jillian to properly greet him. Less than a minute later she obliged, dropping a cup of coffee in front of him and kissing Martin on the cheek, followed by a "How's it going today, honey?"

"Dandy," Martin replied, once again pleased with his response. A girl can make a guy feel good, great, and even fabulous, but how often does a lady hear that her man is feeling *dandy*?

Not often, he guessed.

Jillian moved past Martin and on to a booth where a couple of blue-collar workers were in need of a refill. She deftly poured coffee into each cup without so much as a glance, offering a smile and whispering something that made the men laugh. Martin had always enjoyed watching Jillian work. She was good at her job, and he admired her for this. Competence and efficiency were two of the most admirable qualities a person could possess, and it seemed that Jillian possessed both in great measure.

She was not a bad-looking woman either. Working on her feet all day, navigating the narrow lanes of the diner, had kept her in excellent shape, with long thin legs and curves in all the right places. Her smile was accompanied by a dimple on each side, and her cheeks were gloriously freckled no matter what the season. In Martin's mind, she couldn't be more perfect.

As Jillian made her rounds, Martin took a cursory glance at the menu, though his order rarely changed. Scrambled eggs, corned beef hash, and wheat toast were his standard fare, though occasionally he would try a waffle or some blueberry pancakes if he needed a change of pace. A moment later Jillian had made it back to Martin with order pad in hand.

"The usual?" she asked, extracting the pen from behind her ear.

"Not today," he replied, suddenly changing his mind. "I've got some new business on my plate, and it's put me in the mood for pancakes, I think. Blueberry."

"What's it now, honey? A Flowbee? A blender?"

"Nope," he replied. "A martini set, if you can believe it. Directions on how to hang the glasses from the rack. Pretty hard to mess up, huh?"

When Martin had decided to turn his business into a full-time occupation, he was faced with the dilemma of explaining his source of income to people like Jim and Jillian. His mother had passed away and left him the home and some cash, but certainly not enough to retire upon. His decision to go full-time meant that he would be reducing his hours at Starbucks, just enough to retain his health insurance, so people would naturally be curious about how he was supporting himself without much of a job.

The answer came to Martin on the day that he unpacked his pick guns from their mailing container. As with all tools and appliances, the pick guns had come with a small instruction booklet explaining how to assemble and use the devices. After reading and rereading the instructions three times, it became clear to Martin that whoever had written the booklet lacked a fundamental understanding of English syntax. The instructions were virtually unintelligible, and Martin eventually turned to a website on pick guns for an explanation on how to operate the devices. After retrieving a clear and detailed explanation online and assembling the guns, Martin had decided to write to the author of the instruction booklet, in order to complain about the poor job that he or she had done. Throughout high school, Martin had been an excellent writer and the assistant editor of his school's newspaper. He still considered himself a very good writer and had aspirations of one day making it a career, so whenever he encountered poor writing, it irritated him tremendously. *I should have your job,* he would think. *I could do a better job than this.*

But as Martin thumbed through the booklet in search of an author's name, no name was to be found. It was difficult for Martin to imagine anyone writing something and not wanting attribution for the work, but considering the poor quality of the instruction booklet, he couldn't blame the writer. It was nothing of which to be proud. Still, he wondered why the author's name didn't appear anywhere in the booklet.

In a file cabinet in his office, Martin had a folder containing the instruction booklets for all the appliances and tools that he owned, filed alphabetically by name. Partly out of curiosity (and perhaps because the idea was already taking shape in his mind), Martin went to the cabinet and began examining other instruction books in search of an author's name. Again no names were to be found.

Martin was amazed. While he understood that an instruction booklet could hardly be considered an important piece of writing, it seemed to him that someone should be credited for the work, however poor the end product might be. He had read *Ethan Frome* in high school and had hated almost every page of the novel, but Edith Wharton had still been brave enough to stick her name on the damn thing. Yet with instruction manuals this was not the case, and thanks to this knowledge, the problem explaining his source of income had been solved.

More than two months before reducing his hours at Starbucks, Martin informed Jim that he had received his first freelance writing assignment, writing instructions for the assembly of a twelve-speed bicycle that was manufactured in Japan. He downplayed the news, indicating that he had seen the opportunity in *Writer's Digest*, had submitted a proposal on a whim, and had been shocked upon receiving the acceptance letter. He explained that, in the past, Japanese manufacturers would typically hire Japanese writers who studied English in Japan to write the English section of their instruction manual. This explained why instruction manuals were often impossible to read. Studying English in Japan and growing up speaking the language were two entirely different things. And because instructions were now commonly written in two to four languages (Martin had thrown in phrases like "global economy" and "melting borders" to sound more knowledgeable), he explained that companies were now hiring writers who were native speakers of the language in which the directions were to be written. This was why he had been hired.

Martin spent an afternoon forging the acceptance letter, creating what he thought looked like an authentic piece of stationery. Only when Jim pressed him for the financial details did Martin show him the letter and admit that he was being paid $300 for the assignment, a sum that surprised his frugal friend ("Three hundred dollars for writing a recipe?") until Martin grudgingly admitted that it had taken more than fifteen hours to write and edit the pamphlet.

"Just twenty an hour then, huh?" Jim had said, always quick with mental arithmetic.

A week later Martin informed his friend that the bicycle company had offered him two other assignments.

His writing career was off and running.

"A martini set? I can't believe that people pay you to write that stuff!" Jillian protested, handing Martin's order to Freddy. "You are one lucky man."

Martin watched as Jillian moved to the other end of the counter to take the order of a man named Jeff, another Quaker Diner regular who Martin avoided at all costs. Jeff was a perpetually happy guy who said all the right things and made people laugh almost effortlessly. Sitting next to the man was like sitting next to the sun. It was impossible to be noticed with him blazing away beside you.

Martin looked forward to the day when he and Jillian could enjoy some time away from the diner. Up until now, they had seen each other only within the walls of the restaurant, and Martin had been fine with this arrangement, considering the secrecy surrounding his life.

Lately, however, Martin had grown tired of seeing Jillian only in the diner, with the demands of her other customers (especially the annoying ones like Bob and Jeff) getting in the way. He had been considering asking Jillian to meet him outside the diner, on a more traditional date, but thus far he hadn't found the nerve to do so. He was worried about what the two of them might talk about or do. In the diner, their conversations were public domain, so personal subjects were rarely broached, and Martin liked it this way. In fact, he had been shocked when Jillian publicly declared her affection for him the first time. As he was exiting the diner one day last May, she had shouted out an unaccustomed "Good-bye, Martin!," stopping her constantly moving feet a moment in order to do so.

Taken aback, Martin had managed an uninspired "See you tomorrow."

"It's a date then?" Jillian had asked.

"Yeah," Martin had replied, less enthusiastically than he would have liked in retrospect. "A date."

The next morning Martin had arrived at the diner wearing a tie and sports jacket, the first time he had worn anything other than jeans and a T-shirt to breakfast. Jillian had commented on how handsome he looked as soon as he was seated on his favorite stool, and she had followed up the compliment with a kiss on the cheek, Martin's first from her. He had seen Jillian greet other customers in this manner, usually regulars like Jeff (but never Bob), but Martin knew that his kiss was different. The softness of her lips and the way she had leaned into him ever so slightly had spoken volumes of her affection for him.

The date had gone splendidly. Although Jillian was busy with a restaurant full of customers, she had managed to spend a few extra moments with Martin whenever she could, and Martin had assisted her by consuming five cups of coffee in less than an hour, necessitating her frequent return for refills. Conversation had been light despite her frequent visits to his section of the counter, but he did manage to ask her how she was feeling and if she had any plans for the evening.

"A hot bath and then me and Betty are scheduled for some television on the couch," she had replied with a warm smile.

Martin had assumed that Betty was Jillian's cat or dog but was happy to discover just recently that Betty was actually her longtime roommate. Martin couldn't stand dogs or cats (too unpredictable for his liking) and had dreaded the day that the two would need to broach the subject of pets. But about a month ago Betty had made an appearance in the diner, and Martin had overheard Jillian introducing her roommate to Mr. and Mrs. Sheppard, Quaker regulars. He waited for a similar introduction and had been surprised when he didn't receive one. It had been a busy day, however, and he and Betty had been sitting about eight stools apart.

Martin watched as Freddy, the thankfully bald fry cook (Martin wretched at just the thought of hair in his food), added blueberries to the pancakes that he knew were his. Freddy was the fry cook at the Quaker Diner every day but Monday, and Martin liked him a lot. The two had never spoken, but Martin loved the routine and cadence that Freddy had developed and thoroughly enjoyed watching the man work. Every move that Freddy made was with purpose. No steps were ever wasted in the preparation of an order, and repetition was the hallmark of everything the fry cook did. Eggs always cracked on the same side of the grill. Shells always tossed into the same bucket. Hash browns stirred between every order. Counter spaces wiped almost incessantly. Thanks to Freddy, Martin knew exactly what he was getting when he placed his order with Jillian, because every order was prepared in exactly the same way every time.

Eight minutes later Jillian delivered a stack of blueberry pancakes to Martin, and fifteen minutes and two cups of coffee after that, Martin was ready to leave his tip and pay for his meal. Tipping Jillian had always been awkward for Martin. He wanted to tip her well every day, above the customary 17 percent that he tipped most serving persons. But at the same time, tipping her above and beyond what she deserved felt wrong to Martin, like he was trying to purchase her affection. In the end, he decided to round Jillian's tip up to the nearest dollar, something he never did under ordinary circumstances. This decision had also made things easier for Martin, since the Quaker Diner was one of the few restaurants he frequented that did not accept credit cards. Paying with his Visa allowed Martin to calculate his tips to the penny, which he usually did. Prior to his relationship with Jillian, Martin had been forced to fill his pockets with change prior to coming to the diner, in order to tip properly.

Martin lay two dollar bills down beside his plate (almost a 25 percent tip today) and made his way to the cash register at the front of the restaurant. When time permitted, Jillian would walk the length of the counter in order to collect his payment, but because she was responsible for the rear section of the diner, this was often impossible, as it was today. She was pouring refills and making small talk with a father and daughter sitting at the counter when Martin passed by and said, "See you tomorrow, Jill."

Jillian looked up briefly, smiled at Martin, and said, "Tomorrow it is, my dear" before returning her attention to her newest customers.

Martin loved it when she called him "my dear." Though she said it almost every day to him, he never got tired of hearing those two wonderful words.

Before pulling out of the parking lot, Martin refocused his attention on the business of the day. Client referrals were next on Martin's list, and though he normally disliked everything associated with Housekeeping Day, this was one task that he enjoyed very much. His latest referral had come by way of the Gallos of Kensington, who had proven to be an excellent source of potential clients. As professional chefs, the Gallos were constantly hosting and (more important) being invited to a large number of dinner parties in the area, so their refrigerator magnets were rarely devoid of a new invitation. Almost all of Martin's referrals came from invitations stuck on the sides of his clients' refrigerators or filed away on a desktop, reflecting his belief that like-minded people traveled in the same circles. Married couples befriended other married couples. Couples without children sought couples in similar circumstances. People also tended to associate with others of similar financial standing. The culmination of these suppositions was Martin's belief that the best source of potential clients was his current clients' friends, and the wedding, anniversary, birthday, and dinner party invitations (which usually included the couples' full names, addresses, and telephone numbers) served as access to these people and their lives.

Invitations were also effective at weeding out the wrong kind of client. An invitation to a bar mitzvah, for example, signaled the presence of a child in the home. A daughter's wedding invitation, on the other hand, might signal a child leaving the nest, making that couple a potentially profitable one. Invitations could also effectively signal a family's financial standing. A catered party in the home or the use of the dining room at a moderately priced country club usually indicated a certain level of financial success and lifestyle that appealed to Martin when choosing a client. A dinner party at a beach home on Martha's Vineyard, however, indicated that a client might be too wealthy for Martin's taste. Martin had even taken the time to learn about greeting cards and their pricing, and he could now tell with a cursory examination how much someone had spent on an invitation—a good clue to their financial status.

While all of this information was helpful in identifying potential clients, none of it could replace a site visit and extensive research. The site visit always came first, because just by examining a home and its surroundings from the street, Martin could eliminate 75 percent of all couples referred to him.

Martin's referral of the day brought him to the home of Jennifer and David Hugh of Southington. From the invitation that Martin had photographed two weeks ago, he knew that Jennifer and David were planning a Hawaiian-themed dinner party for an unspecified number of guests in five weeks. The invitation, printed on average card stock in typography, had encouraged the Gallos to "Get into the spirit by dressing like a native! Colorful leis, flowered shirts, and even hula skirts are all welcome!" Martin had taken this as a good sign. Though the Gallos' finances were well within Martin's specifications, he had found that, unlike most clients, the Gallos also had friends who were much wealthier than themselves, and so he was frequently disappointed to discover that a Gallo referral lived in an enormous home along the Connecticut shoreline and maintained a stable of polo ponies nearby. Inviting guests to wear hula skirts did not seem like something that multimillionaires would find amusing, so he held out hope that Jennifer and David Hugh would prove to be potentially profitable clients.

Less than thirty minutes after leaving the diner, Martin pulled onto Ridgewood Road in the quiet town of Southington and began scanning mailboxes for number 32. If the site visit didn't eliminate the Hugh family as clients, his next step would be to research the couple thoroughly, a task from which Martin extracted great pleasure. The Hughs' home turned out to be a large blue Colonial set more than fifty feet from the road and more than a hundred yards from any neighbor, bordered by trees at the rear of the lot. A relatively discreet location on a dead-end street with a probable backyard approach was an extremely good start.

Though Martin typically relished the process of vetting client referrals, he found his mind continually wandering to the last item on his list: *Alan*. He knew that the client referral needed to be addressed first, but he couldn't help but look ahead to the afternoon, when his plan for Alan would be put into place. As he drove past the Hughs' home a second time and prepared to stop, he forced himself to refocus on the task at hand. There would be plenty of time to address the Alan situation after his work was finished in Southington.

Martin brought the car to a halt alongside the Hughs' front lawn and extracted a map from the glove compartment, opening it until it nearly filled the front seat. If anyone ever questioned him (and it had happened once about seven years ago), Martin would play the role of a lost motorist, in search of the road that he was on but in another town entirely.

"I'm looking for Locust Street. Is this the right street?" he had said to the police officer who had pulled up behind him, exited the cruiser, and approached his car. Martin had been parked on a residential cul-de-sac at the time, and no doubt the police officer (or more likely one of the neighbors) had become suspicious of a man sitting in his car in a neighborhood that received few visitors.

"This *is* Locust Street, sir," the officer had said, continuing to look down upon Martin with grave suspicion. "What house number are you looking for?"

"This one," Martin said, indicating the 566 on the mailbox. "Is there another Locust Street in Berlin?"

"This isn't Berlin," the officer chuckled, relaxing his face. "You're in Cromwell, sir. You're on the right street but in the wrong town."

Martin had escaped the encounter (his only one with law enforcement while working) unscathed and had never returned to that neighborhood. More important, he was now secure in the knowledge that if questioned, his strategy would likely work again.

Looking through an irregular-shaped hole in the map about two inches in diameter, located at the junction of Interstates 84 and 684 (there were several of these holes, placed to make it appear that the map was old and worn, rather than deliberately altered), Martin began examining the home more closely. A two-car garage abutted the home, something Martin did not like since it would be impossible for him to tell if there were cars parked inside, but not something that he couldn't work around. The lawn was well kept (a sign of orderliness), the curtains were drawn (always a plus when moving through a supposedly unoccupied home), and there was no blue octagonal sign warning of an alarm system. So far, Martin thought, this was looking good.

Initial inspection complete, Martin then doubled back onto the main road and parked the Subaru about two miles away in the parking lot of a Chinese restaurant. From here he would proceed on foot. Dressed in full jogging regalia (sweat suit, headband, headphones, strap-on water bottle, and pedometer), Martin made his way back to Ridgewood Road, carrying a broken dog

leash in his left pocket and a supply of plastic bags used to re-
trieve dog feces in the right. It had taken Martin more than a
year to build up his endurance to the point that he could run this
far while remaining observant and vigilant, and he took great
pleasure in knowing that another aspect of his career had been
mastered. Though walking would have likely been an effective
means to reconnoiter the referral's home, Martin believed that a
jogger attracted much less attention than a stranger walking
through a neighborhood. A runner could be just passing through
in an effort to squeeze a couple extra miles out of a lengthy run,
whereas walkers tended to stick to their own neighborhoods and
became more a part of the landscape, and a stranger would stand
out considerably more.

After years of training, Martin was able to run more than
five miles with relative ease, and so as he made his way past the
sixteen homes that lined Ridgewood Road on the way to the
Hughs' home, he slowed his pace and paid special attention to
the houses and driveways of the Hughs' neighbors. Too many
cars in the driveways would indicate a concentration of stay-at-
home moms, and if this were the case, Martin might reject the
Hughs as clients. Nosy neighbors were not good in Martin's line
of work, particularly stay-at-home wives with no children. Without children, the women could easily find themselves in the role
of bored housewives, and these were people whom Martin did
not trust. Too much time on their hands spelled a potential disaster for someone attempting to remain unnoticed.

Traffic cameras, ATM machines, and locations like gas stations, where exterior video surveillance cameras recorded auto-
mobile and foot traffic, were also areas of concern for Martin
when evaluating a neighborhood. He had read that the average
American is recorded by no less than half a dozen video cameras
in a single day, at traffic lights, inside stores and banks, and at

hundreds of other locations where video surveillance was routine. If the entrance to Ridgewood Road was manned by a traffic camera, and this was the only approach that he could make to the Hughs' home, Martin would likely eliminate them as potential clients, fearing that his routine visit would be recorded and used as evidence against him one day. Fortunately, Ridgewood Road was an offshoot of an equally residential street, so traffic cameras and local businesses equipped with video surveillance were of no concern in this case.

As he approached the Hughs' home, Martin removed the broken leash from his pocket and allowed it to dangle from his hands while assuming a worried look by furrowing his brows and widening his blue eyes (a routine he had practiced many times in the mirror before today). A few hundred yards from the target, he increased his pace and began darting his eyes left and right, glancing across lawns and side yards and into the copses of trees that separated many of the homes in this neighborhood. He then altered his pace, slowing down briefly, gazing intently at a line of shrubs and a stand of poplars before speeding up again. All of this movement had been carefully choreographed and rehearsed many times before, and Martin had actually videotaped this performance several times in order to critique it. In his mind, his actions were flawless. He was playing the role of a man looking for his dog, and he was playing it brilliantly.

With less than fifty yards to go, Martin looked left, stopped, and then sprinted into the treeline along the south side of the Hugh property, moving far enough into the trees in order to gain a full view of the Hughs' backyard. It was almost noon on a Tuesday, and there was no evidence that anyone was present in the Hugh residence, but for the benefit of someone who might be home, Martin also began shouting "Sandy?" as he closed in on the Hughs' backyard. "Sandy" had been the name of the dog in Martin's first-grade reader, *Bing and Sandy*, and in homage to his first-grade teacher, Mrs. Dubois, he had chosen the name for his ruse.

He didn't need to go far before he was hit with disappointment. Along the rear border of the Hughs' expansive back lawn stood a wooden swing set in excellent condition, a small swimming pool, and several pieces of sports equipment. The Hughs clearly had children, and this immediately invalidated their candidacy as clients.

Less than 10 percent of all his referrals actually ended up as clients, so Martin was accustomed to disappointment. This one, however, was especially difficult to swallow. Ridgewood Road had proven to be an ideal neighborhood, and other than the presence of children, the Hughs' home gave off all indications that they would make excellent clients. It made the jog back to the car seem especially long and painful.

Pessimism was not a common sentiment to Martin, but the disappointment at the Hughs' home was weighing on his mind as he made his way north on Interstate 91. It had been more than ten months since Martin had added a new client to his roster, and in that same time he had lost three others. One of them had moved out of state and two others had added children to their homes, one through pregnancy and another through adoption.

The adoption had been particularly startling to Martin, considering the child had arrived without the usual warning that accompanies a pregnancy (home pregnancy tests, baby shower announcements, ultrasound photos stuck to the refrigerator, and the slow but constant accumulation of pacifiers, high chairs, and the like). Though Martin routinely went through his clients' papers and mail, he had found nothing to indicate that the Brandners had been in the process of adopting a child. Had Molly and Scott Brandner not purchased the furniture for their four-year old son's bedroom and left a photo of him on the dresser in a gold frame, Martin might never have known about the adoption until he was greeted at the door by the Asian boy during one of his regularly scheduled visits. Making this loss even more difficult to accept had been the fact that he had been in the process of acquiring a diamond broach from Molly Brandner at the time, a six-month-long operation that he had been forced to abandon with the new arrival.

Martin had also been denied the opportunity to say good-bye to the Brandners and achieve the degree of closure that he typically managed to attain when releasing a client. During his final visit to a client's home, Martin dedicated much of his time to saying good-bye to the people whom he had come to know so well. He spent a few moments in each room of the house, reminiscing about the time he had passed with his clients and reflecting back upon the relationship they had established. It was a short but important bit of time that he always treasured, but upon discovering the Brandners' newly furnished bedroom, he immediately exited the home, never to return again.

The cancellation of the Brandners had occurred less than two months ago, and part of Martin was still reeling from the suddenness of the situation. This had made the Hughs' home even more appealing than it would have been normally. It had been nearly perfect in terms of what Martin looked for in a client location. With the exception of a two-car garage, he couldn't have asked for a better situation, and so the signs of children were a disappointing blow.

Thankfully, the last item on his list buoyed his spirits considerably.

Following a brief stop at The Corner Pug in West Hartford for a lunch of seafood chowder and salad, and a stop at the dry cleaner to pick up pants, Martin turned his attention to the final item on his list: *Alan.*

Though focused on the tasks at hand, Martin had spent much of his day thinking about this final task. He was excited about the possibilities that it might bring but worried about remaining undetected. He would need to be careful. Choose his course of action carefully. Leave no evidence behind.

He ultimately decided upon a library computer located in Newington, a suburban community where he had once lived, just south of West Hartford. The Newington Public Library was located adjacent to the town hall and was well known for its excellent collection of audiobooks, giving Martin reason to frequent the establishment often. The library seemed an ideal location at which to accomplish his final task of the day.

Computers at the Newington Public Library were assigned on a first-come, first-serve basis, and no identification was required to use them. Each computer was also attached to its own printer, and patrons paid for their printing on the honor system, handing over five cents for each copy to the desk clerk upon exiting the building. This allowed Martin to print anything that he needed without the risk of someone seeing it emerge from a public printer in the center of the library or behind the circulation desk. In addition, the Newington Public Library wasn't equipped with any surveillance cameras, so anything that Martin printed while he was there would be completely untraceable.

In order to avoid the prying eyes of his fellow patrons, Martin typed his letter using Microsoft Word, first reducing the Word window to a two-by-one-inch rectangle so that only a single word or two appeared at any time on the screen. This made composing difficult but not impossible. Once the entire letter was complete, Martin waited until he was certain that no one would pass by his monitor for a moment and then enlarged the window in order to proofread the message in its entirety.

Martin had been composing the note in his head throughout the day, but even with a solid idea of what to say, it took him more than forty-five minutes and eight separate drafts before he was satisfied with the words that were emerging from the laser printer to the left of his computer. As the paper slid its way out of the printer, Martin extracted a surgical glove from his pocket and surreptitiously placed it on his left hand. Once the printer had spit out its sheet, Martin removed it and placed it inside a manila folder that he had brought along with him, careful to handle the letter and folder with only his protected fingers.

Martin then removed an envelope from the same folder (also with his gloved hand) and placed it into the printer. Prior to driving over to Newington, he had stopped at an office supply store and purchased a box of standard envelopes for this purpose. Using surgical gloves, he had removed an envelope from the box and examined it for any distinguishing marks or code numbers that might link it to his purchase. Finding none, he had placed it into the manila folder, which he had carried into the library.

Changing the program's settings so that the printer would address his envelope, Martin typed in Alan Clayton's business address, which he had memorized the previous evening before burning the business card in the fireplace. He took an extra minute to ensure that he had fed the envelope into the printer properly, concerned because he had only brought in one envelope and wanted to avoid a second, more conspicuous trip back into the library. Satisfied, he clicked on the Print icon and was pleased to see that everything was in order.

His work complete, Martin closed Word, clicking the No box when asked if he would like to save changes to each of his documents. He dropped a dime into the basket at the circulation counter and exited the library without anyone taking a second glance, a fact that pleased him immeasurably. Martin was confident that, if they only knew what he had just written, people would be very interested in him.

Martin arrived in Lincoln, Rhode Island, three hours later

and stopped at the first public mailbox that he found, located outside a small retail plaza near a high school. Lincoln had been chosen at random by dropping a die onto a map of southern New England and waiting to see where it might stop. Seeing that it covered parts of the towns of Lincoln and Cumberland, Martin chose Lincoln because of its more convenient access from Route 146, a major north-south highway running through central Massachusetts and Rhode Island.

Parked beside the mailbox, Martin placed two more surgical gloves on his hands and extracted the letter and envelope from the manila folder. It read:

Alan
Bring your wife a single red rose tomorrow. Follow it up with a dozen more next week. It will mean more than you can imagine.
Trust me.
A friend

He was pleased with his creation. One of his first drafts had been more than two full paragraphs long, full of unnecessary details and instructions. In the end, Martin had managed to cut back all but the most essential words. He was especially happy with the use of the word "tomorrow," as it added the urgency to his suggestion that Martin felt was so important.

Martin wasn't sure how Alan Clayton would receive a letter like this, but he was sure that the message would do no harm. With its Rhode Island postmark, he would be unlikely to suspect his wife of sending it herself. And regardless of whether or not Alan Clayton recognized or acknowledged his own flaws, Martin had found that men were generally receptive to advice in the romance department. He might be a bit of a slob, but Martin doubted that Alan Clayton was a fool.

Reading through his letter one final time, looking carefully for anything that might hint at his identity, Martin folded it and placed it in the envelope, sealing it with a wet sponge, also purchased at the office supply store and moistened at the rest area on the Massachusetts Turnpike. No DNA left behind. He then affixed a stamp to the top right corner of the envelope (purchased from a vending machine at the rest area as well) and dropped his letter into the mailbox, checking twice to be sure it had slid into the belly of the blue box.

One his way back to Connecticut, Martin treated himself to a strawberry shake from McDonald's.

He had rarely been more pleased with himself.

If not for an inaccurately marked calendar, Martin might have been able to resume his daily routines without further deviation or incident.

Four days after mailing his letter to Alan Clayton, Martin was visiting the home of longtime clients Daniel and Justine Ashley when he heard a car pull into their gravel driveway.

This was not the first time in his career that a vehicle had pulled into a client's driveway while Martin was inside the house. More than a dozen times in the past, Martin had been inside a home when a UPS or FedEx truck arrived with a delivery for a client. In each of these instances, the driver either dropped a package at the front door or rang the doorbell and, when no one responded, left the package or a note pertaining to the package at the front door. Although these visits were infrequent, Martin was always cautious when passing by windows and doors at the front of a client's home, since deliveries were almost always made to the front of the house.

Once, Martin had been forced to cancel one of his clients, Jim and Joanne Bibeault of Coventry, when he discovered that UPS made deliveries to their home almost every day. Despite their secluded location and a house full of potential long-term acquisitions, Martin canceled the couple within a month of taking them on as clients, deciding that there was too much risk involved continuing to work with them.

Still, the sound of rubber grinding on gravel had always caused his heart to beat furiously, as was the case this time. Though the sound likely signaled a delivery, there was always an outside chance that the client had unexpectedly come home.

Standing in the Ashleys' pantry, Martin froze, trying to control the panic that immediately welled up inside him. Oddly enough, it was his experience in the Clayton household just days before that allowed him to regain his composure quicker than normal and to act without delay. He had survived the worst situation he could imagine, being trapped inside a home with a client, and his success had given birth to a greater degree of self-confidence than Martin could ever have imagined. His attention to detail and training had paid off, and a sense of invincibility had begun to stir within him.

Returning the digital camera to the bag slung over his shoulder, Martin closed the door to the pantry and headed for the stairway to the second floor. If the Ashleys were home, he couldn't risk passing through the kitchen to the back door, his normal point of egress, because the side door of the house also opened into the kitchen and served as the clients' customary point of entry. Although it was very unlikely that the Ashleys were home, it wasn't a risk worth taking.

Standard operating procedure in these circumstances was simple. Evacuate the house if possible, and if not (as was this case this time), take up a position in a predetermined hiding spot until the client exited the home again. Until his encounter with the Claytons, Martin had never found himself in this type of situation, but the possibility had always remained in his mind. For this reason, Martin had identified at least two hiding spots in each of his clients' homes in the event of an emergency.

These locations were chosen based upon his belief that they were infrequently accessed by the clients. The Ashleys, for example, had a closet in their basement filled with Christmas decorations, and a walk-in closet in a second-floor guest bedroom that was entirely empty. Martin felt that either location would serve as an effective hiding place in the event that he became trapped in the home.

In the case of the Claytons, Martin had identified as emergency hiding spots a corner behind the furnace in the basement and a closet in their home office that contained financial records from previous decades. But his rush to return the toothbrush to its proper location had prevented him from reaching one of his predetermined hiding spots in their home.

Yet he had escaped unscathed.

As Martin began to ascend the staircase to the second floor, the screen door on the porch swung open with a whining squeak and was followed by the sound of footsteps. Martin was now certain that this new arrival was neither Justine nor Daniel Ashley. Using the front door, which adjoined the screened porch, was not something the couple did with any frequency. Coat hooks, a bowl for keys, and an umbrella stand were all positioned in the kitchen by the side door, making it clear that the Ashleys used this entrance on a regular basis.

Still not taking any chances, Martin continued to move upstairs, stopping only at the sound of the porch door slamming shut. Though the suspected delivery man hadn't rung the doorbell or knocked on the Ashleys' front door, Martin wasn't surprised. He knew that delivery drivers typically maintained the same route, so if he (or she) had delivered packages to the house before (and apparently he had), he would know that the Ashleys were not home during the day. Martin paused, listening intently for the sound of the would-be delivery truck's engine and was rewarded a few moments later by the expected mechanical growl. Still, he waited a full three minutes before returning downstairs and resuming his normal activities.

There were less than five minutes left before Martin would need to exit the Ashleys' home when the phone rang and a message was recorded on their answering machine, words that would eventually cause Martin to deviate from his routine yet again, and change his life forever.

"Hi guys! It's Laura. Hey, I'm so sorry that I missed the party. I know I said I'd be there, but I got stuck in Philly with my Uncle Bob. He's still pretty sick, you know. I wish I could've been there and I'm so sorry I didn't call. Things just got crazy, if you know what I mean. Danny, I just dropped off your gift on the way to work. It's on the porch next to the swing. Hope you like it! I'll try you again later tonight, okay? Bye!"

As the answering machine beeped, indicating the end of the recording, Martin wasted no time in moving to the front of the house. Standing beside the living room window, he peeked through drawn curtains onto the enclosed porch. Sure enough, a long tubular package was resting against the swing, wrapped in colorful paper.

Standing there, staring at this unexpected surprise, Martin felt the same urge that he had first sensed inside the Claytons' coat closet return. It was the feeling of opportunity, of obligation.

The Ashleys owned a gourmet catering service in their hometown of Southington and kept some of the longest hours of any of Martin's clients, rising before five each morning (Martin always checked the setting on a client's alarm clock in order to determine the time that they awoke) and arriving home well after seven each evening. This rigorous schedule, combined with the success of their business, had made the Ashleys excellent clients.

Three months ago, Daniel Ashley had attended a conference

for the American Bakery Association in Houston, Texas, leaving his wife at home for almost a week. During that time, Justine Ashley, a petite, no-nonsense spitfire of a woman, had transformed their home into Surprise Party Central (actually sticking a Post-it to the dining room doors with this very title). Taking advantage of his absence, Justine Ashley began planning for her husband's fortieth birthday party in late October. During the week a guest list was created, invitations ordered, favors purchased and assembled, and bands interviewed.

Evidence of her plans littered the dining room, kitchen, and office. Copious notes on the various bands that she had interviewed were kept on a clipboard that migrated throughout the house during the week, with a large red circle eventually drawn around a band named "The Degenerates." Clay pots containing miniature putting greens, complete with turf grass and tiny flags and cups (presumably the party favors) were scattered about a makeshift assembly line on the dining room table, eventually disappearing at the end of the week, presumably to the home of a friend or relative for safekeeping. The guest list, tacked to a corkboard above the kitchen sink, expanded and shrank until it finally numbered 156 invitees. Most important, Martin had seen the invitation proofs indicating the date, time, and location of the party, five days from today, on Saturday, October 27, at the Water's Edge Resort in Westbrook, Connecticut. Martin had marked the day on his calendar as well, knowing that Justine Ashley had also planned a surprise golfing and fishing trip to Marco Island in Florida immediately following the party, allowing him unrestricted access to his clients' home for just under a week.

But somehow a woman named Laura, presumably a friend of the couple, had marked the date incorrectly in her calendar and thought that the party had already taken place. If Daniel Ashley were to come home and find the gift on his front porch or listen to the message on the answering machine, all of his wife's work would be ruined.

Martin found himself with an unexpected choice: attempt to help Justine Ashley while risking his anonymity, or ignore the situation and allow the surprise to potentially be ruined.

Had Martin not seen the single red rose standing in a thin crystal vase (one that he had inventoried long ago) on the Claytons' dining room table earlier that morning, during his scheduled visit to their home, he might not have felt compelled to act on Justine Ashley's behalf. But the flower had been there, along with a card that read:

I sometimes forget to tell you how much I love you.
Forgive me.

No large-scale acquisition had ever brought Martin more joy than the image of that flower and the words on the card, scrawled in the hand of a man who loved his wife but had too often forgotten to tell her. His apparent success with the Claytons had brought Martin a remarkable feeling of attachment and goodwill for the couple, and he now felt compelled to come to the aid of Justine Ashley and her cause for the same reason.

In fact, as Martin considered helping his client, he also began to wonder if he hadn't been placed in the Ashley home at that particular moment by fate, in order to hear the answering machine message and take action. Even before Laura's message, Martin had begun to speculate as to whether his career choice had actually been meant to be a vehicle to a higher calling. During visits to the Archambauts and Owens earlier that morning, he had begun envisioning himself as an agent for good, entering his clients' homes in order to make a living, but perhaps to improve their lives as well.

Perhaps Martin had been meant to help his clients all along.

The logical and calculated side of Martin dismissed this notion immediately, and not surprisingly. In the more than sixteen years that he had been in this business, Martin had never entertained any such thoughts. His methodical approach to business had earned him his success, and he was well aware of that fact. Involving himself unnecessarily in the lives of his clients would have been the last thing he might consider. But that rose, and those two simple sentences written on a card from husband to wife, had begun to make him wonder.

And now he wondered if he was somehow meant to help the Ashleys as well.

Without much fanfare, Martin decided that he would try. The only question was how much action he dare risk.

The first decision that Martin made, while still standing in the living room and staring at the gift through the window, was not to allow anything he might do to jeopardize the Ashleys as clients. Helping the couple made sense to him only if it did not place his relationship with them at risk. Whatever he might choose to do, it had to be done without uncovering his identity or his reason for being inside their home.

Next he looked at his watch. 12:35. The Ashleys wouldn't be home until at least 7:00, so he had more than enough time to act. It would mean eliminating scheduled visits to the Sullivans and the Pearls, but those visits could be made up later. This emergency took precedence.

Martin moved to the Ashleys' kitchen and sat down at the butcher-block table, concealed by drawn shades and a dirty window, and began running through his options. The simplest solution would be to erase the message from the machine and confiscate the gift. This would eliminate the immediate danger to Justine Ashley's surprise, but doing so would also leave evidence of his presence in the Ashley home. When Laura and the Ashleys spoke (later that night in all likelihood), the gift and phone call would certainly come up in conversation, and it would quickly become apparent that someone had been in the home.

Even if Martin chose to forsake the Ashleys as clients in favor of protecting Justine Ashley's hard work, erasing the message and confiscating the gift failed to eliminate the danger to the surprise entirely. According to her message, Laura was planning to call later that evening, and if Daniel Ashley answered the phone, the surprise would surely be ruined, even if the message and gift had been eliminated.

Martin saw his options as very limited.

Option #1 was to eliminate the evidence (the message on the machine and the gift) but also to alert Laura to her error, so that she would not call about the party later that evening. He would have to do this without endangering his anonymity, which meant that even if he managed to find and contact the woman, he would have to inform her of the error in a way that would keep his identity a secret and explain how he knew of her error in the first place.

Not an easy task in Martin's immediate estimation.

After some thought, he briefly considered calling Laura (provided that he could find her phone number), posing as the Water's Edge banquet manager. He would tell her that he was calling to confirm her meal choice for Saturday night, claiming that their computer had crashed and the meal choices for the Ashleys' guests had been lost. Martin had seen the invitations (and had even photographed one), and he knew that Justine Ashley had offered her guests three different meal choices. He could even go back to the digital record to determine which three options were available, if necessary. Upon receiving the call, Laura would be alerted to the actual date of the party and would undoubtedly call Justine Ashley and admit to her error, giving Justine enough time to get home and eliminate the message and gift before Daniel found either.

This idea initially appealed to Martin, but in the end he decided that it would not work. A phone call from a banquet manager to a guest would be highly unorthodox and suspicious (and questions as to how the banquet manager acquired Laura's phone number would inevitably arise), but more important, Justine Ashley was likely to see or speak to the banquet manager again before or at the party. Grateful to him for averting disaster, she would likely thank him for the phone call to Laura, explaining how his call had unwittingly preserved the surprise. The banquet manager would deny making the phone call, and Martin would be forced to cancel the Ashleys as clients, since questions as to who made the phone call would necessarily follow.

It was in the midst of this train of thought that the alarm on Martin's watch began to vibrate, signaling the prescribed end to his visit. Only once before had Martin been inside a client's home for longer than he allowed, and that was during his recent Clayton visitation. Though the vibration of the alarm initially sent a shot of panic through his system, Martin focused on his success in the Claytons' home and forced himself to return to the task at hand.

Option #2 was to alert Justine Ashley to the phone message and gift and have her intercept both before her husband could. Again, this would have to be done without exposing his identity to the client and without telling her how he knew about Laura's error. While this option also seemed impossible, Martin developed a plan in which he would call Justine Ashley at work, claiming to be a UPS driver who was attempting to drop off a gift at the home. He would explain that the screen door to the porch was locked and would ask where he should leave the brightly colored gift. Alerted to the presence of a gift at the home a week before the party, Justine Ashley might then find a reason to go home ahead of her husband, in order to determine why a gift had arrived so early. She would then hear the message on the answering machine and be able to eliminate the evidence before her husband arrived home.

He eventually dismissed this plan as well because of the unlikelihood that a UPS driver would know the work number of a homeowner on his route. This too would appear suspicious. There was also no guarantee that Justine Ashley would come home upon receiving the phone call. She might just assume that the gift was from an out-of-state relative who had no plans to attend the party but routinely sent a gift every year. There was also no guarantee that Justine Ashley would check the messages on her machine upon arriving home, and the fact that Laura had not sent the gift by UPS might eventually come up as well.

This train of thought led Martin to consider creating a situation that would force Justine Ashley home. A broken water main, a rock thrown through the front picture window, or an electrical problem were all possibilities that Martin considered but eventually dismissed, finding no way to guarantee that Justine Ashley and not her husband would respond to the problem.

It was at about this time that Martin developed his contingency plan. More than an hour had passed at the table, and without a planned course of action, he had begun to grow despondent. Though he still felt as though he had heard Laura's message for a reason and had been meant to help his client, he was beginning to wonder if he was clever enough to arrive at a solution to the problem with which he had been presented. Perhaps he simply wasn't up to the task, or maybe there was no viable solution. The self-confidence that his success with the Claytons had bred began to wane, and it was amid this growing sense of dread that the pieces of the contingency plan suddenly fell into place.

If no other plan was formulated, Martin decided, he would move the gift underneath a table beside the porch swing, out of sight from anyone who wasn't looking for it. He would erase the message from the answering machine and then trip the circuit breakers in the house, temporarily knocking out the electricity in order to provide the appearance of a local power outage. When he reset the breakers, electricity would be restored, but the digital clocks in the house would begin blinking their preset 12:00 starting point, providing visual evidence of the outage. Martin realized that digital answering machines such as the one the Ashleys owned would not typically lose a recording in the event of a power loss, but he reasoned that the discovery of a missing message combined with the appearance of a temporary power outage would probably lead a homeowner to assume that the two were somehow related, thus dispelling any question or fear that an intruder had erased the message.

Martin liked the plan. He thought it might work. He estimated its probability of success at somewhere near 60 percent. With the incriminating evidence eliminated to a degree, it would all come down to Laura's phone call. If Justine Ashley answered the phone when she called that evening, disaster would likely be averted. But if Daniel Ashley decided to pick up the phone first, or if the couple went out to dinner after work (a not uncommon event), allowing Laura enough time to leave another message on the machine, the surprise would surely be ruined. Martin set the probability for success at 60 percent based upon his belief that women were more likely than men to pick up the phone, and that Laura was more likely to be a friend to Justine Ashley than to her husband. Thanks to the advent of caller ID, Martin found that ringing telephones were often passed to the intended recipient before anyone answered them. Based upon these assumptions, he gave the plan a good chance for success, perhaps as high as 70 percent if the Ashleys came straight home after work.

Not bad for a contingency plan.

Half an hour after he had finalized the details, Martin was ready to make this his primary plan as well. It was almost two o'clock and he was no closer to finding a better solution than when he first sat down at the kitchen table. He had already spent more time in the Ashleys' home than at any other client's in history, and though he was certain that the Ashleys would not be home for another four hours or more, he was becoming nervous just the same.

As with many of his ideas, it was when Martin had stopped struggling for a breakthrough that one arrived. He was standing in the Ashleys' basement, examining the circuit breakers, when his mind took an unconscious leap out of the box and awarded him with a possibility.

The plan, as it developed in his mind, involved a certain degree of danger, and its success would depend on Martin's ability to acquire critical pieces of information, but if it worked, Justine Ashley's surprise would most assuredly be saved. Oddly enough, the danger in the plan appealed to Martin in a way that it never had before. He had always been painstakingly methodical, and this had allowed him to become as successful in his career as he had been thus far. But while trapped in the Claytons' home, Martin had demonstrated an ability to think quickly and to adapt to a pressure-filled situation, and these were qualities that he hadn't known that he possessed. As he reflected back upon that episode, he couldn't help but be impressed by the rapidity and wisdom of his actions. Though frightened at the time, his quick thinking had kept him safe from any real danger. His years of planning and experience had paid off, and though the plan that he was formulating now included some risk, it was no more dangerous than what he had faced while trapped behind the Claytons' sofa. Most important, the risk that he might face in no way jeopardized the Ashleys as clients. Even if his plan failed,

Martin felt that he would be able to return to the Ashleys' home the next day, his anonymity still intact.

So now Martin had another decision to make. With a solid contingency plan in place, he would have to decide whether this new plan was worth the risk. Did it afford him a greater chance of success than that of tripping the breakers and proceeding with his contingency plan? If his new plan failed, would there be time to come back to the Ashley home and put his contingency plan into place? If that were the case, was he willing to reenter the Ashleys' home for a second time in a day, something he had always tried to avoid throughout his career? Were there any other dangers that he hadn't yet considered? Could he do what needed to be done in order to make the plan work?

Martin ran through the plan in his mind, attempting to visualize his actions and the potential obstacles that he might face. The plan involved doing things that Martin had never done before, yet he had never been trapped in a home with two clients before either, and that situation had turned out exceptionally well. The plan also depended on several factors over which Martin had no control, but he felt that those factors would be determined early enough to allow him to abandon course and return to the Ashleys' home to enact his contingency plan, if necessary. He attempted to estimate the amount of time it might take to complete his new plan, breaking each task down into pieces and adding up the minutes to determine if he might complete his plan (or fail) before seven o'clock, and if so, how much before that hour.

Martin spent more than ten minutes standing by the fuse box, his hand unconsciously holding the latch on the box's door, visualizing, timing, assessing, and predicting.

Once his decision was made, he moved without hesitation.

Closing the fuse box, Martin headed back upstairs and toward the Ashleys' office, located in a spare bedroom on the second floor. The first thing he would need was Laura's full name and address, and he thought he knew where to find it.

The office was a study in dichotomy. Two identical desks dominated the west and east walls of the room, facing away from each other. The desk closest to Martin was used by Daniel Ashley, a tall, thin man who cared little for organization or appearance. Piles of paper littered the desktop and computer keyboard, with no attempt to neaten or even out the stacks. Junk mail and circulars were piled in one corner, moved only when the pile threatened to topple over. His computer hummed quietly, always turned on, with more than half a dozen programs open and running. Photographs of Justine Ashley, most of which featured her in an apron, armed with a spatula, or decked out in some other cooking accoutrement, were displayed across the top of the desk, curling rectangles propped against a stack of cookbooks, a softball trophy, and a dish containing coins, cufflinks, and dozens of keys, none of which had ever moved from their round, yellow home. A two-drawer file cabinet stood beside the desk, unlocked as always, one drawer open, with file folders stacked inside. The drawers of the desk were filled with a mishmash of office supplies, birthday candles, golf tees, aging check registers, and more.

In opposition to this mess stood Justine Ashley's desk on the far side of the room. Not a single item other than her small wireless keyboard and flat screen monitor occupied any space on the desktop. Along a shelf mounted above the desk were several framed photographs of Daniel Ashley looking perpetually distinguished despite his long, somewhat goofy face, along with smaller images of friends and relatives. A larger photo of the couple hung on the wall above the shelf, their difference in height (nearly two feet) painting a startling contrast. An identical file cabinet stood beside her desk, but this cabinet remained locked at all times. Martin had successfully picked the lock years ago (without the use of a pick gun, he was proud to recall) and had found it to be a study in organization. Files hung alphabetically in color-coded folders and everything seemed to have a place. Most of the material contained therein pertained to the finances of the business, but there were also files for recipes, vacation plans, and documents such as college transcripts and income tax returns. She even had a file set aside specifically for her birth certificate (something Martin had as well). The drawers to her desk were also neatly organized, containing many of the same types of office supplies that could be found in her husband's desk, but with greater ease. Martin knew that Justine Ashley's address book was located in the top drawer of the desk, and that it too was meticulously well kept.

Martin began on the first page of the book and started thumbing through the dozens of names that each page contained. Justine Ashley knew a great many people and appeared to save addresses and phone numbers for years. Because he did not know Laura's last name, he would have to flip through the entire address book, hopeful that the couple had only one Laura in their life. If more than one Laura were listed in the book, there would be no way of determining which one had called the house that afternoon.

On the page containing surnames starting with G, Martin found a listing for a Laura Green, including an address and telephone number. The number was the third of more than twenty names listed on the page, indicating that the Ashleys had known this woman for some time. Less than ten minutes later, Martin completed his search of the WXYZ page, finding no other Laura in the book. He returned to the page containing Laura Green's name and photographed it, recording the address and phone number on his digital camera but committing the information to memory as well. He then returned the address book to the drawer and made his way back to the kitchen.

Lifting the telephone off its cradle (the first time Martin had ever touched a clients' phone), he activated the caller ID feature by pressing a button imprinted with an arrow pointing down, bringing up the incoming calls on the phone's digital readout and allowing the user to scroll through them. He noted the first number to appear on the listing and confirmed by the time stamp that it had been Laura Green's call. In place of a name, the words "Wireless Caller" appeared, indicating that she had called from her cell phone. He wasn't sure whether to be pleased or disappointed. Had Laura Green called from home, Martin's course of action would have been difficult, but at least it would have been clear. Adding her unknown locale to the equation added a great deal of uncertainty.

Nevertheless, Martin felt as though he had found the right person, and the first task in his plan was complete.

Before exiting the house, Martin completed a meticulous survey of each room that he had entered. In all, he had spent more than two hours in the Ashley home, a record for him (and one he had never intended on setting), and though he had spent the majority of that time at the kitchen table (purposely, so as to avoid leaving any accidental trace of his presence), he still wanted to be sure that he had left everything in its place. The disturbance to his routine worried him, and demanded an extra degree of vigilance.

Satisfied that everything was in order, Martin exited through the back door and cut across the Ashleys' backyard and into a line of trees along the northern border of the property. Less than five minutes later he emerged onto the baseball field of Southington High School, empty on this warm and bright day, and five minutes after that Martin was on the road and heading for Manchester, a town about thirty minutes north of Southington, and the one that Laura Green called home.

chapter 8

Laura Green's home was a nightmare. Located on West Middle Turnpike, a busy two-lane road running through the center of Manchester, number 280 was a white and tan Colonial adjacent to similar houses on three sides and all set less than fifty feet apart. A narrow driveway winded beside the house and into a single-car garage at the rear of the property, a building so small that Martin wondered if a large lawnmower would fit inside. Though a tall wooden fence ran along the rear of the property, no fencing or shrubbery protected the front or side doors from the view of the neighbors. Accessing this house would be difficult, if not impossible.

Insane, Martin thought as he examined it further.

Adding to the insanity was a driveway marked by chalk drawings of flowers, cats, tic-tac-toe boards, and several large, shining yellow balls (presumably the suns of some multistarred solar system). Laura Green appeared to have children, and though the house looked quiet and no car was parked in the driveway, the thought of small children terrified Martin.

Martin took in all these details as he stood in front of the home, tying his purposefully uncooperative shoelaces. Pretending to struggle with the laces made him think about Mrs. Carroll, the kindergarten teacher who had once warned him that he would not graduate to first grade until he had learned to tie his shoes and recite his telephone number by heart. He recalled the stress that her demands had placed on his six-year-old psyche and smiled.

This task would prove to be infinitely more challenging than anything Mrs. Carroll could have thrown at him.

Martin had hoped for a better situation than this. Had Laura Green been referred to Martin as a potential client, he would have dismissed her following the drive-by without a second thought. This was simply not the kind of home to which Martin would ever attempt to gain access.

Until today.

With his troublesome shoe finally tied, Martin continued his jog around the block, reviewing the situation in his mind. It was October and the house appeared empty. Two of the adjacent neighbors appeared to be absent as well, but the third neighbor had two identical Volkswagen Beetles parked in the driveway and fans running in the upstairs windows. This was also the neighbor closest to the Greens' side door, the most likely point of entry for Martin. Though it was apparent that children lived at the residence, it was unlikely that they were home alone during the day while their mother worked. Since it was October, Martin assumed that they were probably at school or daycare, safely out of the way.

Martin considered all of these factors while also reminding himself that Laura Green was not a client, nor would she ever be a client. Certain precautions and routines that he took with a typical client might be avoidable in this case, but which of these could be omitted while still avoiding detection remained a question.

Next he checked his watch. 3:03. If he was going to make his move, it would have to be soon. If Laura Green left work before Martin could act, he would be forced to abort his plan. She would have to be in a public location in order for him to have even a chance at success. Of greatest concern to Martin was the visibility of the front and side doors of the home. He had no doubt in his mind that he could gain entry, but he worried that one of the many neighbors might see him doing so.

As Martin turned back onto West Middle Turnpike, he removed the broken leash from his pocket and began yelling for Sandy, assuming the lost-pet-owner persona that had become second nature to him. When he reached Laura Green's driveway, he bolted left past the side door and into her backyard, where he stopped, looking left and right, continuing to shout for Sandy but quickly taking in all that he saw at the same time.

Martin first noted that the backyard was littered with large, colorful plastic toys, additional indicators of the existence of the Green children. A Fisher-Price picnic table, a plastic lawn mower that popped plastic balls around like a popcorn popper, and a variety of rubber balls were strewn from the house to the edge of the fence. More important, Martin noted two additional entrances to the Green home, one through a sliding glass door adjacent to a patio and another through a hatchway leading into the basement. Though sliding glass doors were nearly impossible for Martin to pick, the hatchway held potential. One of Martin's clients in Glastonbury kept their hatchway unlocked at all times, and Martin had used it as a means of entry for years.

Still shouting out the name of his lost dog, Martin moved toward the metallic doors of the hatchway, feigning interest in a copse of shrubs growing alongside it. Even with the fence at the rear of the property, Martin noted, it was possible for someone in the backyard neighbor's home to see him if he or she were on the second floor, looking out of one of the three windows that faced the Green property. Peering over his shoulder to ensure that those windows were vacant, Martin gave a pull on the hatchway doors and found them to be locked.

His only access would need to be through either the exposed front or side door.

With time of the essence, Martin left the property and ran back to the Subaru at an unaccustomedly fast pace. The Subaru was parked three blocks away at a Bally fitness center, where he had initially donned his jogging disguise and made his way into Laura Green's neighborhood. If he decided to enter the house, he would need his pick gun, which meant that he would have to decide how he was going to reapproach the Green home. He could continue in his present disguise, or he could switch to another.

In addition to his jogging paraphernalia, Martin owned a Northeast Utilities uniform, a mixture of store-bought pants matching those worn by the utility workers, a blue cap, and an actual NU work jacket, left behind by workers at a job site about seven years ago. Martin had seen the jacket slung over a set of flashing barricades one evening on his way home, and had immediately recognized its value. Though he wore it infrequently, he currently had two clients (including the Pearls) whose homes were more exposed to their neighbors than most, and he made a point of donning this costume from time to time before approaching these locations.

After a moment of consideration, Martin decided to keep with his original uniform, concerned about the suspicion he might arouse if one of Laura Green's neighbors had already seen him jogging in the neighborhood.

Better to remain consistent.

Less than ten minutes later, a breathless Martin was reapproaching the Green home for the third time, now paying careful attention to the neighbors' homes as he closed in. If he saw a face in a window or anyone outside one of their homes, he would abort the mission immediately.

There are moments in life when a person cannot believe what he or she is about to say or do, but for one as measured and methodical as Martin, this might have been the first time in his life that he'd had such an experience. As he jogged back down the hill toward Laura Green's home, closing in on the moment of truth, he was momentarily stunned by the reality of his current situation. He was about to enter the unmapped home of an unknown woman in order to gather information that would help him execute a plan that was outlandish at best. He was risking his safety and his freedom for a woman he had never actually met. Despite all this, he knew with certainty that his actions were right and just. Justine Ashley needed his help, and there was no one else with the skill, knowledge, or ability to come to her aid. He was meant to be her savior. That single rose, a gift from Alan Clayton to his wife, had confirmed it. His success with the Claytons had signaled to Martin that there were times when his considerable skills could be used for good, and that the affection he had begun to feel for his clients was not as ridiculous or purposeless as it might have previously seemed.

Boldness was what Martin believed had saved him in the Clayton home, and so boldness was what he decided upon as a course of action today. Without slowing at all or assuming the pretense of a lost dog, Martin turned up the Green driveway once again, this time ascending the three concrete steps to the side door. Though the front door was slightly less exposed to the neighbors' homes, Martin knew that the locks on side doors were consistently less complex and therefore easier to pick. Also, homeowners tended to lock, dead-bolt, and even chain their front doors but leave their side doors and other frequently used entrances relatively unprotected. In this case speed was critical, considering his exposed position. Martin did not want to run into a tricky dead bolt or multiple locks.

Pick gun already in hand (having pulled it from his waistband like a gunslinger), Martin opened the screen door and began to work on the lock. Though the door was equipped with a dead bolt, it had not been engaged, and Martin successfully unlocked the door in less than twenty seconds. Taking one final peek at Mr. and Mrs. Matching Volkswagen's home and seeing no sign of life, Martin entered the Green house, closing the door and relocking it.

Even before the attack, Martin knew that something was wrong.

The side door of the Green home opened up into a long, rectangular kitchen. As Martin scanned the room from one end to the other, he realized that his assessment of Laura Green had been completely wrong.

Had he been asked, Martin would have said that it was the refrigerator that gave it away, but in reality, he had detected a number of clues on an unconscious level that quickly led him to the same conclusion. The lack of dishes in the sink. The kitchen table pushed up along the far wall, leaving room for only one person to sit comfortably. The single place setting on the table. A raincoat and a sweater hanging alone on coat hooks mounted next to the door. The cleanliness of the linoleum.

But the refrigerator had been the dead giveaway. A stainless-steel model, devoid of fingerprints of any kind, the only magnets attached to its surface lined in a neat row along the top of the door. Half a dozen plastic vegetables, aligned in perfect symmetry, with not a single scrap of paper beneath them.

This was not a home in which small children lived.

Had Martin managed to avoid assuming otherwise, he might have remembered to ring the doorbell before picking the lock. He always rang the doorbell of a new client, finding it an effective determinant of dogs in the home.

Had the possibility that Laura Green might be single entered his mind, Martin would have most assuredly rung the bell, knowing that women who live alone often kept pets, and if the woman was at all nervous about being alone, that pet was usually a large dog.

These thoughts and observations rushed into Martin's mind in the seconds before he heard the first angry bark and saw the black Labrador retriever come bursting through the entranceway into the kitchen and toward him.

"The Attack," as Martin would henceforth refer to it (referencing a chapter from one of his favorite novels, *Treasure Island*), was not as violent or as painful as the previous attack he had suffered, as a child, the one that had led to his lifetime fear of dogs.

Martin had been pedaling his bike down a long, winding driveway to the home of David Durand, one of his few friends at the time. Martin was twelve years old and had been over to the Durands' home many times, and he was very familiar with their Doberman pinscher, Valerie. Despite her ferocious appearance, Valerie had proven herself to be a gentle and fun-loving dog—until that fateful spring day.

David and his tall, balding father were standing at the end of the driveway, peering at the engine of one of the Durands' many fixer-uppers, this one an ancient Ford Mustang, as Martin glided across the pavement atop his knobby-wheeled Huffy. As he closed to within fifty feet of his friend, Valerie burst out of the open garage, hurling herself toward Martin at a furious pace. Though he had spent many an occasion with the animal, Martin took one look at the dog and knew that something was wrong, in much the same way he knew that something was wrong from the moment he entered Laura Green's kitchen.

As Valerie closed the gap between them, Martin turned his bike left to avoid the attack, but was too late. The dog leapt into the air, connecting with Martin's right leg and biting down hard.

The collision caused the bike to topple over and threw Martin to the pavement with the dog still clamped onto his throbbing leg.

Upon striking the ground, Martin screamed, feeling the gruesome tear of skin off his right elbow as he struggled to free his leg from Valerie's ironclad grip. David's father ran over, his son trailing close behind, and the two of them bent down to examine the carnage. As Mr. Durand attempted to remove the dog's jaws from Martin's leg, Martin watched as David carefully examined Valerie, never giving his wounded friend a second glance. In fact, minutes later, when David finally looked up and made eye contact with his friend, Martin detected a hint of blame in those small, gray eyes. Blame and a lack of concern for anything but his dog. The two had taken a severe fall onto the pavement, but in Martin's mind, if the dog was still holding on tight, she was doing better than he was.

It took Mr. Durand an agonizing five minutes to coax the jaws of his dog open, finally managing to do so by tickling the dog's underbelly. Martin was immediately rushed to the hospital in the back of Mrs. Durand's station wagon. The wounds were deep and fourteen stitches were required to sew up the holes, but Martin was released from the emergency room that same afternoon.

Though the animal control officer (and Martin) had wanted Valerie to be put down, Martin's mother prevailed and the animal was allowed to live. Martin was initially angered by his mother's defense of the dog, unable to understand her lack of concern for such a dangerous animal, but in time he understood and even came to respect her decision. In an age of overindulgent parents, she had gone against the grain and allowed a boy's beloved dog to live. She placed the needs of a young boy and his dog ahead of the anger and fear of her son, and that could not have been easy. Besides, her decision made sense. Valerie had never bitten anyone before. Ultimately, Mr. Durand chalked up the incident to "one of those things that can't be explained."

Though Martin eventually understood his mother's decision, he had found himself unable to forget the lack of concern his friend had shown him that day, and their friendship slowly dwindled to an occasional hello in the middle-school hallways. Eventually even those moments disappeared entirely.

David had been Martin's only real friend besides Jim, and the incident had led to Martin's extreme fear of dogs.

As the Labrador bounded into Laura Green's kitchen, Martin turned back toward the door, every muscle of his body bent on exiting the house as quickly as possible. Panic had once again seized him, but as he reached for the knob he saw the door to Mr. and Mrs. Matching Volkswagen's house opening and a woman (older and therefore nosey, Martin thought, despite his haste and panic) emerging from within. Trapped between a dog and a possible witness, Martin did the only thing he could: He ran.

Turning right, Martin ran out of the kitchen and passed through a small dining room, taking in details such as the loose Oriental rug on the floor and a collection of snow globes filling a glass display cabinet as he ran by. Only four chairs around the table, Martin noticed. Laura Green was probably not a frequent entertainer of guests. Once out of the dining room, Martin found himself in a short hallway that ended with a darkened room directly ahead before turning left into what he presumed was a living room.

Martin was running on instinct now, thoughts firing in his brain as he moved as quickly as possible, a combination of adrenaline, experience, and training working together seamlessly. Martin had already mapped the Green home without conscious effort, identifying it almost immediately as a roundabout, the type of home in which the rooms were positioned around a central staircase, allowing for continuous movement through the home without hitting a dead end. The staircase to the second floor was not on his left as he passed through the front hallway and by the front door, as he had expected, leaving him to assume (correctly) that it was on the inner wall of the living room. All of these thoughts flooded his mind instantaneously, his experience and preparation paying off in ways he'd never known it would.

Hearing a thump behind him (probably the dog slipping on the loose rug and running into one of the aforementioned dining room chairs), Martin decided that he might have time enough to enter the room directly ahead and slam the door shut after him. His only other choice was to continue around the house, through the theoretical living room, back into the kitchen, and out the side door for his escape. But there was no telling where Mrs. Matching Volkswagen might be, making this alternative too dangerous.

Besides, the dog might also be upon him before he ever reached the kitchen.

In a final burst of speed, Martin flung himself into the room at the end of the hall, simultaneously reaching for, missing, reaching, missing again, and then finally grasping and closing the door behind him. As the hallway disappeared from view behind the rapidly closing door, he saw the Labrador attempting to slow down before slamming its muzzle against the door's wooden base.

Had it not clicked shut in time, Martin doubted whether he could have held the door closed against the weight and speed of the large animal.

Seconds later the barking came, a constant stream of yelps, complete with scratching and pawing, further terrifying an already shaking Martin. If the barking continued for too long, a neighbor might become worried and call the police, especially if Cujo (the name he had already assigned the beast) was not in the habit of making this much noise during the day.

Unsure what to do, Martin turned to take in the room that had now become his prison. It appeared to be a sparsely furnished sitting room of sorts, with a sofa, an easy chair, a barren coffee table, and a small television. Two things immediately eased his mind: a pair of windows that might serve the need for a possible escape and a home-office area along the far wall, complete with desk, filing cabinets, and a computer. Had Martin not been attacked by Cujo, this was the room that he would have ultimately sought out.

This meant that his plan was still possible.

But first, Martin thought, something needed to be done about the barking. More than a minute had passed and Cujo showed no signs of letting up.

Martin's only other experience similar to this had been with Alfredo, and in that case Martin had quieted the bird (and eventually befriended it) by giving it what it wanted: conversation. In this case, giving Cujo what he wanted might mean offering himself up as a human sacrifice, which would not do.

Martin wondered if speaking to the dog might help as it had for Alfredo. Using the most soothing voice possible, Martin began talking to the dog, assuring it that he was a friend and only here to help (which ironically was true).

"It's all right, boy . . . I'm not here to hurt anyone. I'm just here to help."

Though he knew that he was breaking his rule about speaking inside a client's home, he didn't hesitate a bit, reminding himself once again that Laura Green was not a client but simply a person in need of assistance. He would never be inside this house again, so in the unlikely event that listening devices were recording his voice, there was little danger that this evidence would ever be used against him.

Remarkably, the talking worked, at least to a degree.

Martin found that as long as he was speaking to the dog, it wouldn't bark. It might growl or whine a bit, but as long as he continued to talk, the dog was relatively quiet. When he stopped talking, the barking resumed, louder and angrier than before.

Switching to a soothing and repetitious rendition of the ABCs in order to allow him to refocus his concentration, Martin readjusted the rubber gloves on his hands, checked that his hairnet was still in place, and resecured his pick gun under the waistband of his sweatpants.

Ready to move, he thought as he covered the last four letters of the alphabet before starting again. Calmness was returning quickly as he began to fall back into habit and routine.

Martin had conducted searches like this many times before and had the process down to a science. Be thorough and fast. Work from top to bottom. Don't ignore items in plain sight. Remember that the absence of information can be just as valuable as information itself. Assume that every item holds value.

In this frame of mind, he began his search.

He began by taking three photographs of the desk, each from a different angle, to be used in the event that he couldn't remember where an object belonged. He would do the same for each drawer that he opened as well.

Photos secured, Martin started his search by scanning the top of the desk, taking in the absence of photos as a further indication that Laura Green had no children and likely no husband. The chalk drawings and toys littering the grass might have belonged to a visiting niece or nephew, or perhaps to some neighborhood kids she permitted to access her large backyard, but definitely not to children of her own.

A cup containing a dozen identical black Bic pens (no fancy colors, indicating she was a woman without pretense), a stapler, and a three-hole punch were lined up on the left side of the desk. A letter organizer on the right-hand corner of the desk contained several unpaid bills, electric, gas, phone, each addressed solely to Laura Green. The envelopes were already affixed with return address stickers (black and white, no frills) and stamps, awaiting the checks that would be deposited therein. A quick scan indicated that none of the bills were yet overdue.

Based upon what he had already seen, he was surprised that someone as organized and efficient as Laura Green might have gotten the date of the party wrong. An unlikely occurrence in her life, to be sure.

Next he opened the three drawers in the desk, searching each one carefully. The first contained an organized selection of office supplies: staples, tacks, Post-its, etc. This continued evidence of organization boded well for his search. Organized people kept meticulous files and maintained orderly records of their business and financial transactions, all of which might eventually lead Martin to his ultimate goal.

The second drawer contained envelopes, stamps (eight books in all, a gold mine in a regular client's home), and half a dozen boxes of thank-you cards in a variety of designs. Though lacking pretense, Laura Green apparently believed in the importance of etiquette.

In the third drawer Martin hit pay dirt. First, a box of personal checks, with only her name appearing on top, indicated to Martin that she was certainly unmarried. Also, there were no business checks to be found, indicating that it was likely she did not own a business but worked for someone else. Beside the box of checks was a box of business cards, and this alone was all that Martin would need to continue with his plan. The business cards indicated that Laura Green was a notary for the Town of West

Hartford and listed her business address as 50 South Main Street in West Hartford, Connecticut. Not surprising to Martin, the box appeared nearly full. Lacking pretense, a woman like Laura Green would find little reason to pass around business cards unless specifically asked. Conveniently, it appeared that she worked in Martin's hometown, and based upon the address, he had an idea of where her place of employment might be.

This was all Martin needed to proceed. The business cards had been a lucky find, but had they not been there, he was certain that he could have found pay stubs, performance reviews, an employee award of some kind, letterhead from her place of business, a URL bookmarked in her Web browser, or a dozen other artifacts that would have led him to her job site. Though tailing clients had proven to be an effective means of identifying their occupations, the truth was that Martin had already determined many of their jobs long before he ever left his home. As had Laura Green, clients often left mountains of evidence behind indicating their place of employment.

And if Martin's guess as to where Laura Green worked was correct, things were looking up.

As long as he could escape her house alive and undetected.

Using the digital images as a reference (though he didn't need them), Martin returned the desk to its original state, the whole time singing his alphabetic melody and committing Laura Green's place of employment to memory. Normally he might have photographed the business card as well, but memorizing a simple street address was something that Martin was sure he could handle.

With Laura Green's desk back in order and the address of her place of employment memorized, it was time to examine his means of escape. He had been holding off on inspecting the windows, fearful of the disappointment that it might bring, but Martin could no longer afford to wait. While continuing his soothing rendition of the ABCs, he examined the room's two windows, one facing the side yard and the other facing the back. His hope was that one of them would be unlocked. If not, he would be forced to leave one open during his escape or face Cujo once again.

Neither prospect was at all appealing.

This time Martin got lucky. The first window, the one above the sofa and facing the side yard, was locked tight, but the other, facing the backyard and obscured by a tall row of hedges, was unlocked. A window fan sat on the floor beneath the window, still plugged in, an indicator as to why the window may have been left unlocked.

He had found his means of escape.

Not only was the window unlocked, but it was a large window, tall to be precise, and he thought that, with a bit of crouching, he could probably kneel on the sill in the rectangular space that the bottom pane of glass currently occupied.

Only one piece of evidence indicating his presence in the house remained. The door to the room in which he was trapped was closed, but it had been open prior to his entry. In order to restore the home to its original state, he would have to open the door before exiting.

Even with the ABCs, Martin doubted if Cujo would remain still once the door was opened. Though quiet, the dog continued to occasionally whine and growl. But this wasn't a bad thing. Martin was banking on the dog's continued anger, and desire to eat him alive, in order to get the door open again.

First, he raised the bottom pane of glass and examined the area outside. Because Laura Green's property sloped down toward the backyard fence, the window was unusually high off the ground, perhaps as high as six feet. The bush obscuring the window was nearly flush against the house, promising Martin a prickly but concealed escape. The area beneath the window was free of debris, and the drop to the ground, though farther than he would have liked, was manageable. The bush would probably slow his fall a bit. An electric meter was jutting out of the siding to the right of the window frame, about two or three feet from the ground, but Martin thought it would be easily avoided. With the window now open, it was also clear to Martin that he would be able to jam his crouching body into its space. His knees would be none too happy, supporting his full weight atop the sill, and his head and neck might not appreciate the degree of bending that would be required, but the space was large enough. This would be the first time in his career that Martin used a window as a means of exit, but as he examined his landing zone and the cover that the bush would provide, he felt confident that it would work.

Next came the dangerous part of his escape plan. Returning to the door, Martin raised the volume of his ABCs as he reached out and grasped the doorknob. His goal was to open the door just enough for the knob to release from the catch without the dog noticing any change. In order to cover the expected click of the knob, he increased the volume of his ABCs even more. Turning slowly, he twisted the brass knob until he felt the door release from the jamb. He then turned the knob back to its original position, hoping that the door would remain unlatched but in place. As he loosened his grip a bit on the knob, it seemed like his plan would work, but the test would be to release the knob entirely; he hoped that the door didn't swing inward.

About fifteen feet separated Martin from his escape window. Keeping his right hand on the knob, continuing his passage through the alphabet, Martin positioned himself for a diving leap through the window in the event that the door moved too much and Cujo became aware of his intentions. He envisioned himself leaping over the sill, grabbing hold of the bush, and sliding down.

He thought it could be done rather easily, albeit painfully, if necessary.

Taking a final deep, relaxing breath, Martin released the knob and moved backward, watching the door as it opened inward less than half an inch before stopping, still well within its frame. He was already at the window now, ready to jump if necessary, but it appeared that the dog hadn't noticed.

Luck continued to be on his side.

Climbing onto the windowsill, Martin prepared for his escape. Kneeling on the sill, his chin tucked into his chest, he managed to fit his entire body into the bottom half of the window. Martin turned his body so that he was still looking into the room, his eyes affixed on the door, his shins and feet extended outside the house, pressing into the bush. His knees were already beginning to ache, but if things went as planned, he would be on the ground in moments.

Reaching up, Martin grasped the bottom edge of the window, preparing to pull it closed in front of him, leaving just enough room on the outside of the sill for his knees to remain perched as the window came down. With everything in position, he at last stopped his ABCs on the letter G and waited.

A moment later the first bark came, followed by another, and a second later the dog scratched on the door once again. This time the door swung halfway open and Martin could see the dog's eyes brighten, its nose lifting from the floor just inches from where the door had been. Reenergized, the Labrador bolted upright and, upon seeing Martin in the window, surged forward, shoving the door entirely open on his way into the room.

Martin pulled down on the window, trying to put glass between himself and the dog, and he suddenly wished that he had practiced this final maneuver before he had stopped his singing.

The window didn't budge.

Whether it was stuck or the angle at which he was attempting to close it was creating the problem, the window would not move as the dog reached the wall and launched its front paws onto the sill. Angry teeth snapped at Martin's exposed knees, forcing him to drop them off the sill and outside the house. As he hung by only his fingertips, Martin's sneakers scrambled against the siding until he managed to catch hold of the electricity meter with his left foot, halting his fall. His head and shoulders were now just outside the open window, gloved hands still gripping the inside of the top of the frame, his lower torso now below the window, feet perched precariously on the meter. He looked like a man preparing to do chin ups, using the window frame in place of the customary bar.

With the dog now staring him in the eye, Martin strengthened his hold on the inside of the window and pulled down even harder, with no more success than he had the first time. Sweat beginning to bead up on his forehead, Martin watched the dog's front paws disappear from the sill just before it leapt into the air, targeting his hands this time. The dog's jaws snapped shut inches away from his left wrist before disappearing below the sill once again.

Though Martin could have jumped to safety at any moment, closing this window was critical. Leaving it completely open would surely signal the presence of an intruder.

The window had to be shut.

Martin continued to pull frantically at the window frame as the dog's paws returned to the sill, its muzzle rising up until he and Cujo were nearly face to face. The dog snapped again, this time almost catching hold of Martin's chin. Martin leaned back as far as he dared, still pulling with all his might.

Cujo barked and snapped again at Martin, this time managing to grab hold of the collar of his shirt. With his hands clinging to the window frame, Martin was defenseless as the dog tugged at the fabric, pulling him back into the house, refusing to let go. If he released his hands, Martin knew that he would fall backward into the bush, but it was unlikely that he would be able to climb back up the side of the house to the window again.

If he let go now, the window would be left open.

And if the fabric of his shirt was strong enough and the dog didn't let go (as Valerie had refused to do, so many years ago), Cujo would likely come spilling out of the house as well, atop his prone and defenseless body.

Despite the hot breath of the dog on his face, its angry growls, and the tug of war taking place between the two of them, Martin suddenly realized that had he simply continued chanting the ABCs until the window was closed, this never would have happened.

Breaking routine, violating his rules, was continuing to haunt him.

The dog growled and continued to tug, snapping up more fabric, pulling Martin even closer, and as the neckline of his shirt shrunk, the dog gathering more and more fabric in its jaws, Martin felt his airflow begin to constrict. He wondered if Cujo might choke him to death before the dog ever managed a bite.

With fear and frustration rising from his belly, Martin lashed out, head-butting the dog in the muzzle with the center of his forehead. The dog let out a piercing whine and released the shirt, tumbling back into the room and out of view.

Martin's victory was short-lived, as seconds later the dog made another attempt at his wrist, leaping into the air and coming even closer than before. Realizing that the angle of his pull on the window was likely the problem, Martin used the brief respite in the battle to reverse his hands so that they were grasping the outside of the window rather than the inside. Using the full weight of his body, he pulled as hard as he dared, fearful of ripping the window from its frame, and this time he was rewarded with the rapid descent of the glass. As his hands passed the sill, the dog made one final attempt at grabbing hold of his wrist, and Martin actually felt the dog's hot breath on his skin just before the window sealed shut, knocking him and the dog back in opposite directions.

Martin released the window just as it slammed shut, falling backward into the bush behind him. Prickly limbs lashed at him as he descended to the ground, his fall broken by a combination of the bush's branches and the mulch piled beneath.

He had survived.

Feeling more tired than he ever had in his life, Martin marshaled his energy and picked himself off the ground, pushing past the branches until he emerged into Laura Green's backyard. Free of the house and dog, he expelled a premature sigh of relief.

"What are you doing?" a voice announced from behind him.

Martin spun, adrenaline still coursing through his veins, and saw a young, blond-haired girl, perhaps six years old, sitting at the Fisher-Price picnic table that he had mentally inventoried earlier. She was staring up at him, her brows furrowed as if a question mark had lodged in her throat.

"Hello?" she said, louder this time. She appeared to be friendly but dreadfully curious, and in possession of a distinct accent, English or perhaps Scottish.

Martin thought about turning and running, getting back to his car as quickly as possible, but instead he stood his ground and replied with a hello of his own, adopting the hitherto-undefined accent of the girl.

He hadn't meant to speak in the accent. It just came out that way.

"Are you still looking for your dog?" she asked.

"My dog?" Finding Cujo in the backyard was the last thing that Martin wanted to do. And again he had replied in an awkward facsimile of the girl's accent, as if he'd been suddenly saddled with Alfredo's verbal limitations.

"Your dog," the girl repeated emphatically. "I heard you calling for him a wee bit ago. Andy, right?"

It took Martin ten painfully long seconds to make sense of what this girl was saying. The only dog that he could think of was Cujo, the one who had nearly strangled him to death just seconds before. But then it came to Martin. In a flurry of words, still mimicking the girl's accent as best he could, he answered. "Oh, you mean Sandy. Sandy is my dog. Yes, I'm still looking for Sandy. You heard me calling for Sandy, right?" As he spoke the words, he began scanning the backyard, looking for Blondie's parents. He assumed that they were close by.

"Is Sandy a boy dog or a girl dog?"

Remarkably, Martin didn't know. He had never assigned his fictional dog a gender. He thought about the Sandy in his first-grade reader and couldn't remember if the author had ever distinguished a gender. So he said the first thing that came to mind. "A girl dog. Sandy is a girl dog. Sandy is my girl dog."

"My dad says girl dogs are bitches. I can say 'bitches,' but only if I'm talking about girl dogs. Did you know that girl dogs are bitches?"

Martin marveled at the way this child spoke, using words that he said his entire life but twisted in a remarkably new vernacular. His astonishment over her accent allowed him to relax a bit.

"Yes, I knew that. But I don't call my Sandy that word. That wouldn't be nice." As he replied, Martin smiled. That was something his mother might have said.

"But Daddy says it isn't bad, because it's grammerly correct."

"Where is your daddy?" Martin asked, the inquiry suddenly making him feel like a child molester.

A child molester with a ridiculous Irish accent.

"Daddy's in San . . . San something. He comes home soon. Me and Mum are staying with Auntie Bea until Thanksgiving. Where do you come from?"

The scope of the question baffled Martin. Was the little girl asking what town Martin lived in or what country? Did she want to know where he had just been or where he had been born? At that moment Martin realized that he was trapped in an unrehearsed conversation. For so much of his life, probably starting the moment he left the driveway after being scolded by his stepfather, Martin had spent much of his life rehearsing for all future conversations. Practicing them in his mind. Running through word choices, sentence combinations, and possible retorts. Whether it was paying for gas at the Mobil or explaining his latest writing assignment to Jim or visiting with Jillian in the diner, he was prepared for whatever he might need to say.

But never in his life had he prepared for a situation like this.

"I come from here," he finally said. "I live in America."

"Oh," Blondie replied. "You talk funny for an American."

He did. Though he was doing a fair job of imitating the words that Blondie was saying, he was guessing at the others, the ones she hadn't said, and he was certain that those words weren't sounding good.

More important, he was talking too much. It was time to move.

"I have to go. Okay?" And as the words came out of his mouth, he realized how ridiculous they sounded. He was asking a child for permission to leave, and his question hadn't been rhetorical. Had Blondie answered in the negative, told him to stand his ground with a "Stay put, buster," he might have done just that. Without a rehearsal, Martin had no way of gaining control of the conversation, making it more important for him to leave now.

"Where's *your* daddy?" the girl asked.

This was perhaps the most unrehearsed question of Martin's life.

"I'm not sure," he answered with blind honesty. Martin's mother and father had divorced when he was in second grade, and though he had visited his father quite frequently for a year or two after the divorce, their communication had become less and less frequent as his mother became more publicly involved with the future stepfather who had broken up the marriage. He wasn't even sure how he had finally ended all contact with his father. The Sunday afternoon visits to the apartment behind the liquor store evolved into Christmas Day drop-bys and second-rate birthday parties with just Martin, his father, and an occasional girlfriend sitting around a table, eating cake and searching for something to say. Eventually even these visits faded until one day Martin had stopped seeing his father entirely. It wasn't a conscious choice, at least on his own part, but in fairness, he couldn't remember clamoring to see his namesake either. Though Martin could recall missing his father for quite a while, he also knew that in his heart he had allowed his new father to replace the old. He had embraced the new life that his stepfather had brought into the household, a life of slightly fewer arguments and slightly more money. More presents under the tree and a new pair of sneakers whenever needed. Martin despised his father for leaving as only a seven-year-old could, and blindly pledged his allegiance to his father's usurper, unaware of the man's potential for cruelty and selfishness. Eventually Martin learned that his stepfather had purposefully kept him away from his father, wielding his influence as a psychiatric social worker to reduce his father's visitation rights, hoping to eliminate the influence that the man might exert on his son. But Martin had apparently made it easy.

Had barely put up a fight.

For that reason, Martin hadn't seen his father in years. Even after Martin's stepfather had left his mother for a younger woman, two or three years prior to her death, Martin made no attempt to reconcile with his father. A healthy dose of guilt and remorse, combined with the awkwardness that two decades apart can create, had kept them apart.

Of course, Martin's career had a lot to do with their continued separation as well.

In addition, Martin was still angry with his father. Though he was willing to accept some of the blame, he also knew that, for whatever reason, his father had let him down as well. Martin could not remember even a single time when his father had fought for his right to see his son. Though Martin had allowed a strange man to fill the shoes of his father, his father had allowed it to happen without so much as a peep.

"Do you *have* a daddy?" Blondie asked, impatient for an answer. Her first question had stymied Martin, and there was no telling how long he had stood there, allowing the question to hang in the air, before the girl had asked her follow-up. But this question forced Martin into action.

It was time to go.

"Look at the time," Martin said, glancing at his wrist. "I have to run." And just that quickly, Martin felt in control of his movements once again. Dodging a question was a strategy that Martin employed quite often. Finally his training had kicked in.

"Okay," the girl said with disappointment filling her face.

"Well," Martin replied apologetically, "I've got to find Sandy, right?"

"Can I help?" the girl asked, leaping up from the picnic table in excitement.

"Sure you can," Martin replied, firmly in control of the situation now. *And speaking without the accent,* he noticed. "But you'll have to ask your mum, okay? Run along and ask her if it's all right, and I'll wait here for you."

Without answering, Blondie turned and sprinted for the door of Mr. and Mrs. Matching Volkswagen, faster than Martin would have expected. As soon as she turned the corner and passed from view, Martin turned and began jogging back in the direction of his car, using a slightly faster pace than normal. Before Blondie had even entered the neighboring house, Martin was well up the street and out of view.

Once back inside his car, Martin permitted himself a few minutes to regroup. First he allowed himself to relax, waiting for the quiver in his hands to subside and his breathing to return to normal. He couldn't quite believe what had just happened. Yet the pride that he had been feeling from his experience in the Clayton household was beginning to suffuse this situation as well. Though he had blundered badly, he once again had managed to escape unscathed.

Next he took a moment to retrace his steps, looking for any evidence that he might have left in Laura Green's home. Though his escape had been harried and nearly disastrous, he was sure that the desk had been left in order and that the window had been returned to its original state. For a moment he wondered if Cujo had managed to tear any of his shirt loose, but a quick visual inspection showed that, although torn and slightly frayed, all the fabric seemed to be present.

Next he examined the clock on the dashboard. 4:11. He would need to be in West Hartford before 5:00 if he wanted any chance of success. That might be tough. Traffic through the capital city was often bumper-to-bumper at this time of day, and if this were the case, he didn't have any time to waste. Throwing his car into drive, he headed back down West Middle Turnpike and toward Interstate 84.

As he wound his way through traffic, Martin began rehearsing his lines, looking for a way to convey the necessary message in a realistic and natural way. He would have only one chance to nail this performance, and rarely had he found himself forced to perform under such pressure. Developing a mental script had always been easy for Martin. Words had always flowed naturally from his mind, and he was the master of internal dialogue. It was rare when he didn't have a conversation of some sort running through his head. He was also quite adept at anticipating the responses of others and therefore often had rebuttals, retorts, and counterpoints at the ready. Though his contact with other people was somewhat limited beyond his exceptionally small circle of friends, he was quite the wordsmith.

Where Martin required more preparation was in his actual performances. He was by no means a natural actor, and so his prepared speeches often came across as unnatural and insincere. With a great deal of rehearsal, he had found he could sound believable, but in this case the only rehearsal he would have would take place while behind the wheel of his Subaru, darting between traffic. He found himself almost hoping that he wouldn't make it to West Hartford on time, so that he wouldn't be forced into an unprepared performance.

This ended up not being the case. At 4:42 Martin pulled into the parking lot at 50 South Main Street in West Hartford, the location of West Hartford's town hall (as Martin had suspected). With time to spare before the 5:00 closing, Martin rehearsed his lines a few more times, trying to find the right combination of words and inflection. Still feeling unprepared but with no more time to spare, Martin climbed out of his car at 4:50 and headed for the front doors to the large brick building.

Martin had been inside this building before, for a variety of business including the payment of excise tax and the filing of his mother's death certificate, but he wasn't sure in which office Laura Green might be working. Stopping for a moment beside the directory, he quickly thought better and went over to the information desk, where he was informed by a blue-haired lady that he was looking for room 207 on the second floor. With no time to waste, Martin bypassed the elevators and took the stairs, two at a time.

West Hartford's town hall had originally been constructed as a high school, and though decades had passed since the last student had roamed its halls, the building had nonetheless retained its institutional feel. Following signs, Martin was soon standing outside the door to room 207, marked with a sign stating TOWN CLERK.

His heart began to beat faster with the knowledge that Laura Green was likely behind this door.

Thankfully the hallway outside the town clerk's office was empty, so Martin took a full minute to compose himself. He wasn't sure what to expect once he entered the office, but he tried to steady his breathing and focus on the task at hand. *One chance*, he reminded himself. *I've got just one chance to get this right.*

At 4:54, Martin opened the door and entered the office of the town clerk. The room was larger than he had expected but customarily stale. To his immediate right, a high counter separated the public side of the office from the employees' side, where three large desks were evenly spaced along the far wall. A woman was sitting behind each desk, head down, busy at work. Martin approached the counter, removed his wallet from his back pocket, and waited patiently to be acknowledged. A moment later a middle-aged woman looked up, smiled, and made her way over to Martin at the reception desk.

"Can I help you?" she asked in a pleasant and friendly tone.

Martin immediately wished that he had paid better attention to Laura Green's voice as she had spoken on the Ashleys' answering machine. He hadn't expected there to be three women from which to choose, and he had no way of knowing if this was Laura Green. Had Cujo not attacked, he would have taken the time to locate a photograph of the woman somewhere in her home, but being restricted to the single room had made this impossible.

"Uh, yes please," Martin responded, searching for a name tag on the woman's purple blouse and finding none. "I need to have a copy of my driver's license notarized."

About four years ago, Jim had needed a notarized copy of his license in order to be paid for some out-of-state consulting that he had performed. Apparently the people for whom he had done the work had failed to secure the proper identification before he flew home, and as a result, Jim had to jump through several hoops in order to get paid. The process had taken more than a month, and Jim had complained about it each step of the way, even arguing that he should've been paid for the time it took him to get paid. The incident had stuck in Martin's mind.

Thankfully.

"No problem," the woman replied. "I'll just need the copy of your license and another form of identification."

Martin had anticipated this response. "Oh. I'm so sorry. I didn't make a copy. Could you please make one for me? I'll pay whatever it might cost. I'm just having one of those days, if you know what I mean."

The woman chuckled. "No problem. I'm having one myself. Let me see your license."

Even if Martin had found the time to photocopy his driver's license, he still would have asked this woman to do it for him. He knew that the longer he remained in this office, the greater his chance of success.

Martin handed the license over and watched as the woman made her way to the far end of the office, where a large photocopier waited, humming away. With a moment to himself, Martin risked a glance at the other two women sitting behind desks. The nearest was a young, red-headed girl, probably in her early twenties, wearing a plunging V-neck sweater and large hoop earrings. She was shuffling papers on a disorganized desk and chewing gum with a vigor Martin had rarely seen. All instincts told him that this was not Laura Green.

The other woman, seated the farthest from Martin, appeared to be in her thirties and was dressed conservatively in a dark business suit. Her blond hair was pinned back and she had yet to look up from her computer screen. A large bobble-head doll, appearing to resemble herself, rested on the edge of her desk.

His instincts were less certain when it came to this woman.

Martin had begun to compare the desks of his two candidates, looking for still more clues as to their identity, when the woman who was helping him returned, handing back his license and sliding a sheet of paper across the counter to him.

"I'll need you to sign at the bottom of the page, and I need another form of identification, please."

Martin reached into his wallet and removed a credit card, asking if it would suffice.

"That's fine," the woman replied, examining it for a moment before handing it back.

"Thank goodness," Martin said with a relieved sigh, beginning the series of lines that he had rehearsed more than two dozen times in the car. "Another thing off my list. It's been crazy today."

Before he could finish his monologue, the woman jumped into the pause between sentences and said, "Please raise your right hand and repeat after me. I, Martin Railsback, Junior, swear that the information I have provided is the truth."

Martin raised his hand and repeated the woman's words, suddenly concerned that his window of opportunity was closing. Desperate, he lowered his hand and began his rehearsed lines again, this time louder in hopes of avoiding interruption. "Thank goodness. Another thing off my list. Now, if I can just find a good gourmet caterer, I can go home and relax."

Martin waited for a reaction from the woman but saw none. The woman stamped the sheet of paper and slid it back across the counter to him. "That'll be five dollars, please."

With that, his hopes plummeted.

Martin was reaching into his wallet for the money when the

woman seated farthest away stood up, causing her bobblehead to bobble, and made her way over to the counter. "I'm sorry," she said. "Did you say you're looking for a caterer?"

"Boy am I ever. Not just any caterer," Martin replied, trying to suppress his excitement and stick to the script. "I was told by my sister to find a gourmet caterer for our parents' fiftieth wedding anniversary. She hired someone over a year ago and it turns out that they're out of business. Didn't bother to call us or anything. The party is on Saturday, so now I'm stuck. And my sister isn't coming up from Virginia until Friday night, so she's thrown this problem in my lap."

It wasn't great, Martin knew, but it didn't sound bad either. Wordy for sure and a little unnatural. A day of rehearsing would have made a world of difference, but he thought that it might have been good enough to get by.

"I know a great caterer," the woman said with the exuberance of someone who is excited to help. "A friend of mine. I don't know if she's available on Saturday, but if you'd like, I could give you her name and number."

"That would be great," Martin answered. "Really great. Thank you."

Martin completed his transaction with the first woman, signing a receipt for the money that he had passed over the counter while the second woman wrote down the name and number of the catering service on a sheet of stationery. Though Martin knew what she would be writing, he was still shocked to see the words *Ashley Gourmet Catering* on the slip of paper.

Up until this moment, he had never believed that his plan would work.

Transaction complete, Martin took the notarized copy of his license and folded it carefully before sliding it into his pocket. As he took the slip of paper with the number of the Ashleys' catering service, he looked up and said, "Thanks so much. You're a lifesaver."

"No problem. I'm Laura, by the way," the woman responded, allowing her smile to linger a moment longer than necessary.

"Oh. I'm Martin. Nice to meet you, Laura."

Martin said good-bye and exited the office with a spring in his step, feeling more confident than he had ever felt before.

Ten minutes later, he was sitting in his car outside the town hall, rehearsing what he hoped would be his final performance of the day. This one would be considerably easier. First, he'd be speaking over the phone, a means of communication that Martin typically preferred (whenever e-mail was not possible). Second, this call would be more natural and expected, the type of call a caterer might expect at any time of the day. *A welcome call*, in fact. As long as he got Justine Ashley on the line and hit a couple of key points, his plan would be complete.

Taking another deep, relaxing breath, Martin dialed the phone number from the sheet of paper, though it would have been just as easy to call Information for the number.

It wasn't the phone number that he had been seeking when he'd entered the office of the town clerk.

It was Laura Green's recommendation that he had needed.

The phone was answered on the third ring by a girl with a youthful-sounding voice. Maybe even a kid, in Martin's estimation. "Ashley Gourmet Caterers. Can I help you?"

"Yes, please," Martin answered. "Could I please speak to Justine Ashley?"

Had Martin been told that Justine was unavailable, he was prepared to tell the person on the other end of the line that he was looking for a caterer but had been referred specifically to Justine Ashley and would speak to her only. Though the request might have seemed a bit strange, he couldn't see Justine Ashley not making herself available for new business. Thankfully, the voice on the other end of the phone asked Martin to wait a minute while Justine came to the phone.

Moments later, Martin began his first conversation with a client.

"This is Justine Ashley. How can I help you?"

"Hello Mrs. Ashley. My name is Martin. I was referred to you by Laura Green. I'm in need of a caterer for Saturday for my parents' fiftieth anniversary and she told me that you might be able to help me out. She said to ask for you personally. Are you available?"

"This Saturday?"

Martin liked the tone of the question already. "Yes, I'm afraid so. I know it's last minute, but I'm afraid the caterer we booked a year ago is now out of business. We're really in a jam."

"I'm afraid we're not available this Saturday," Justine Ashley answered. "It's our annual staff picnic." Then a pause, followed by, "Are you sure that you told Laura that your party was *this Saturday?*"

"Absolutely," Martin answered, buoyed by her response. He then recited the lines that he had rehearsed the most. "In fact, she told me to try to get you and your husband to handle the party personally. She said that your staff is excellent but that you are the best. But I guess she didn't know about your picnic."

"Yes, I guess so," Justine responded almost absently. "Sorry I can't help. Would you like me to recommend another caterer who might be able to help you out?"

"Sure," said Martin, and he pretended to write down the name and number as Justine Ashley relayed the information.

"Thanks anyway," Martin said, sensing the call was coming to an end. "Please tell Laura that I appreciated the referral. The next time you speak, I mean. Okay?"

"Right," Justine Ashley answered. "Sorry we can't help you out. Have a good day."

And with that, she hung up.

The final phase of Martin's plan was now in action. With luck, Justine Ashley was placing a call to Laura Green at this very moment, inquiring as to why she might refer someone for the day of her husband's surprise party. Martin thought that his chances were good that she would place the call immediately. Justine Ashley was an obsessively organized and diligent woman who would not want to leave any loose ends dangling. She would also need to speak to her friend out of her husband's earshot, and she probably had a better chance of that at work than in the quiet of their home. Most important, Martin knew the lengths to which Justine Ashley had gone in preparing this party (scheduling a counterfeit staff picnic for the same day in order to avoid conflicts and allow employees to attend the party), so if any part of Martin's call had roused concern or suspicion, she would want to eliminate it as soon as possible.

And he had tried to arouse as much suspicion as possible.

However, Martin also knew there was a chance that the call might not be placed in time. Perhaps Justine Ashley didn't know Laura Green's cellular telephone number, or maybe Laura Green's phone was turned off. Any number of circumstances might delay the call, and if so, Martin would need to know this so that he could enact his contingency plan if necessary. His plan was to drive back to Manchester and stake out the Ashley home, ready to reenter the house if the call wasn't placed. In that case he would, as planned, trip the breakers to the home, erase the message on the machine, and move the gift underneath the porch swing, out of view.

But if luck remained on his side, all that would be unnecessary.

Once in position outside the Ashley home, he would call Justine Ashley once more to claim he had lost the number that she had just given him. Had she called Laura Green and averted disaster, she would likely thank him for his fortuitous inquiry, or he would be told by the catering staff that she had left early for the day. Once he confirmed her arrival home ahead of her husband, he would know that the plan had worked and could head for home.

As he pulled out of the parking space and turned his car toward the exit, he noticed Laura Green exiting the town hall through the same doors that he had exited minutes ago. She saw Martin in his car and waved at him, motioning for him to stop.

Oh God, Martin thought as he slowed the car in front of the woman. *What did I do?* A wave of heat rippled through his body and he felt his hands begin to shake. Though barely able to focus his thoughts, he tried to imagine what he might have done to cause this sudden encounter. Nothing came to mind, but Martin knew that he had been swimming in new waters all day long. There was no telling what kind of mistake he might have made. Less than two hours ago, he had been battling this woman's dog in her house. What might she know?

Laura Green took a few steps over to his car and waited a moment, staring at him through the window glass. She looked even better now that she was out from behind the counter. A thin woman with an athletic build, she was wearing a pair of well-worn jeans and a green and white striped top. No more conservative business suit. But it was her hazel eyes and slightly crooked smile that Martin couldn't help but notice.

What does this woman want? Martin wondered, staring back at her. He attempted to adopt the look of someone who was both innocent and befuddled, and waited for her to make the first move.

After a moment, Laura Green raised her hand and motioned

for Martin to lower the driver's side window. Feeling incredibly stupid, he did so.

"I'm sorry," he said. "I don't know what I was thinking."

"That's okay. One of those days, right?"

"Yeah."

"I just wanted to thank you. You saved my life. My friend was planning a surprise party for her husband this Saturday, but like a dolt, I confused the days. Not like me at all. When you called her about Saturday, she got worried and called me."

Laura Green paused for a moment, but when Martin failed to fill the silence, she continued.

"You see, I had dropped off a present at their house this morning and left a message on their machine about the party. I felt so bad about missing it. But it turns out that I didn't miss it, and if her husband had gone home and heard the message or seen the gift, the surprise wouldn't've been ruined. And you don't know Justine. She would've killed me. She's put so much work into this thing."

"Well," Martin said, still looking awkwardly up from his place behind the wheel. "I'm glad that it all worked out."

"Thanks to you," Laura Green quickly added. "Did you find a caterer for your party yet?"

"I think I did," Martin lied. "That's why I'm still here. Your friend gave me a number and I gave them a call. Looks like I'm all set."

"Great. Then it worked out for both of us."

"It sure did," Martin answered, exhilaration mixed with a sudden feeling of sadness. This woman would never know the lengths that he had gone to to help her.

"Hey, if you're not busy, would you like to get a bite to eat? My treat. It's the least I can do for you. You really saved the day."

I'm busy.

I have plans.

I'm meeting a friend.

I have a dentist appointment.

I have a girlfriend.

I'm married.

I'm gay.

Any one of these excuses would have allowed Martin to avoid dinner with this woman, and under normal circumstances he would have used one of them immediately. Though Martin rarely attracted the attention of women, there had in the past been rare occasions when he had been asked to have coffee or drinks, and each time he had deftly avoided the situation. But Laura Green was an attractive woman, and Martin had saved her day. For the first time in a long time, he felt appreciated, so he wasn't so surprised to hear himself say his next few words.

"That sounds great. Where would you like to go?"

With that, Martin was on the first real date of his adult life.

Martin had learned early on that people loved to talk about themselves. All his life, he had been uncomfortable around others, never sure what to say, so he quickly adopted the strategy of listening and probing rather than sharing and contributing. When trapped in a social situation that required him to speak, he would often allow his conversational partner to do most of the talking, asking questions when it seemed as if the person was running out of steam and encouraging him or her to share as much as possible.

Once he began his career, Martin found himself wanting to share less and less of his life, so he employed this strategy even more effectively. Martin rarely interacted with people, other than his few close friends, without thought and preparation. And when he did, he encouraged them to speak as much as possible.

Thus far this strategy was working well for him, but Laura Green had been doggedly persistent. Though willing to talk about her own life, she repeatedly attempted to turn the conversation back in his direction, and each time, Martin was forced to return her volley like a tennis player being chased around the court.

She had chosen the Elbow Room for their dinner, a relatively upscale restaurant within walking distance of the town hall that afforded rooftop dining, though the evening chill kept the couple indoors on this night. During their brief walk to the restaurant, conversation centered on Justine and Daniel Ashley and Martin's fortuitous need for a caterer. She had thanked him at least half a dozen times during their five-minute stroll through the center of town, which Martin found pleasant but surprising. Laura Green should have been under the impression that fate had intervened and saved the day, using Martin as its unwitting instrument. He rightfully deserved the praise that this woman was lavishing on him, but she had no way of knowing it.

And yet she had thanked him just the same.

Dinner had begun with wine and bread while Laura shared the prescient details of her life. Single and never married, she was living in Manchester with a dog named Boxer and several house plants.

Cujo still seemed like a more appropriate name for the dog, Martin thought, but Boxer wasn't bad.

Laura had bought her house about five years ago, and though she liked it, she was hoping to find a place with a larger yard and a bit more privacy. She had been working in the town clerk's office for nearly a decade and found the job to be stable and boring. She had an accounting degree from the University of Connecticut but had become interested in interior design over the past few years, and was considering opening a business of her own.

"I can't imagine myself trapped in that office for the rest of my life. I'll go crazy. The problem is that the job pays well and is so damn secure. The pension is terrific and the benefits can't be beat. But the job is as boring as you can get. I just can't spend my life in that room, you know?" She paused and took a sip of her wine, as if considering what she had just said. "So how about you? Do you think you'll still be writing in fifteen years?"

Martin had told her that he was a writer of technical manuals but hoped to one day write more creatively. This last part was actually the truth. She had been impressed to hear that he was a professional writer, but Martin was working hard to temper her enthusiasm.

"*Technical manuals,*" he insisted. "I write instruction booklets. That's all."

Despite Martin's attempt to avoid the question, Laura asked again. "Seriously . . . where do you see yourself in fifteen years?"

"I'm not sure," he answered honestly. "Maybe still writing instruction booklets. I don't know. Writing creatively takes more bravery than I think I have."

"What do you mean?"

"When I write an instruction booklet for a blender, I'm not really doing anything that you couldn't do. Be clear, precise, and specific. Write in complete sentences. But if I were to start writing a novel, let's say—well, that would be coming straight from me. It would be all me. And if it wasn't any good, that would be a tough thing to face."

"That sounds like a terrible reason to dodge a dream."

"Yeah, but it's true," Martin replied, once again finding remarkable truth in what he was saying. "Rejection is an ugly thing."

Laura leaned across the table and looked Martin directly in the eyes. "Look, Martin. I'm going to be honest. I could tell you not to worry. I could tell you that whatever you put on the page will be great. But you're right. It might not be very good. I don't know you and don't know if you have any talent. But you don't strike me as a coward. So do me a favor, even if we never speak again after tonight, which I hope isn't the case. Go home tonight and start your novel. Write the first page and see where it takes you. Okay?"

"All right," Martin answered, not meaning it. Though he dreamed of being a novelist one day, he couldn't imagine it happening anytime soon.

"I'm serious, Martin. Don't just say it. Do it. Start it tonight. Just one page. Okay?"

"Okay," he answered, trying to sound more sincere. Surprisingly, he was. No one had ever been so direct with Martin before about his writing, and he was surprised to find that he appreciated it. Just listening to this woman call him by his first name sent his heart racing a little faster.

"I'm sorry. I must sound a little crazy. It's just that I've been stuck in a dead-end job for longer than I care to remember, and I can't stand watching other people spin their wheels like me. You know?"

The next sentence shocked Martin, even though it came from his own mouth.

"Then you need to do something too, Laura." It was the first time he had referred to her by name, and it felt both delicious and dangerous at the same time. "You want to design homes. The insides, I mean, right? So do it. I'll go home tonight and write my first page, but you need to go home tonight and do something too. Whatever interior designers do. What could you do tonight to get your business moving?"

Laura smiled. "You're sweet."

"I'm serious," Martin countered, both because it felt right and because it gave him something to talk about. No need to grapple for the next sentence when you can badger the woman and still be perceived as sweet. "When you get home tonight, what could you do?"

"Fine," she said. "I could get online and find a degree program? How's that?"

"It's a start," Martin answered. "I'll write my first page, and you'll choose a degree program." And just like that, Martin sensed that this line of conversation was coming to an end. He could already feel the pressure returning.

"A toast to beginnings," Laura said, raising her glass.

"To beginnings," Martin repeated and tapped her glass. He suddenly felt more like an adult than ever before in his life.

Salads came as Laura finished her wine and ordered another. Martin still had more than half a glass of wine left and suddenly felt an inexplicable need to catch up. By the time he had finished his own salad, a Caesar with dressing on the side, he was in need of another glass as well. Though he occasionally drank beer or wine at home with dinner, it was never more than a single glass. He reminded himself to be careful as he took the first sip from the new glass.

"So tell me about your parents' party. It's an anniversary party, right?"

"Yeah, it's their anniversary," Martin said, suddenly wishing that he didn't have to lie to this woman. Something remarkable and unexpected was happening to him. The longer he spent with Laura, the more relaxed he became in conversation, but the more anxious he became in wanting to impress her. He couldn't remember the last time that he had felt either way, and now he was experiencing both feelings simultaneously. He wished he could just be honest with Laura. Not completely honest, of course, but more than he was being right now.

"So tell me about it," she persisted. "How many years? Where's the party? Give me the details."

"Well, they turn fifty this year. I mean, they are celebrating their fiftieth anniversary this year. This month. My sister made the plans for the party, but she lives out of state, so I'm stuck handling the details. The problems with the caterer and all."

"So where's the party going to be?"

"My sister's house," Martin blurted out, grasping at the first thought that entered his head. He didn't want to name a restaurant or banquet hall in case Laura chose to follow up on his statement, send a gift, or whatever. So he went with the only option floating around in his brain.

"But I thought you said that your sister lives out of state."

"She does," Martin answered. "But she has a house on the shore, too. A summer house, I mean. The party is going to be there."

"How nice. What town?"

"Westbrook," Martin answered.

"What a coincidence," Laura said. "Did you know that Daniel's party is in Westbrook too? At the Water's Edge Resort. Right on the shore. This is a day full of coincidences, huh?"

Martin was sure that he had said Westbrook because the town had been on his mind earlier that day when recalling the Ashley invitation. He would have to be more careful with what he told this woman. Fabricating stories had become part of Martin's daily existence, but he had always had time to prepare. Not only was he creating family history on the spot, but he would need to remember this history or risk being caught in a lie. So far he had a fictional set of married parents celebrating fifty years of marriage, and a fictional sister who owned a second home along the Connecticut shoreline.

At the moment he felt like a skydiver without a parachute.

"It's a day full of good luck," Martin added.

"I agree," Laura said with a smile. "So what's the party going to be like?"

"To be honest, I'm really not sure. My sister is taking care of everything. Except the caterer, I mean. She's always been the planner. I'm just along for the ride."

"She's older than you?"

"Yup. By half a dozen years." Martin had always believed that it was easier to recall a concept like "half a dozen years" rather than the number 6, so his fabrications tended to be full of these types of expressions.

"What's her name?" Laura asked.

Thankfully Martin had just placed a slice of bread into his

mouth, so he had a moment to consider the question before answering. The first name to enter his mind was Jillian, but it didn't seem right to give his fictional sister that name. He took an extra moment to chew before deciding.

"Wendy," he answered, placing the image of the character from the Peter Pan stories into his mind. Associating the thought with a mental image would help to keep the idea fixed in his mind. "How about you?" he asked, looking to redirect the conversation away from himself. "Any siblings?"

"Nope. Just me. My father died when I was ten, and my mom lives in Coventry. Same house I grew up in."

"I'm sorry about your father."

"Thanks. But it was a long time ago."

Once again Martin desperately wished that he could be more honest with this woman. Having lost his own mother, he knew how much it could still hurt from time to time, and he wanted to tell Laura that he understood how difficult it was to lose a parent. But his fictional parents were alive and well, still married, and preparing to celebrate their fiftieth wedding anniversary together. The empathy that he felt for this woman, who had brushed off his condolence with a timeworn expression and a touch of sadness in her eyes, was useless to him.

It had never hurt Martin so much to lie.

This time Laura turned the conversation away from thoughts of her father and onto travel. Martin had never traveled outside New England, so he was able to turn the question back toward Laura rather quickly. Thankfully, she had seen much of the United States as a child and had recently been skiing in Cortina, Italy. Without much prompting, Laura was happy to spend more than fifteen minutes extolling the virtues of the Italian Alps.

As their entrees arrived, Martin excused himself to use the restroom. He had needed to urinate for some time and had hoped to avoid using the public restroom, but the discomfort finally became too much.

Martin despised public restrooms and avoided them whenever possible. Even in the finest establishments, he thought of them as germ-infested closets. As he approached the men's room, just past the kitchen, he was pleased to see that the door opened out, necessitating a pull on the handle in order to gain entry. This meant that after washing his hands, he would be able to push the door with his foot or elbow in order to exit, allowing him to avoid the skin-to-handle contact that made him want to retch.

Not that the washing of his hands appealed to him, either. Though Martin wanted every other human being in the world to wash his or her hands after using the bathroom, this was because of a lack of trust in the personal hygiene of others. His own, he knew, was impeccable. As a result, Martin never understood the need to wash his hands after touching his penis. After all, his penis was clean, probably cleaner than his hands or any other part of his body that had been exposed to the world. He had washed it, dried it, and then covered it by underwear and pants. Two layers of protection that remained firmly in place throughout the day. This was the same penis that women would theoretically come into contact with during sex (Martin hadn't had sex since high school, and even that had been a poor effort at best). A woman might touch it with her fingers, place it in her mouth, or allow it inside her vagina. Yet it wasn't clean enough for Martin to touch it without immediately needing to wash his hands? In fact, Martin thought, his penis might well be the cleanest part of his body. Yet after urinating, he was expected to wash his hands thoroughly. This meant that he would need to touch faucet knobs and soap dispensers that had previously been touched by men who had just spent ten minutes sitting on a toilet touching their own disgusting penises.

Surely his penis was more germ-free than these bacteria farms.

But if Martin was able to avoid the restroom door entirely, by trailing behind another man or pulling it open with a napkin, he found that he could often enter, sidle up to a urinal, and complete his business without coming into contact with anything save the his pants buttons and his penis. On these occasions, if the restroom was empty, he would exit without washing his hands.

Sadly, this didn't happen very often.

On this particular evening, two older men were occupying the restroom with Martin, discussing the degree to which they hated their boss, so he was forced to use the faucets and soap dispensers lest the men see how "unsanitary" he was. Because of an absence of paper towels (the restroom was equipped with hand dryers), Martin chose to leave the water running when finished rather than placing his clean hands on the faucet knobs once again. Someone else could turn it off after he had left. Using his foot, he pushed the door open without coming into contact with any part of it, and made his way toward the front of the restaurant.

As Martin approached the table, he noticed that Laura was speaking on her cell phone. As he came closer, she looked at him and smiled, unable to contain her excitement. "Just a minute," she said to the person on the other end of the line before asking Martin, "What time is your parents' anniversary party on Saturday?"

Unsure of what might be the best answer, Martin answered "Noon," sticking with his strategy of avoiding numbers while fabricating.

"So you'll be done by seven?"

"Yeah, I should be," he answered, almost immediately wishing he hadn't. "Why?"

"You've just been invited to Daniel Ashley's surprise party. A guest of honor of sorts. The man who saved the surprise from ruin."

Martin sat down and placed his napkin back in his lap, trying to contemplate what had just happened as Laura finished her call.

"Okay, Justine. Let me run . . . I can't. We're still having dinner. I'll call you tomorrow . . . Okay, okay. I'll call you tonight. Bye."

Martin waited until she had closed her phone before beginning. "Laura, I can't . . ."

"Yes you can," she interrupted. "You'll be my guest. It's perfect. You're already going to be in Westbrook, so why not? If it hadn't been for you, Justine's planning would've been ruined and I would be in the doghouse. Justine wants you to be there, and I want you to be there, too."

It was the mixture of her gratitude, combined with the words *I want you to be there, too* that made refusing her invitation impossible. He couldn't believe how fast his heart was racing.

"Okay, I'll go. It sounds like fun."

As they ate and chatted about their lives, Martin tried to assess the damage that might come from attending the Ashley surprise party and meeting a client face-to-face for the first time, but he found himself unable to focus, distracted by the woman across the table whom he couldn't take his eyes off of. Other than his fictional family and career, he had managed to stick to the truth throughout the rest of dinner, telling Laura about his home, his friends, and answering questions about religion (he was a nonpracticing, skeptical Christian) and favorite films (*Field of Dreams* and *As Good as It Gets*). When the check came, Martin made a perfunctory attempt to pay the bill but knew that Laura would insist. He allowed her to pay without complaint, wishing that he had thought ahead and found a way to hand the waiter his credit card before the bill had ever hit the table.

Had there been time to prepare, he would have found a way.

As they left the restaurant, Laura suggested ice cream at a shop less than a block down the street and on the way back to the town-hall parking lot. Martin agreed. Laura ordered a double scoop of chocolate in a waffle cone, and though Martin never ordered ice cream in a cone because of the mess that it typically made, he said, "The same for me" when the tattooed teenage girl asked him what he wanted.

He wasn't even sure why.

Laura allowed Martin to pay for the ice cream, and the couple licked double scoops of chocolate while strolling past the window displays that lined Farmington Avenue and the newly developed section of the town center. Familiar with this area, Martin pointed out Vintage Vinyl, a record store owned and operated by two of the most unfriendly brothers ever to walk the face of the earth. Martin had been in their store on several occasions, and though he had managed to avoid their venom so far, he had heard the owners responding rudely and sarcastically to several customers, both in person and over the phone. One look at their front door, plastered with signs warning against cell phones, dogs, unattended children, and ice cream, and you knew that this was not an accommodating merchant.

"Why do you shop here if the owners are so rude?" Laura asked.

"It's entertaining. I never know what they might say next. And I'm kind of hoping that they come after me someday. I'm ready for them."

"Ready for them?"

"I've practiced my one-liners and zingers. I'm ready to put them in their place and make a scene. Someday I'm going to walk in there, yapping on my cell phone, with a melting ice cream cone in one hand, two dogs in the other, and trailed by three random kids from the street. I can't wait to see what they say."

"I'd like to be there when you do."

"I'll let you know," Martin assured her.

Laura smiled.

As they crossed Main Street, Laura reached out and took Martin's hand, a move that startled him so much that he dropped his ice cream in the middle of the street. He paused in the crosswalk, staring at the upside-down cone before Laura tugged on him, offering to share the rest of hers with him.

It was a moment that Martin would never forget.

As they turned past the town hall and began walking down the hill toward the parking lot, Martin suddenly grew panicky. They were still holding hands, which Martin could barely believe, and now he wasn't sure what might happen next. Should he walk Laura to her car, or should they separate at the most logical spot, halfway between the two vehicles? Should he open her car door? Could he, considering he didn't have the key? Should he attempt to kiss her? The last girl that he had kissed had been Katie Neelon, a girl who had been working at Dunkin' Donuts around the same time that Martin was employed there. She had just graduated from college, was a couple of years younger than Martin, and was working the overnight shift while trying to find a teaching job in the local school district. Katie had asked Martin out after the two had spent an evening together in the drive-thru, pouring coffee for bleary-eyed plow drivers and scores of young people who disregarded the foot and a half of snow that had already fallen on the roads. After an evening of chili dogs at Doogie's and a movie (*Four Weddings and a Funeral,* which Martin had adored and Katie had not), he had managed an awkward kiss on Katie's parents' doorstep. Martin could remember feeling the same way then as he did now. Unsure. Afraid. Desperately wanting to do the right thing. He wanted to kiss Laura, that was certain, but he was also terrified about where that first kiss might lead.

More uncertainty, to be certain.

Fortunately for Martin, Laura didn't leave the decision making to him. Still holding his hand, she led him past his Subaru and over to her Honda Accord. Stopping beside the door, she turned, took hold of his other hand as well, and smiled. "Thank you for a delightful evening, Martin. And thank you for keeping me out of trouble with my friend. You really saved the day." And with that, she leaned in and briefly kissed him on the cheek.

"Thanks," was all that Martin could manage at first, but after Laura giggled at his response, he added, "I mean, thank you for a terrific evening, too. I mean it. I'm not just repeating."

"You're welcome," Laura said with a smile and kissed him one more time on the same cheek. The two exchanged phone numbers and a promise to speak in a day or two. Martin wasn't quick enough to open the car door for Laura, but once she was inside, he closed it for her before attempting to walk back to his car with as much ease as he could muster.

It had been one of the finest days of his life.

Sitting in front of his computer later that night, he began to type.

The means by which Matthew Stock had managed to become trapped inside the home of Jane and Tom Casper was a long story, and one worth telling, but for the moment, Reader, suffice it to say that Matthew Stock was hunkered

down behind a couch while the homeowner, the aforemen-
tioned Tom Casper, was crunching on Doritos and watching
television. Little did he know that our hero sat less than
three feet away, desperately awaiting an opportunity to
escape.

Martin had kept his promise and begun his novel.

Martin's excitement over his dinner with Laura had begun to wane during the week. Though his enthusiasm had reached an all-time high during the date, the return to his environment and routines had brought a sobering reality to his circumstances. In thirty-six hours, he was to attend a surprise party for one of his longtime clients, and his date was a woman whose house he had entered without her knowledge. Though he was enjoying the new sense of adventure, he was also becoming concerned about where these changes might lead. Chaos led to unpredictability, and Martin's life was becoming more chaotic than he could remember it ever having been.

Yet at the same time he had managed to help his second client, and within a week of the first. His risky, improbable plan had worked, reinforcing the feeling that he was doing the right thing.

Still, he had violated several rules to do so, and he feared that this would eventually catch up to him.

Despite this growing sense of dread, he couldn't stop thinking about Laura. She had called him the evening after their date, and after some small talk, they had decided upon a place to meet about an hour before the Ashley party. They were going to stop for a drink at a local pub about a mile from the Water's Edge and then head over to the party together. Martin had inquired about what he should wear and was given an inadequate "whatever you want will be fine" answer. He had decided upon a collared shirt, cotton slacks, and sports jacket. He was still debating the tie.

Martin had even called Jim for advice, turning to his friend as he had many other times in his life when in need. Unlike Martin's life, Jim's had followed a more traditional trajectory, complete with loving parents (still alive and married), four years of college, a well-paying job, a marriage, and children. Though he hadn't suffered through the family difficulties and low-paying jobs that Martin had been forced to endure, Jim had sympathized with his friend to a degree that Martin had found amazing, and in many ways had done more to help him survive than his parents ever had. When Martin was twenty-three and unable to acquire a credit card, it was Jim who ordered a second card, adding Martin as an authorized user and allowing his friend to use it in case of an emergency. On his twenty-first birthday, Martin had been struck by a car in the parking lot of a Boston Market, and Jim had been the first one to arrive at the hospital, a full thirty minutes ahead of his parents. But in Martin's mind, Jim's most remarkable quality was his willingness and ability to forge friendships with the most diverse group of people imaginable. His Sunday afternoon picnics (one of Jim's summertime staples) were populated with business executives and convenience store clerks, accountants and janitors, flag football teammates and Dungeons and Dragons aficionados. Though none of these people had become Martin's friends, he had gotten to know a few of them through Jim and had found them to be warm, kind people for the most part. Jim was willing to befriend people from all walks of life, and Martin felt incredibly fortunate to have such a friend.

Unfortunately, Martin had been unable to turn their phone conversation in the direction of Laura, sidetracked by Jim's concern about his daughter's recent bout with pneumonia. In truth, Martin wasn't sure how to even begin talking to his friend about a girl. When he was younger, Jim had tried to set Martin up on several dates, but all had ended in awkward handshakes and the purposeful avoidance of eye contact. Probably sensing his friend's frustration, Jim had eased off on the attempts to find Martin a girlfriend, and conversation on the subject of women had dried up entirely. Springing questions about Laura on Jim at this point therefore seemed impossible. As a result, Martin was on his own in regard to his plans on Saturday. He was flying blind and dreading every minute of it.

Since his date, Martin had made every effort to return to his normal routine, to bring some semblance and structure back to his life.

Even that had been difficult.

Though his work routines were falling back into place, Martin had not returned to the Quaker Diner since meeting Laura, unsure of how to handle his relationship with Jillian. Though he knew that the bond that he and Laura had was already more significant and meaningful than anything that he had with Jillian, he couldn't bring himself to reenter the diner knowing that he might have to lie to the girl who had been serving him eggs and referring to him as "honey" for years. Part of him wanted to sit down on his stool and tell Jillian everything he knew about Laura, but he feared that such news would come as a devastating blow to the girl he still cared about a great deal.

Even more difficult, Martin had been forced to locate a new restaurant for breakfast and had yet to settle on a replacement (albeit temporary, he hoped) for the Quaker Diner. Though places like Mo's Diner, Effie's Place, and even Friendly's had served decent meals, none had possessed the charm of the Quaker.

Thankfully, work routines had been easier to reestablish.

Martin had scheduled makeup visits for the clients that he'd missed while preserving the Ashley party, and he fell right back into his regular schedule with refreshing ease. A week of uneventful work leading up to the party was what he'd hoped for, but this hope was dashed this morning when he arrived at the home of Sophie and Sherman Pearl of Newington. It was just over a month ago that Martin had acquired the diamond earring from Sophie Pearl's jewelry box, but a lot had happened since that day.

It seemed like ages ago.

Martin was jogging across the park adjacent to the Pearls' backyard, closing in on the invisible line that separated the Pearls' property from the park, when he saw something that caused him to stop in his tracks.

The rear door to the Pearls' home was slightly ajar. Not enough for the casual passerby to notice, but Martin's attention to detail was anything but casual. The door wasn't open, but it wasn't fully shut either.

Something was up.

Martin bent over, pretending to tie his troublesome shoe while reviewing a checklist in his mind. Before parking in the lot adjacent to the tennis courts, he had driven by the Pearls' home and confirmed that there were no cars parked in the driveway. Though the Pearls owned a two-car garage, at least one car was usually parked in the driveway overnight. Though it was possible that the Pearls had accidentally left their back door unlatched, this would be the first time in their more than nine years as clients.

Unsure of what action to take, Martin chose to wait and watch. Entering the house on this day was now out of the question. Even if the door had been accidentally left open, any change in routine was enough reason to abort a visit. Still, Martin wasn't ready to leave just yet. Instead, he limped about fifty feet south to a set of benches and sat down, feigning a muscle pull. While rubbing his quadriceps, he never took his eyes off the Pearls' home.

Martin's patience was rewarded less than a minute later when he saw movement at the back door. A moment later a man emerged from the home, pulling the door shut behind him. Looking left and right, the man then began walking across the backyard and into the park, the same escape route that Martin would have taken had he entered the house. The man was moving with the speed of someone who wanted to move quickly but remain inconspicuous.

Martin knew that pace well.

For years, Martin had wondered if he would ever run into someone else in his line of work. He knew that they were out there, smash-and-grabbers for the most part, but he couldn't help but wonder if he was the only one who specialized in the business the way that he did. Being alone in his career choice, the only person on the planet operating as he did, was both an exhilarating and a lonely feeling. It allowed Martin to think of himself as an innovator, a unique, one-of-a-kind guy, but at the same time, the nature of his business forced him to remain silent on the matter.

Without colleagues of any kind.

Alone.

Perhaps.

Considering this man's quiet and careful exit from the house and seeming empty-handedness (no flat screen television or laptops in his arms), it appeared as if Martin might have found someone in his line of work after all.

Intrigued, Martin decided to follow the stranger. He rationalized that knowing as much as possible about the intruder would be crucial to his continued success with the Pearls, but underneath the logic, the decision to follow the man was born primarily from a desire to know if this intruder operated his business in a way similar to Martin.

Curiosity had its sticky grip on him like never before.

Of course, following the man would only be possible if he had parked his vehicle in the same lot as Martin had. If the man was parked on the other side of the baseball field, or in the shaded lot below the footbridge, there wouldn't be much of a chance of following him. He'd be in his car and driving off before Martin could even find him.

But fortune was on Martin's side. As the man crossed the field, less than a hundred feet from Martin's position on the bench, he veered left toward the nearest parking lot, the same lot in which Martin had brought the Subaru to a halt less than ten minutes ago. As the man passed, Martin looked up from his crouch and stole a quick glance. He was a tall, bulky man in his late thirties or early forties, built with more muscle than fat, though a generous portion of both seemed evident. He was wearing a pair of black jeans, a long-sleeve, nondescript black T-shirt, and a baseball cap. His face was angular and featureless except for the nose, which appeared off-kilter, as if it had been broken one too many times.

Most notably, the man looked mean to Martin, the kind of guy you would want to avoid in an alley late at night. He was big and tough and had the type of face that projected anger at all times. He moved with a confidence that made Martin wonder if he himself had ever moved with as much self-assurance.

He doubted it very much.

Martin waited until the intruder was twenty paces from the parking lot before standing up and limping toward his car, ensuring that he was limping on the same leg as he had been moments ago. As he crossed the field, following the intruder's footsteps through the morning dew, he noticed that the man was wearing gloves, not the latex kind that Martin wore while working, but brown leather gloves. They seemed terribly out of place on this warm day, but Martin knew that they would be just as effective as the latex variety that he wore. Daring a more careful examination of the man, he realized that the intruder's shoes were covered with a white rubberlike material, similar to his latex moccasins. It didn't take Martin more than a couple of seconds to realize that whatever it was around his shoes, it was worn by the man in order to avoid leaving footprints behind.

Martin was impressed. This man clearly knew what he was doing.

Martin watched the man climb into a dark blue pickup truck, start the engine, and pull out of the lot. Quickening his pace, he managed to reach his Subaru in time to see the pickup turning left out of the parking lot and heading up the short side-street that connected to a main road. Moments later, Martin was turning left as well, onto Audubon Avenue, less than two hundred feet behind his quarry.

The chase was on.

Though Martin had tailed clients before, his previous endeavors were always preplanned and carefully staged. Prior to tailing a client, Martin would locate the client's home and probable place of employment (whenever possible), and then map the likely routes between the two, allowing him to follow with ease. Occasionally a client might make an unexpected stop or detour, but in these cases it wasn't critical for Martin to maintain his tail. If he lost the client in traffic or if he feared detection, he could always call off the chase and try again the next day. But in this case, he had just one chance. If he lost the intruder or was detected before he could identify the man's home address, it was unlikely that he would have a second chance at uncovering the truth. And without this information, he would surely have to cancel the Pearls as clients immediately and leave his burning curiosity unsatisfied.

At the end of Audubon Avenue the pickup turned right, heading up the road toward the center of Newington. Martin had parked the Subaru in the center many times (it was one of his random parking spots for the Pearls' home) and knew the area well. He was relieved. There would be plenty of traffic in which to conceal his car, and only one or two traffic lights to potentially interrupt the chase. At the next intersection, the pickup turned left onto Main Street and began a three-mile trip out of Newington and into neighboring West Hartford. Martin waved on the driver of a red Toyota Corolla before pulling onto Main Street, effectively placing the Corolla between his car and the pickup. This three-car procession continued for the entire drive into West Hartford, breaking up only when the Corolla made a right onto New Britain Avenue, heading toward Hartford, and the pickup made a left, proceeding further into Martin's hometown.

Without the cover of another car, Martin immediately grew more anxious. He had read about vehicle surveillance in several criminal investigation texts and understood how difficult it was to follow a suspect alone. In order to avoid detection, police manuals suggest multiple units should participate in the surveillance, traveling on routes that are parallel to the suspect so that the surveillance vehicles can rotate as the suspect changes directions. Alone, Martin knew, the likelihood of following the intruder very far would depend upon his ability to put traffic between him and the pickup truck without losing his visual of his suspect.

Less than half a mile north on New Britain Avenue, the pickup turned right onto Quaker Lane. As Martin approached the intersection, he noticed a dark sedan in the opposite lane, its directional indicating the desire to turn left onto the same road. Though Martin had the right of way, he waved the sedan on, placing it between himself and the pickup.

One of the dangers of this tactic is falling behind your quarry if the driver of the middle car fails to drive fast enough, which quickly became the case now as the pickup began gaining ground on Martin and the sedan over the next half mile. Martin surmised that if he didn't pass the slower-moving sedan soon, he would lose visual contact with the pickup altogether. Fortunately, the traffic light ahead split Quaker Lane into two. Martin waited until the sedan chose the left lane before pulling right in preparation to pass it. Before he could arrive at the next intersection, however, the traffic light turned yellow. Martin watched as the pickup passed underneath it and knew that he would have to run the light or lose the intruder entirely. Steeling himself, he accelerated, searching for oncoming traffic from the west and eastbound lanes and seeing none. The light had been red for five full seconds when he passed through the intersection, but without any crossing traffic, he made it safely through.

This was the most severe moving violation of Martin's life.

Less than thirty seconds later, Martin was within five car-lengths of the pickup, resuming his tail. Had this been an ordinary client, Martin wouldn't fear detection as much as he did now. Ordinary people weren't typically concerned about being followed, and rarely would someone suddenly become aware of the same vehicle in the rearview mirror for an extended period of time. But in Martin's business, the threat of being followed was a constant concern. He imagined that the intruder might feel the same way.

Martin maintained a safe distance for the next two miles before the pickup made a left turn onto what Martin knew was a residential street. Had the pickup continued on for another three blocks, the intruder would have reached Park Road, a main thoroughfare through town. Turning off prior to Park Road probably meant that the intruder's destination was somewhere within the twelve to sixteen blocks that made up this middle-class neighborhood. Wary of following the pickup into the residential area (tailing a car on a main road was one thing, but doing so on a side street might draw suspicion), Martin continued past the turn (Ascension Street), taking the next left instead, hoping to reacquire the pickup as it crossed through the neighborhood.

This is when Martin's luck failed him. By the time he rounded the block and was at the intersection of Gates Road and Ascension Street, one block north of Quaker, the pickup truck was nowhere to be seen.

Martin was not immediately concerned. There were obvious explanations for the absence of the truck. There could have been an additional side street dividing Ascension: a cross street, a dead end, or a cul-de-sac. Or the intruder's destination (and perhaps his home) might be somewhere on Ascension Street. As long as he didn't park his truck in a garage, finding it would be only a matter of time.

Martin quickly decided to turn right onto Ascension, continuing north on the same street where he had expected to find the pickup. As he rolled slowly through the neighborhood, he scanned both sides of the road, looking for the blue truck or a side street where it might have turned. After less than a block, Martin spotted it, disappearing behind the automated door of a garage set behind a small white Cape. As he pulled past the property, Martin spotted the intruder walking up the driveway toward a side door. Martin took note of the house number, 414, before continuing past the house and circling back to Quaker Lane.

414 Ascension Street. That was probably all he needed in order to identify the intruder.

By late morning, Martin had finished processing the day's acquisitions (managing to visit the remaining three clients on his list in near-record time), and with his workday complete, he was now ready to identify the Pearls' intruder.

This process had occupied his mind all day.

Though determining a client's identity was sometimes necessary, he often knew the client's name long before entering their home. However, it was standard operating procedure for Martin to identify his clients' neighbors as well (hoping to identify law enforcement officers, stay-at-home moms, and the like), and for this purpose, Martin had a system in place. Sitting at his kitchen table with a tall glass of lemonade (courtesy of the Reeds, who purchased more Country Time lemonade than a person could ever consume), Martin began his online detective work in the property records for the town of West Hartford. Within minutes, he had the particulars for 414 Ascension Street on his screen, including the owner's name (Clive Darrow), the date of the home's most recent purchase (two years ago), and a basic blueprint of the house (useful to Martin when scouting potential clients and their homes).

Unless the man lived with a roommate or was renting the home, Martin was relatively sure that he had identified the Pearls' intruder by name.

Next, Martin conducted an online search for the name Clive Darrow, hoping to turn up any information on the man. After scanning several websites containing the name (including one on which a Cayman dive-master by the same name frequently posted in the scuba forums), it did not appear that any matched the Clive Darrow who had visited the Pearls' home earlier that day. None of them seemed to have any recognizable connection to Connecticut.

In possession of the intruders' probable name and address, Martin next went to an online directory in order to secure his telephone number. In less than a minute, he had this bit of information as well. A well-timed call from a nontraceable phone would likely give Martin the confirmation of the intruder's name, either by tricking the man into confirming his name

(Martin would falsely represent a charity in this case) or by listening for the intruder to identify himself on his answering machine (which most people did).

Next, Martin logged onto a website that provided in-depth background checks for a monthly fee. There were dozens of these websites in existence, and after extensive research, Martin had found the service that he thought was best. Simply enter the client's name and at least one other identifying piece of information (current address or Social Security number, for example), and in minutes Martin would receive a report that included up to ten years of address history with all listed phone numbers, a marriage and divorce history, an instant criminal background check, a Sex Offender Registry check, as well as a list of bankruptcies, tax liens, and small claims judgments. The report would also include a local and national Web-based search of more than five hundred sources, including major U.S. newspapers and magazines, trade publications, websites, and newswires.

As he waited for the report to arrive in his e-mail box, Martin conducted a search of eBay for Clive Darrow's name, turning up no further information.

At that moment the phone rang, startling Martin. Though he was engaged in nothing illegal, he couldn't help but think that the intruder was watching him, tracking his every move. He involuntarily glanced at the open kitchen window just to be sure.

Martin picked up the phone during its third ring, as he always did, and was surprised to hear Laura's voice on the other end. "What are you doing right now?"

Laura had a way of dispensing with formality and getting right to the point. This both excited and unnerved Martin. The absence of formality made Martin think that the two were becoming close despite the short amount of time that they had known each other, but at the same time, the lack of a standard greeting and other social rhetoric flustered Martin, not allowing him time enough to develop an appropriate response.

"Just getting ready for lunch," Martin managed to answer after a moment. "Why?"

"I've got an hour for lunch. Want to meet me someplace?"

"Sure." Martin hadn't thought he'd see Laura before Saturday, so this was quite a treat. Their conversations on the phone had started out awkward and stilted, with Martin taking notes on everything Laura said and reviewing them later for future conversational topics. But in the past couple of days, he had found himself able to speak to her with less and less mental exertion. In fact, he had inadvertently stopped taking notes for more than ten minutes during their last phone call before realizing his gaffe and attempting to remember what had been said in order to jot it down. It had been his most relaxed conversation with her so far, and the prospect of seeing her in person thrilled him. "Where?"

"Max's in the Center makes a great Caesar salad with oysters," she said hopefully.

"Sounds good," Martin answered, though he despised oysters. "When should I meet you?"

"Can you be there in thirty minutes?"

"You bet," he answered, pleased with his quick response.

"Great!" Laura said with genuine enthusiasm. "I'll see you there. I'll be the pretty girl at the bar."

"Okay," Martin answered, shaking his head in disgust as he hung up the phone. " 'Okay?' Is that the best I can do?" he wondered aloud. He'd think of something clever to say on the way over to the restaurant to make up for the blunder.

After a quick trip to the bathroom to straighten his hair, floss, and brush his teeth, Martin was ready to walk out the door when he heard the chimes that signal the arrival of an e-mail.

Glancing at the clock and seeing that he had a few more minutes before he needed to leave, he sat down in front of the laptop, unable to contain his curiosity about the intruder. He double-clicked on the e-mail and began skimming the text, not expecting to find much. These reports tended to be full of addresses and previous work history, and little more. He was about halfway down the page when his eyes fell upon a piece of information that he had seen only once before.

Martin was suddenly very afraid for Sophie Pearl's safety, and a few moments later, when the rest of the puzzle pieces clicked into place, his fear rose exponentially.

Sophie Pearl was in grave peril.

The drive to Max's Oyster Bar was torture for Martin. He had gone from absolute glee over Laura's invitation to a desire to dispense with the lunch as quickly as possible. There was much to do if Sophie Pearl was to remain safe, and he had no idea where to begin.

Adrenaline raced through his extremities, causing his hands to shake and his fingers and toes to tingle. His ears were filled with the sound of rushing blood. His heart raced like never before. As he turned onto South Main Street, in the direction of West Hartford Center, his fear grew as he began to comprehend the type of man with whom he was dealing.

The intruder, Clive Darrow, reminded Martin of himself. Meticulous, clever, and cautious.

Halfway down the page, Martin's eyes had found Clive Darrow's criminal history:

First-degree sexual assault.
Assault and battery with a deadly weapon.

A few lines past his criminal record, Martin saw that Clive Darrow was a registered sex offender, and it was this bit of information that allowed Martin to grasp the ingenuity of this man's plan.

Only once before had Martin encountered a registered sex offender while conducting background checks. This had been Noah Blake, the man still living next door to the Pearls. Martin had allowed this fact to register as a coincidence for all of three seconds before the genius of Clive Darrow became apparent to him. Martin realized without any doubt that Clive Darrow, in search of a new victim, was targeting the home of a woman who lived within close proximity to a known sex offender. With a sex offender registry available online for anyone to access, Darrow would have been able to locate the homes of hundreds of these convicted criminals in the area. If his plans for Sophie Pearl were timed properly and executed without leaving any physical evidence behind, this would give the police a prime suspect for whatever crime Darrow might commit. And if Darrow was capable of breaking into the Pearls' home undetected, he was more than capable of gaining access to Noah Blake's home as well, in order to collect DNA evidence to leave behind at the scene. Hair from a drain or comb would be simple enough to obtain. In fact, he might have already gathered the necessary evidence and spent the morning dispersing it around the Pearls' house. And since Noah Blake was a registered sex offender, his DNA would already be on file with law enforcement agencies.

Just as Martin was meticulous and ingenious in his work, it appeared that Clive Darrow was equally capable, and this was a dangerous combination in Martin's estimation. Sophie Pearl was in great danger, and Martin knew that he would have to stop Darrow before it was too late.

What he should do was unclear, but as he pulled alongside a parking meter a block from the restaurant, he tried to rid his mind of this new problem, at least until his lunch with Laura was finished. Filling the meter for one hour and hoping he wouldn't be there any longer, he walked briskly into Max's, spotting Laura where she said she would be.

She hadn't been lying when she told Martin to look for the pretty girl at the bar. In Martin's opinion, no one in the bustling restaurant came close to Laura's beauty. She was wearing a green sweater and blue skirt, and her hair was pinned up and away from her face, the way Martin would have her wear it every day if it were up to him. She spotted Martin almost immediately, walked over with a glass of seltzer water in her hand, and kissed him lightly on the cheek. He smiled and wondered if he should kiss her back in the same fashion but refrained, rejecting the mental image of such an attempt and feeling foolish for even considering it. The two were quickly seated by the window at a small table for two. As soon as he sat down, Martin's thoughts returned to Sophie Pearl.

He tried to push them away.

"How is your day going?" he asked, attempting to fire off the first question to avoid being blindsided by Laura's randomness.

"Better now. What were you going to have for lunch?"

"Huh?"

"You said you were about to have lunch when I spoke to you on the phone," she reminded him. "What were you going to have?"

"Oh. A grilled cheese sandwich, but this is much better." Though he liked the line (it had made Laura smile), Martin knew that the excitement and joy that he typically felt when speaking to her was gone. His hands were still shaking beneath the table when the menus arrived and drinks were ordered.

"Caesar salad with oysters for me," she declared, pushing the menu aside. "It really is the best here."

"I'm not a big oyster fan," Martin admitted, hoping this news wouldn't disappoint her too much. "But the French onion soup looks good." He placed the menu down and returned his hands to his lap, where they continued their nearly imperceptible trembling.

"So . . . are you excited about tomorrow?"

"Of course. I mean, I still feel a little odd about going to your friend's party. I didn't really do anything. Just got lucky."

"I'm the one who got lucky," Laura said, staring him directly in the eyes.

Martin blushed. "Yeah, well I feel the same way. And as long as I'm going with you, I'll be fine."

"Good," she said, the shortness of the word signaling an end to this part of the conversation. "So how is the novel coming?"

In truth, Martin had continued to peck away at the thing over the last few days, but he still had only a couple of thousand words written. He had begun by writing about his own life, but he knew that if this were to be a successful novel, he would need to begin fabricating new characters, settings, and storylines soon, otherwise he'd end up with a tell-all memoir that might some-day land him in prison. Besides, Martin knew that his life wouldn't be interesting enough to carry a reader for three hundred pages, so fabrication would be essential.

"I've worked on it every day," Martin answered truthfully. "Slow and steady. But you first. Any news on the interior design front?"

"Not since the other day. I've got a list of three schools that I like, but no way to pay for any of them. I'll need to look into financial aid, I guess."

"I'm going to stop writing if you don't get a move on," Martin chided, lifting a piece of bread from the basket. He loved pushing Laura this way, because he knew how much she appreciated it. Seemed to need it even. And yet it came so easily to Martin, a man who didn't like to waste a moment.

"No, you won't," she said, laughing. "You're not a quitter. You're a writer, and someday your book will be sitting on one of the front tables of one of those bookstores around the block. Maybe you can even arrange to do a signing, and I'll sit beside you and tell your readers that I am the Laura who the book is dedicated to. That would be great! Now please, can't you tell me what the book is about? Please?"

Martin shook his head. "Even I don't know. I'm just writing what comes to mind."

"Well, what have you written so far?"

"Nothing good. Honestly. When there is something worth reading, you'll be the first to get a copy. Okay?"

"Okay. But I don't like it."

The waiter arrived at that moment and took the couple's order. While they waited for their lunch, Laura tried to engage Martin in conversation, but without his full attention on the task at hand, Martin was failing miserably to carry his end.

"Is there something wrong? You seem a little down. Not yourself exactly. Did I say something wrong? You don't really need to dedicate the book to me."

"No, it's not you," Martin answered, almost laughing at the thought that Laura Green could ever do anything wrong. "I got news this morning from a friend who is in a bit of trouble, and I'm not sure how to help."

"Do you want to talk about it?"

Martin paused for a moment, unsure of how to proceed. In his heart, he wanted to tell Laura everything. The burden of Sophie Pearl's safety was already feeling like too much to bear. But without telling her everything about his life, he wouldn't be able to explain his dilemma.

"She asked me to keep this confidential. But let me ask you this: My friend is in trouble, and I don't know what to tell her. I've never dealt with a situation like this before. What do you do when you want to help a friend but don't know how?"

Laura thought for a moment and then answered. "That's a tough one, buddy. But if I can't help my friend, I usually go to someone who can help and ask for their advice. If it sounds right and I can support it, I pass it along. Do you know someone who might be able to help with your friend's problem?"

"Yeah, I know someone. But he's not the easiest person to talk to."

"Well, if you care about your friend and she needs your help, you'll manage."

Martin had already considered this option and dismissed it. But perhaps Laura was right. If it kept Sophie Pearl safe and unharmed, he might have to speak to a man he hadn't seen or spoken to in nearly two decades.

He might have to speak to his father.

After lunch, Martin walked Laura back to her office and received another kiss on the cheek before returning home. Though he had decided upon his next course of action, he wanted to take another look at Clive Darrow's criminal history and check to see if he had missed anything of importance.

According to the report, Clive Darrow had been convicted of assault and battery with a dangerous weapon and first-degree sexual assault seventeen years ago, when he was twenty-two years old and living in Pittsburgh, Pennsylvania. It appeared that he had been in prison for fifteen years before being released less than two years ago, when he moved into the home on Ascension Street. Since his three previous addresses were all within the Pittsburgh city limits, Martin could not discern the reason that the man had moved to Connecticut. He had no current employment history listed, and there were no marriages or divorces on record.

But the one thing that Martin could be certain of was that this man was intelligent. His plan to implicate Noah Blake in his own crime (and Martin had no doubt in his mind that this was Darrow's plan) was brilliant in its simplicity. The only two things Clive Darrow needed to do in order to guarantee its success were to leave no DNA evidence of his own inside the Pearls' house (something Martin knew that the man could avoid) and to make sure that Noah Blake had no alibi for the time of the attack. If Sophie Pearl was home alone at a time when Noah Blake was also alone, Darrow could strike. And considering the frequency with which Sophie Pearl's husband traveled on business, and the fact that Noah Blake lived alone, the opportunities for Darrow would be plentiful.

The fact that Darrow had been in the Pearls' house that morning, likely planting DNA evidence to implicate Blake while mapping out the home for his next break-in, indicated that the man planned to make his move soon. He would likely wait until he was certain that Noah Blake was home alone, probably late in the evening or sometime over the weekend, but regardless, the time was near.

Martin could not waste a minute in formulating a plan.

He spent the next three hours planning the conversation that he would have with his father. Ideally, Martin would drive over to the house, acquire the information desired, and leave. But considering that father and son had not spoken in so long, Martin worried that the topic of family history would inevitably arise. He needed to be prepared.

With the script set firmly in his mind, Martin drove to his father's apartment in East Hartford, arriving outside the apartment building shortly past five o'clock. The sun was low in the sky as he parked the Subaru in the shaded parking lot behind the building, reminding Martin of how quickly time was passing. Having not visited the Pearls in almost two weeks (missing his previously scheduled visit in order to preserve the Ashleys' party), he couldn't be sure when Sherman Pearl's next business trip was planned for, or even if he was out of town right now. Though Martin was keenly in tune with his clients' vacation schedules, business trips taken by one spouse were less critically tracked, since these trips rarely provided him with additional opportunities for entry into the client's home. For all Martin knew, Clive Darrow could be hiding in a closet in Sophie Pearl's bedroom right now, waiting for the moment to strike.

Martin's father rented an apartment behind a barbershop on Silver Lane, and though it was small, it appeared clean and well maintained on the outside. Martin had always known where his father lived, and had kept close tabs on the man since their separation, cruising by occasionally to see if his father was still driving the 1990 Ford pickup that he seemed unable to rid himself of.

He was. Martin's Subaru was now parked alongside its battered exterior.

Though he had never actually been inside his father's apartment, Martin had driven by the building hundreds of times over the past ten years, always wanting to stop and knock on the door, but never able to bring himself to do it. "Next week," he'd say to himself, until next week became one year and then five, and any hope of reconciliation seemed impossible.

But now he would have to knock on the door and face the man who hadn't bothered to fight for his wife or son, who had left his home more than twenty years ago with little more than a whimper.

When his father finally answered his knocking after more than a minute, Martin barely recognized the man. His once black mustache was now wispy and gray, his thick black hair was almost gone, and what remained was gray and lifeless. He had put on weight since Martin had seen him last, most of it in his belly, and he held a cane in his right hand for support. It was clear from his father's furrowed brow that the man did not recognize the son standing before him.

Martin hadn't anticipated this, and as a result he froze.

"Yes?" his father said. After a moment, he repeated himself, curiosity quickly turning to annoyance. His voice hadn't changed a bit in nearly two decades, and for that, Martin was relieved. It was as if one piece of his childhood father still existed.

"Can I help you?" the man asked, becoming more perturbed by the second.

"It's me, Dad. Martin."

The man's blue eyes opened wide, and a second later Martin saw recognition in his father's face. "Martin," he said after a moment, a sigh more than a word. Then again. "Martin. I can't believe it. Look at you."

"Do you mind if I come in?" he asked, this line rehearsed.

"Of course. Come in." His father backed away from the door, clearly requiring the cane for support, and Martin entered a kitchen in serious need of remodeling. Though the room was clean and organized, the yellowing wallpaper and the ancient linoleum gave it a depressed, hopeless appearance. The appliances were old, the cabinets were old, and the man standing before him was older than Martin could have ever imagined. He looked nothing like the father who had taught Martin to bait a hook, steer a canoe, and ride a bicycle, all in the same day. He was tired, used up, lacking the spark that Martin so fondly remembered. They stood facing one another for a moment, each man taking measure of the other until Martin's father gestured to a small kitchen table opposite the appliances and cabinets and took the seat closest to the door. Martin sat down across from him.

"How have you been, Dad?"

The old man smiled. "You looking for a summary of my life, son?"

"No," Martin said, amused. His father was still as quick as ever. "I'm just wondering how you're doing."

"Better than most of my friends, I can tell you that. So not too bad. I've managed to stay alive and out of the nursing home so far, which is more than I can say for most of my buddies."

"What's with the cane?"

"Arthritis," he answered with a growl. "Bastard disease. I haven't been able to golf or even walk much for, what?, at least three years now."

"Sorry," Martin said and meant it. He hadn't seen this man since he was a child, and yet he loved his father all the same. He had never really known it until this moment, but now he was sure. Despite the anger and disappointment that he felt toward his father, the thought that the old man couldn't walk the golf course or even to the corner store anymore pained Martin more than he would have expected.

"Yeah, I'm sorry too," the old man laughed. "So what brings you here? You in trouble?"

Martin was both surprised and hurt at the implication, but he couldn't deny its veracity. "Not me, but a friend. I'm not sure how to help her." This line had been rehearsed.

"What's that got to do with me?"

"I thought you might be able to tell me what to do." This line had also been planned on the drive over.

"I can't see how an old man who can't walk straight might be able to help, but if you pour me a cup of joe from that pot over there, I'll give you an ear."

Martin was relieved. His father would at least listen to the problem, and that's more than what Martin had expected. He rose, moved over to the counter, took a mug from a rack hanging above the sink and poured from an ancient coffee pot. "Black?"

"Yup. Only way I'll drink the stuff. You remember that from when you was a kid?"

Martin remembered but chose to lie. "Nope. Just a good guess. You seem like a guy who would like his coffee black." Admitting that he remembered how his father drank his coffee might open up the door to that long-forgotten past, and Martin wanted nothing more than to keep that portal shut. At least for today.

Martin returned to his seat, slid the mug across the table to his father, and waited for him to take a sip. Then he began. "Listen, Dad. I'm going to tell you some things that you might not want to hear, and I'm not going to tell you the whole story. Just enough so that you can get a picture of how much trouble my friend might be in. I can't tell you everything, and like I said, I don't think you'd want to hear it. But I can't trust anyone else with this, and you're the only person I know who might have a clue about what to do. Do you understand so far?"

"No. Not yet," his father said, taking another sip. "But from the sound of things, you're in some trouble yourself, or else you'd be telling me everything. But I'm guessing that your friend might be in even more trouble. So I'm going to listen and help if I can, because I get the feeling that this is some serious business. But son, let me ask you something first. Why me? Why in hell do you trust me? You ain't seen me in twenty-five years."

Martin had rehearsed the answer to this question dozens of times. He had planned on explaining how the bond between a son and father transcends time and space, and that he had always known his father to be a decent, honest man. He was going to tell his father that he had always felt a connection to him, even during the many years that they had been apart. But instead, this came out:

"I don't know, Dad."

"Well, there's got to be a reason you came here. What was it?"

"I dunno, Dad. I guess that you're the only family I have left."

"After twenty years, I'd hardly call us family. I certainly haven't been much of a father."

"You're the only family I've got, Dad. You let me down, for sure, but I think I probably let you down too. Our relationship got messed up pretty badly, but it wasn't because either of us wanted it to. We were just stupid. A couple of cowards without a brain between us."

"Ain't that the truth," his father agreed.

"But we were never mean to each other, Dad. Never intentionally cruel. I've always loved you, Dad. I just did a lousy job loving you. And I'm guessing, maybe hoping, that it's the same for you. The apple doesn't fall far from the tree, right?"

Martin's father took another sip of coffee, either to stall in case his son had more to add or to consider what had been said. When it was clear that Martin was finished, he placed the cup down and nodded. "Good enough, son. Someone had to say it, and you're probably right. I was probably too stupid and afraid to be the one. You can trust me. Go ahead with your story."

Martin nodded, took a deep breath and began. "I came into possession of some information today while doing something that's not exactly legal. I wasn't hurting anybody, and it has nothing to do with drugs or guns or anything like that, but it's something that could land me in jail if I'm not careful."

"Tax evasion?"

"Huh?"

"Tax evasion," his father repeated. "Let's think about your illegal activities as tax evasion. Okay? I can get behind that. Unless that don't sit right with you."

Martin thought for a moment and then answered. "Yes, tax evasion. That's good. Okay, so while I was evading my taxes, I discovered that a registered sex offender is stalking someone I know. Not exactly a friend, but someone I care about. Someone who I don't want to see get hurt."

"How do you know he's a sex offender?" his father asked, placing the mug down and leaning forward.

"After I saw him leave my friend's house, I followed him to his home. Got his address, and from there, it was easy. He's got two counts of assault, one sexual, and did fifteen years for it. He's been out about two years and is living in West Hartford."

Martin's father leaned in even more, placing his glasses, which had previously been hanging by a cord around his neck, on his nose. "You saw this man inside your friend's house?"

"I saw him leaving the house," Martin answered.

"How do you know that your friend wasn't home? How do you know she hasn't already been assaulted?"

Martin had wanted to avoid this question, but he decided to answer it truthfully. "She wasn't home. I'm sure of it."

"So you were watching your friend's house, even though she wasn't home, and you saw this man leave the house, and you followed him. Correct?"

"Exactly," Martin replied, but he didn't like the way the old man seemed to be putting the pieces together so quickly.

"But you can't tell your friend about this man because if you do, the IRS will find out about your tax evasion and lock you up, right?"

"Yes," Martin answered, feeling a little ashamed. He had lost control of the conversation. His father seemed to already know too much.

"How do you know that this man isn't one of many who live in the house that you followed him to? How do you know that he isn't renting from the owner, who is the actual sex offender?"

"The sex offender registry includes a photo. It's the guy, Dad."

"Oh."

Now it was Martin's turn to lean forward. "So what should I do?"

"Listen, son. If you know that a convicted criminal is stalking anyone, you need to let the police know right away. But I'm guessing that if you told the police, you might get prosecuted for tax evasion. Yes?"

"Yes," Martin answered, trying to think of a means of ending this interrogation.

"How about an anonymous tip? A phone call or note?"

"That's what I was thinking. But do cops pay attention to that kind of thing?"

"When I was on the job, we would get tips all the time. Some were real. Most were bogus. But we followed up on each and every one. I used to tell the young guys that it's the tips you ignore that will bite you in the ass one day."

"But what if there's no evidence against this man?" Martin asked. "Just my anonymous word against his. What if he hasn't left any evidence inside the house? Won't the police just tip him off and point him at another victim?"

"Two things, son. First, if that man was in your friend's house, they will find evidence. There is always evidence. No one is that careful. If he jimmied the door or picked the lock, there are guys on the job who can tell. If there are traffic cameras in the area, they might be able to spot him casing the house. There's skin and hair and footprints. All kinds of DNA evidence. Trust me. There's always physical evidence to be found. Second, even if the cops tip this guy off, the worst you've done is protected your friend. Maybe saved her life. If this guy can't stop himself, he's a whack job. He'll do it again unless he's locked up, but now the police will have his name. His address. If he isn't caught, he will probably move to another part of the country and try again. But your friend will be safe regardless."

Martin didn't like any of these statements. First, he didn't believe his father when he said that physical evidence would undoubtedly be left behind. Though his father had been a police officer for twenty years, the last dozen or so as a detective, Martin didn't believe that all criminals were stupid. He was confident that he had never left a trace of physical evidence behind in the Pearls' home, and if Darrow was as clever as Martin suspected, he would have left nothing behind either. From what Martin had already seen, the man was smart.

And if his father was right and there was physical evidence left behind, some type that Martin had yet to consider, then the police would most certainly find evidence of his own presence in the house as well, and this would not be good.

Finally, if Darrow was tipped off by the police, his father was right: Sophie Pearl might be spared, but the next woman whom Darrow targeted might not be so lucky. The prospect of saving one woman while damning another did not appeal to Martin. He had come to believe that he was supposed to help Sophie Pearl, even more than Cindy Clayton or Justine Ashley. But he wasn't supposed to simply redirect the bullet that was aimed at her. He had been placed outside the Pearls' house so that he could stop that bullet cold.

"What about some kind of sting operation?" Martin asked. "Catch him in the act?"

"A possibility," his father answered. "But unlikely. Too dangerous for your friend, and it requires too much manpower. Too much time. If you send in a tip, the cops will probably pick this guy up immediately. Try to get him to confess. That's what I would've done."

"And if he doesn't confess?"

"They can usually get a guy to confess to something, and being a two-strike guy, it won't take much to put him away for life."

Martin doubted that Clive Darrow would confess unless shown evidence that directly implicated him in the break-in of the Pearls' home. He feared that his father had put away too many stupid criminals over the years and never realized how many clever ones had slipped through his grasp.

Clever people like himself.

"Anything else?" Martin asked, still in search of a better solution.

"Not really, son. Send in the tip and let the cops do their job."

"All right. Thanks, Dad."

"My pleasure, son. You know, we should do this more often. Except next time, maybe we can talk about the Sox. Or have some lunch together."

"Yeah, we should," Martin answered, fearing that his father didn't mean what he had said. His father now knew that his son was engaged in illegal activity, and he probably had a good idea of what that activity was. Why would he want a criminal visiting his apartment, even if it was his son?

"Martin, I mean it. I'd like to see you again. I know that things have been rotten between us, and there ain't much we can do about the rot but try to brush it away and start over. No use in shining up a piece of shit, right? You just toss it away and try to find some gold."

"That sounds good, Dad," Martin said with sincerity. "A fresh start."

"You were right, son. I've always loved you. I just did a piss-poor job of it."

"I know." Martin stood up to leave, but his father reached across the table and pulled him back down by the arm.

"And Martin, you'll send in that tip to the police today? Right? I've seen a lot of girls get hurt and it ain't pretty."

"I will, Dad. Today. As soon as I get home."

And with that, Martin's fresh start with his father began with a lie.

Before Martin tipped off the police, he wanted evidence, or at least the location of the evidence, so that Darrow could be put in prison for life. With that in mind, there was only one thing that he could do.

As he turned onto the on-ramp for Route 84, heading back in the direction of West Hartford, he glanced at the clock in the dashboard display. 5:30. The Pearls would be home in fifteen minutes, if they weren't already.

Martin drove into the capital city and took a downtown Hartford exit, winding his way past the train station and through traffic along Farmington Avenue until turning into a gas station on the Hartford–West Hartford border. This particular gas station had a pay phone, a disappearing fixture on the American landscape, and no traffic cameras, ATM machines, or security cameras within view of it. It was a phone that Martin had used before when calling a client to verify that no one was home.

Martin had never called the Pearls' before (he rarely called a client to ascertain their location), but their phone number, along with those of the rest of his clients, was located on a sheet of computer paper inside the same first-aid kit that contained his clients' keys. The phone numbers were coded, of course, and the code necessary for deciphering each phone number was different. Cracking the first code would yield you the first number, but that same code could not be applied to the rest of the phone numbers on the page. A separate code was needed to identify each specific number, and Martin had memorized the means of deciphering each one. All of this had taken a great deal of time and research on Martin's part, including the reading of several code books in a variety of Connecticut libraries, but the result was a highly complex series of letters and numbers that Martin could decode in minutes.

Placing gloves on his hands, Martin put a quarter in the pay phone and dialed the Pearls' home. Mrs. Pearl picked up on the second ring.

"Hello?"

"Yes, hello. May I please speak to Sherman Pearl?"

"One moment please. May I ask whose calling?"

"I'm sorry," Martin said, moving the phone away from his mouth and garbling his voice. "What did you say?"

"May I ask who is calling," Sophie Pearl repeated, slower and louder this time.

Martin moved the receiver more than a foot away from his mouth and said, "I'm sorry. It seems . . . bad connection. Call back . . ."

Then he hung up.

A moment later Martin dialed a second number but was informed by the ubiquitous female voice inhabiting every telephone system when a number was no longer in service. Disappointed, he returned the receiver to its cradle and headed back to the Subaru.

Clive Darrow's phone was no longer working.

Back in his car, Martin removed his gloves and placed them in the concealed area beneath his dashboard and breathed a sigh of relief. Sherman Pearl was home, so Sophie Pearl was safe for at least another night. Darrow wouldn't dare risk a home invasion with a potential combatant and eyewitness at home.

Turning back onto Farmington Avenue, Martin pointed the Subaru in the direction of West Hartford. With his client safe, it was time to put the second part of his plan into action.

Less than fifteen minutes later, Martin was turning onto Ascension Street, driving slowly enough so that as he cruised by Clive Darrow's home for the second time today, he could take in as many details as possible. The garage in the rear of the property was closed and the lights inside the house appeared to be off. There was still enough daylight to explain this, however, so Martin couldn't take it as a sign that the man wasn't home. The house appeared to have two entrances, a side door that likely opened into a kitchen and a front door that probably opened into a living room or hallway. The side door was the one that was probably used more often, and would therefore have the easier lock to pick.

Martin continued up Ascension Street, turned his car at the next intersection, and then made his way back down the street, passing by the house one more time, hoping to spot anything else that might help him decide on his next course of action.

He saw nothing.

At the end of Ascension, Martin turned right and traveled four blocks north and then east, parking the Subaru in the lot at Smith Elementary School. There he donned a hat, sweatshirt, and running shoes from the backseat and placed his pick gun, surgical gloves, rubber moccasins, and a hairnet into a small backpack that he strapped to his back. Once ready, he began his walk back in the direction of Clive Darrow's home.

Martin had decided that, in order to guarantee Darrow's incarceration, he would need to locate evidence that implicated the man in the stalking, break-in, and planned attack on Sophie

Pearl. He knew that the police officers' hands were often tied when it came to obtaining search warrants, so he thought that if he could specifically identify evidence in Darrow's home in his tip to the police, that might be enough to secure them a legal search of the premises.

Entering Clive Darrow's home would be dangerous, Martin knew. First, he didn't have much information on the man, so he had no knowledge of the type of schedule he kept. Because Martin had seen him exiting the Pearls' home this morning, he reasoned that Darrow was either unemployed or worked odd hours, perhaps the night shift. If Martin could be certain that the house was empty, he might be willing to risk entry, even though he wouldn't be sure when Darrow might return home. Sophie Pearl's life could be at stake, and if not Sophie's, then that of the next woman. For this, he was willing to take the risk.

In addition, Martin had little to fear from police intervention in the event that he was caught by Darrow inside the home. In the planning stages of a violent crime, Darrow would be unlikely to seek police attention, so he would be more inclined to deal with the situation on his own. This might mean Martin's own life would be in danger, but that was a risk he was willing to take. If he was careful and planned his escape carefully, Martin was confident that he could exit the house safely, even if detected.

Martin's plan was to maintain surveillance on Darrow's home until he could determine if the man was home. Walking up and down Ascension Street and the side streets that made up the block that Darrow lived on, Martin would watch for lights to come on or other signs of life until he felt confident in his assessment of the situation. If it became clear that Darrow was occupying the premises, he would head home, pack an overnight bag, and park in the lot close enough to the Pearls' home so that he could maintain surveillance on their rear door. Sacrificing a good night's sleep would be problematic considering that the Ashleys' party was tomorrow, but he would have to manage. This was serious business. If Sherman Pearl left the house for an early round of golf or a morning of boating and fishing, Sophie would be alone and Darrow might attempt to strike. This was especially true since tomorrow was Saturday and it was likely that Noah Blake would be home, asleep, without an alibi. Once Sophie and Sherman Pearl had left their home for the day and Martin was certain that Sophie was not home alone, he would return to Darrow's home, looking for an opportunity to gain entry.

Hopefully all this could be accomplished before the party.

Martin began his walk, wondering how many times he might round the block before he could determine if Clive Darrow was home. Realizing the number might be high, he slowed his pace and steeled himself for a long evening.

Despite his high level of physical fitness, Martin felt uncommonly tired as he turned the corner and headed back up Ascension Street, this time on foot. Though the sun was still blazing on the horizon and it was not yet dinnertime, it had been a long day. The investigation into Clive Darrow, his impromptu lunch with Laura, and his visit with his father had been more excitement in one day than Martin was accustomed to, and he felt both physically and emotionally drained. Nevertheless, he was also feeling hopeful and optimistic. The visit with his father had gone better than he ever could have expected, and he chided himself for not making the effort sooner. It was remarkable how a fear of the truth and an unwillingness to be honest had kept the two men apart for so long. Regardless of the awkwardness that might still exist between them, Martin vowed to call his father soon and plan for another meeting.

Remarkably, he found himself looking forward to it.

Martin had been walking the block for more than an hour in

the dimming light when he spotted the blue pickup coming down Ascension Street toward him. He was standing at the corner of Ascension and Quaker, ready to approach Darrow's home for the tenth time when the truck, with Darrow at the wheel, came to a stop less than five feet away. Martin watched as the man looked left and right, a cigarette dangling from his mouth, and then turned right onto Quaker Lane. Had Martin's car been close by, he would have tailed the man to his destination, but since the Subaru was more than four blocks away, this was impossible. Instead, Martin turned up Ascension Street, walking briskly toward Darrow's home while transferring the pick gun from his backpack to the waistband of his sweatpants. Though he couldn't be sure how long the man was going to be gone, Martin knew that this might be the best chance he had of gaining entry to the house.

He had to try.

As he approached 414 Ascension Street, he liked what he saw. Though the neighbors' homes were situated uncomfortably close to Darrow's house, the lights in all three were out and there appeared to be no cars in the driveways. Across the street stood a row of two-family homes, and though lights were on in some of the units, Martin always preferred renters to homeowners when it came to his clients' neighbors. Renters never cared about the neighborhood to the degree that someone who actually owned a home did, and therefore they were less likely to be suspicious of a stranger approaching a neighbor's home. Besides, Martin had an inkling that Clive Darrow was not the friendliest of neighbors and had probably made few allies on his block during the past couple of years.

Moving with as much confidence as he could muster, he then turned up the driveway and climbed the five steps to the concrete landing on the side of the house as if he owned the place. The door was made of wood with a pane of glass filling the top half, but maroon curtains concealed the space behind. There were two locks on the door, a locking mechanism in the doorknob and a dead bolt. By quickly examining the crack between the door and the frame, Martin could see that the dead bolt was not engaged.

More good news.

After slipping on the surgical gloves, rubber moccasins, and hairnet, Martin reached out and rang the doorbell three times, waiting for the sound of a barking dog but hearing none. He tested the knob and found the lock to be engaged. Taking one final glance and finding no one within sight, he removed the pick gun from his waistband, inserted it into the lock, and turned it on. In less than ten seconds, the lock was disengaged. Martin took one final look behind him and entered Clive Darrow's home.

For a man who had been living in the home for almost two years, it was apparent that Clive Darrow had no interest in decorating. The kitchen in which Martin found himself standing was nearly empty. A single wooden chair was pushed up against an open TV tray, with the remains of a Taco Bell dinner covering the wooden surface. The countertops were nearly bare except for a pair of salt and pepper shakers and a dirty frying pan, and nothing hung on any of the three bare walls. Before exploring any of the rooms in more detail, Martin moved from the kitchen, through a wide archway, into a carpeted, nearly unfurnished living room. A single sofa chair resided in one corner, and flanking it was a rack of wooden TV trays, two slots vacant. Otherwise the room was startlingly empty.

On the far end of the room, opposite the stairway to the second floor, stood the front door to the home. Martin checked the locks on this door and was surprised to find both disengaged. Preparing for the possibility of a quick exit, he opened the front door slightly so that a quick pull, rather than a turn of the knob, would gain him access to the front yard and street. He then moved past the door and into the adjoining room, presumably meant to be a dining room, now empty, and into a hall that connected the kitchen with the bathroom and another room at the end of the house. This room was also empty save for a stack of empty boxes, another TV tray stacked with mail, and an upright, rotating fan.

Martin moved back down the hallway toward the kitchen, opening a closed door opposite the bathroom and finding an empty closet, leaving him to assume that the house was built on a slab and had no basement. More important, there was also no other exit to the outside. If Clive Darrow arrived home, it was the front door that Martin would use for his escape.

With the layout of the first floor set in his mind, Martin ascended the stairs to the second floor, where he found two empty bedrooms and a small, unused bathroom. No beds, no bureaus, no clothing of any kind.

As he returned to the first floor, Martin grew concerned. Though town records indicated that Clive Darrow had lived in this house for almost two years, the house was barely furnished, with no living room furniture, no television, and no telephone to be found. Other than a room full of cardboard boxes and a couple of TV trays, the house was nearly empty, as if someone had broken in and stolen everything of value from the place.

Martin moved back to the kitchen and took a peek through the window above the sink, which looked out onto the backyard and garage, and saw no sign of Darrow. He hoped that if the man returned, he would hear the sound of the truck moving up the driveway and past the house or the noise of the garage door opening and closing, but he wasn't sure if this was possible. The garage was set to the rear of the property and there was no telling how loud the door might be. In order to aid his cause, Martin opened the window above the sink about four inches, hoping that this might be enough to allow some sound indicating Darrow's return to waft into the house.

With little to investigate, Martin made his way back down the hall and into the room of boxes at the end of the house in order to examine the stack of mail on the TV tray. As he entered the room, he noticed three rolls of packing tape, still encased in cellophane wrappers, stacked in one corner, along with several cardboard boxes not yet assembled into cubes.

It appeared that Clive Darrow was in the process of moving.

Martin began sorting through the stack of mail, which was more than a couple of inches high. On the top of the pile were envelopes that Darrow had previously opened, and beneath them junk mail and other unopened envelopes. The light was dim inside the house now and, not daring to turn on any lights, Martin drew each sheet of paper close to his face for inspection. The first opened envelope contained a letter from Wachovia Bank, indicating that foreclosure proceedings were to begin in less than a week as a result of Darrow's failure to make the monthly mortgage payments on the property. Several other opened letters from Wachovia, going back more than six months, indicated that Clive Darrow hadn't paid his mortgage for quite some time. Martin also found a shutoff warning (two days from now) from the electric company with an outstanding balance of $818.45, and similar notices from the gas and water companies. By the end of next week, Darrow's home would be without electricity, gas, or water if he failed to make payment on these bills. A letter from Comcast, the local cable television provider, indicated that Darrow's cable television, telephone, and Internet service had already been disconnected almost a month ago, yet there was no television, telephone, or computer in the house.

Beneath these bills and warnings, Martin found a letter from the Trust Realty Company of Virginia Beach, Virginia, indicating that first and last month's rent plus deposit had been received more than a week ago and that "Mr. Darrow could move into his townhouse" on November 1, a little less than a week away.

Clive Darrow was moving to Virginia in less than a week, and for about six months prior to his move, he had stopped paying his bills entirely. It was as if he were preparing to flee the state.

Martin finished shuffling through the stack of mail and found little more of interest. A great deal of junk mail, a couple of late notices from Jordan's Furniture (late by eight months) and Target (late by two months), and several envelopes addressed to Darrow by hand but no longer containing any letters and lacking return addresses. Nothing more. Most important, there was no evidence indicating that Clive Darrow had any intention of harming Sophie Pearl.

Still, Martin had the sense that something was wrong.

Finishing up with the mail, Martin made one more pass through the house, opening drawers and cabinets in the kitchen and bathroom and finding nothing. Not one plate, fork, or cup. Not even a toothbrush or sleeping bag. Martin began to wonder if Clive Darrow had any intention of returning to this house, and this began to make him worry even more.

Forgoing his usual final inspection of a house, Martin closed the front door completely before exiting through the side door. Though he didn't expect to find much, a cursory examination of the garage also yielded nothing. It was as empty as the house itself. Back on the move, Martin walked down the driveway and back onto the street, breaking into a jog once he was past Darrow's house. He wanted to get to his car as quickly as possible and make a phone call.

Perhaps Sherman Pearl had gone out for the evening, leaving Sophie Pearl home alone.

Because Martin was in his hometown, finding another public phone proved rather simple. Less than a mile away, across the street from Kennedy Park, was a 7-Eleven with a pay phone that Martin had used in the past. Again, no cameras were in view of the phone, making it a safe place to call from, though his own personal safety was becoming less of a concern as the minutes passed.

Martin came to a screeching halt in the parking lot, and after nearly forgetting to don another pair of surgical gloves, he managed to push his last quarter into the phone's slot despite his trembling hands.

The phone rang five times before Martin heard Sherman Pearl's prerecorded voice inform him that no one was home at this time. Martin hung up the phone before the beep and walked back to his car, attempting to assess the situation.

It was perfectly conceivable that Sherman and Sophie Pearl had gone out to dinner or a movie tonight, and that was the reason they had not picked up the phone. According to Martin's watch, which was set to the online atomic clock in Greenwich, subtracting four hours for time-zone differences, it was 9:35, making it still relatively early for a couple out on the town. It was also Friday, a night when people traditionally went out to dinner and a movie, so this assumption was certainly within reason. In all likelihood, the couple were sitting in a darkened theater at this moment, watching some indie film, if he knew the Pearls well. No big-budget action adventure epics for them.

It was also possible that Sherman Pearl had gone out on his own tonight, to a poker game, a business dinner, or anything else that a guy like him might do. Therefore, it was possible that Sophie Pearl was sitting at home alone this evening, unaware of the danger that she might be in, but Martin didn't think so. From what he knew about the couple, he thought it highly unlikely that Sherman, devoted husband and best friend to his wife, would leave her home alone on a Friday night.

What continued to plague Martin, however, was the nagging thought that Clive Darrow was ready to move to Virginia *tonight*. Though he could imagine Darrow stopping by his home one more time, perhaps to pick up his mail, leave his keys, or gather the remaining pieces of furniture, he couldn't imagine the man sleeping there for the night, with no sleeping bag, toothbrush, or pillow to be found. Something told Martin that Clive Darrow intended to hit the road for Virginia tonight, with the few possessions that remained in Connecticut tossed into the back of his pickup truck. But if this were the case, why would Darrow go through the trouble of locating a victim like Sophie Pearl, and put himself in the position to implicate Noah Blake in the crime?

For a moment, Martin began to wonder if Darrow's plan was nothing more than a figment of his own imagination. Perhaps Darrow, a convicted felon, had burglarized the Pearls' home earlier that day. Perhaps Darrow had left the house with Sophie Pearl's jewelry collection stuffed in his coat pocket. Martin supposed that it could simply be a coincidence that Noah Blake, a registered sex offender, lived next door to the people whom Clive Darrow, also a registered sex offender, had robbed earlier that day. Perhaps in need of traveling money, Darrow had burglarized several homes this week, taking just what he could safely carry in his pockets.

Though this scenario seemed entirely reasonable to Martin, it nevertheless did not feel right.

Martin started the car and pulled out of the 7-Eleven parking lot in the direction of Newington. He would take a peek at the Pearls' house, make sure that Darrow's pickup was nowhere to be found, and maybe even keep an eye on the place for the night.

He would at least ensure that Sophie Pearl was not home alone.

Martin pulled into the parking lot alongside the basketball courts at 10:17. The lights of the park were turned off and the park was technically closed, though nothing could stop a guy from parking his car and shooting a few hoops, save the absence of illumination. Martin was relieved to see that the blue pickup was not parked in the lot as it had been earlier that day, and that the lights of the Pearls' home, visible across the swath of grass that separated the park from the Pearls' backyard, were off except for a single light in their kitchen window, probably over the sink. The Pearls were either asleep or still out on the town.

Prior to pulling into the parking lot, Martin had driven past the front of the Pearls' home and down the block, making sure that Darrow's blue pickup wasn't parked anywhere in the neighborhood. Sherman Pearl's Audi was parked in the driveway (a good sign), but there was no sign of Sophie Pearl's Explorer. Though it could easily be parked in the garage, Martin had no way of telling from the street. He also drove to the parking lot adjacent to the tennis courts, one block down from his present location, and found that lot empty as well.

All seemed quiet.

Martin reclined his seat back a couple of clicks and relaxed. In all likelihood, the Pearls were on their way home from a night of dancing or were already sleeping soundly in their bed. Either way, as long as Sherman Pearl was with his wife, Sophie would be safe tonight. Tomorrow he would prepare a letter for the Newington and West Hartford police, explaining everything that he knew about Clive Darrow and his possible plans for his client. Unable to locate any incriminating evidence in Darrow's home, he had no other option. He would have to hope that the police would find something to implicate Darrow, and that Martin wouldn't be implicated at the same time.

He didn't think he would be. Even if he had left a stray fingerprint or piece of DNA evidence in the Pearls' home (which he highly doubted), Martin's fingerprints and DNA coding were not on file with law enforcement. In his mind, he had already canceled the Pearls as clients, but that was a small price to pay for the safety of Sophie Pearl.

As the clock glowed 11:03, Martin thought about calling the Pearls again. If he could confirm that they were both safely home, he too could head home and get some sleep. But placing the call on his cell phone was out of the question, particularly at this hour. A random hang-up during the day could be ignored by most homeowners, but a mysterious and potentially frightening call in the middle of the night might cause someone to involve the police. If the Pearls' phone had caller identification capabilities, it would not be difficult to trace his number back to him.

Still, he wished that he knew if his clients were home and together.

At that moment Martin realized that a quick visual inspection of the garage, to determine if both cars were present, would yield the information he desired. The Pearls' garage was attached to their home and had two windows facing the backyard. Though they were obscured by the tree line that ran along the border of the park and the Pearls' neighbors, Martin could see the dark outlines of both windows through the shadows. If he were able to look through one of them, he was sure that he could see if Sophie Pearl's Explorer was parked inside. With both cars present, Martin could be certain that both of his clients were home and that Sophie Pearl was not alone.

Slipping on a pair of surgical gloves, more out of habit than necessity, Martin turned off his car, slid his keys into his jeans' pocket, and exited the Subaru, walking along the tree line that perpendicularly intersected the property line between two of the Pearls' neighbors. As late as it was, Martin doubted that anyone would be awake, but many homes were equipped with motion-activated spotlights in their front- and backyards. Though he couldn't remember ever seeing one in the Pearls' backyard, he had no desire to set off any floodlights in their neighbors'.

At the edge of the tree line, Martin turned left, walking along the invisible property line that separated the Pearls' neighbors' backyards from the park. He passed by a total of three houses, including Noah Blake's, and found them all to be dark and quiet. When he reached the Pearls' property line, he took a quick turn into their backyard, across their well-manicured lawn, and over to their garage. Though the windows were higher up than he expected, Martin was able to grab the bottom sill and hoist himself up, feet no longer touching the ground as he looked into the garage.

Parked inside the garage was Sophie Pearl's Ford Explorer. Parked beside it was Clive Darrow's blue pickup truck.

Spotting the pickup caused Martin to gasp and lose his grip on the sill, dropping him to the grass below. He landed with a thud, smacking his elbow into the dirt and jamming his keys nearly out of his back pocket and into the small of his back. The instantaneous sensation of panic, marked by the trembling of his hands and arms, the loss of peripheral vision, and his inability to focus on any one object, consumed him like never before. For more than a minute, he was incapable of anything but erratic breathing and a breathless, nearly soundless "Oh my God. Oh my God." Clive Darrow was here, inside the house, and so were the Pearls. Both of them. Martin had assumed that Darrow would wait until Sophie Pearl was alone before attacking her. He had been certain of it. His mistake had placed his clients in grave danger. As these thoughts raced through his mind, they incapacitated him to an even greater degree.

Nearly two minutes passed before Martin was able to regain control of his breathing, though the violent shaking of his arms, his legs, and even his head continued unabated. He reached into his right pants pocket, hoping to find his cell phone before realizing that he had left it behind in the Subaru. He had taken his keys with him, something he would never have done normally, but had left his cell phone in the compartment above the gear shift. *Never enter a home with incriminating evidence on your person.* This rule, which had become habit, had done him in.

Struggling to bring himself to his feet, Martin turned and began running for his car. He would call the police and then wake the Pearls' neighbors, including Noah Blake. Flood the neighborhood with light and sound. Scare the bastard off if the police didn't arrive first.

Martin had taken three strides across the Pearls' back lawn when he heard something shatter inside the home and a female voice shout, "No!" before being muffled and then silenced. Martin froze in his tracks. His hands ceased to shake. His peripheral vision returned. He was able to clearly focus on his Subaru, more than two hundred yards away on the other side of the park. His legs felt strong and steady again. He heard something else shatter in the house, a vase, a lamp, a plate, and another cry, though softer and more in pain than in terror, as the first had been. There was a struggle taking place inside the house.

Martin turned and walked to the Pearls' back door.

The door was unlocked, as Martin had expected. Clive Darrow was not as cautious as Martin had once thought. He opened the door, stepped inside, and then closed it behind him, trying not to make a sound. Standing in the kitchen, under the pale light of a single bulb above the sink, Martin looked into the living room and saw Sherman Pearl stretched out across the floor, motionless. He was lying face down, with lengths of black cord wrapped around his feet and binding his hands behind him.

Martin was relieved. The man was probably still alive, or else Clive Darrow would have had no reason to tie him up.

Still motionless, Martin waited by the door for a moment, listening and examining every shadowy corner of the kitchen and living room for possible danger. He could hear movement upstairs; a man's muffled voice, and footsteps.

He couldn't believe how calm he was.

"Mr. Pearl," Martin whispered. "Can you hear me?"

No answer. Martin tried again with the same result.

Next, he looked to the far end of the countertop, where the recharging base of the Pearls' telephone was located. Martin spotted the number 2 flashing in red, indicating that the Pearls had two unheard messages. He moved closer and saw through the shadows that the phone was not resting on its base.

Freezing again, trying to listen and look and think at the

same time, Martin scanned the kitchen for any signs of the Pearls' cordless phone. The kitchen table, the countertops, the end tables adjacent to the sofa.

Nothing.

Martin knew that the phone could very well be down the hallway in the couple's office, or upstairs on a nightstand. Or even in the bathroom. Clive Darrow might have removed it from the base himself. There was no way of knowing.

Martin decided to move on, remaining watchful for the phone as he did so. Had he thought that there was time to search for a telephone and call the police, he would have run back to the Subaru, grabbed his cell phone, and done it there. But there was a struggle of some kind going on upstairs, and Sophie Pearl was in grave danger. Every second counted. He had been standing inside the Pearls' home for a full minute now, and Martin knew that he had already wasted too much time.

Knowing the Pearls' kitchen as well as his own, Martin slid open the drawer closest to him and removed a knife from its tray. The eight-inch blade gleamed in the sixty-watt light, its tip looking impossibly sharp, and Martin shivered at its menace. He didn't think he could bring himself to stab another human being, but he wanted the knife just the same.

Next he moved into the living room, walking as quietly as possible, passing by the unconscious Sherman Pearl. At the fireplace, he removed one of the four perpetually unused logs from the hearth stand, making sure that the other three didn't shift in the process. Though he couldn't imagine plunging a knife into the chest of another man, he thought he was perfectly capable of bashing the son-of-a-bitch over the head with a chunk of wood if necessary.

This was not Alan Clayton, loyal client who had done no wrong. This was a dangerous criminal with a full head of hair.

For a moment, Martin thought about cutting the cords that

bound Sherman Pearl's wrists and ankles, in case the man regained consciousness, but quickly decided against it. Martin had entered this house knowing that Sophie Pearl's life was in imminent danger. His Hedgehog Concept was perfectly clear. Rescue Sophie Pearl.

There was not a moment to waste.

At the landing, Martin paused to look up the stairs. The second floor was dark. There were bedrooms to the left and right of the stairway and a bathroom directly opposite the stairs. He could still hear the faint sound of a male voice, emanating from the left of the landing, leading him to believe that the door to the Pearls' bedroom was probably closed.

This was both good and bad.

A closed door meant that Martin's ascent of the stairs would likely go undetected, but it also meant that surprising the intruder would be much more difficult. Had Martin been able to creep into the darkened bedroom undetected, he could have landed at least a couple of good blows on Darrow's head before the man had a chance to respond. But if he had to open the bedroom door first, his opportunity for surprise would be seriously compromised.

Martin ascended the stairs as slowly and quietly as possible, regardless of the probable closed door. As he took each step, he desperately tried to formulate a plan. In his entire life, Martin had been in exactly one fight, and he had won. When he was in ninth grade, several seniors had grabbed him and another kid named Paul, brought them into an empty classroom, and instructed them to fight like two roosters in a cock fight. Martin had thought that their demand was lunacy and refused until one of the larger seniors, Eddie Meeres, landed a punch in Martin's gut, knocking the wind out of him for a full minute. "Fight or we beat you up ourselves," Martin was told. Not wanting the same treatment, Paul lifted his fists and charged at Martin, swinging in desperation. Martin dodged the first few punches until Paul managed to land a right hook on Martin's jaw. He could remember seeing stars for a moment as he wobbled back and forth, marveling at the reality behind what he had previously seen only in cartoons. An instant later, a rage that Martin had never known consumed him, and he charged at his opponent with fists flying. Eventually it took three seniors to pull Martin off the boy, whose nose and lips were bloody and raw.

Martin still regretted that momentary loss of control, born from fear and anger, and since that day he had never committed another act of violence. Now he had a piece of lumber in one hand and a knife in the other, and the only question was how he was going to use them.

It was Martin's near disastrous fall that brought him the answer.

Three steps from the top landing, with his mind consumed in thought, Martin missed a step. Rather than coming down on the next stair, his foot caught the front of the step and slipped back down, causing him to stumble backward. Reaching out with the hand in possession of the knife, Martin managed to grasp the wooden railing, but as he did, the knife momentarily slipped from his grasp. He reached out and was able to pin the blade between his palm and the railing, preventing it from falling, but in doing so he was forced to grab hold of the sharp side of the blade, slicing through the surgical glove and cutting his palm open down the middle.

With his adrenaline at epic heights, he barely felt any pain.

Once steadied, Martin froze, listening for any signs that his near fall had been heard inside the bedroom. He could still hear a man's voice, speaking on and on but in what sounded like whispers. Threatening, ominous whispers. And he could hear something else now too. Whimpering. The soft, quiet cry of a woman in trouble.

It was at that moment that Martin, suddenly recalling Jim's lateral-thinking puzzle about the burglar who fell down the stairs and broke his leg in the midst of a robbery, knew exactly what needed to be done.

As quietly as possible, he regained his grip on the knife and ascended the final three stairs. Once on the top landing, he confirmed his suspicion. The bedroom door to the left of the landing was closed. Directly across from the stairs, the bathroom's door was open. Martin entered and placed the knife in the sink, knowing that he would no longer require it. He then slowly closed the bathroom door, stopping just before the latch engaged with the jamb. Holding it in this position, as he had done the day he'd been caught in Laura's house with Cujo, Martin turned on the bathroom light, hoping that the high carpeting in the hall would block any residual light filtering into the bedroom through the base of the door. He wanted to give his eyes time enough to adjust to the light before executing his plan. If the light was off in the bedroom (as Martin suspected it was, since no light had shown from any of the upstairs windows), this meant that he might be able to get Darrow to step out of near total darkness into light, which might temporarily blind him.

Martin needed every advantage he could get.

He allowed his eyes thirty seconds to adjust, for his pupils to fully contract. He then opened the bathroom door and moved quietly to the back wall, farthest from the stairs. Positioning himself so that he was facing the stairs, he lifted the log and held it out in front of his chest like a battering ram, and began.

"Sherman? Sophie? Is anyone home? I thought I heard noise." Martin spoke these words in an airy whisper, attempting to make it sound as if the noise was coming from downstairs. He also spoke in his strange version of Blondie's Irish accent, for reasons he didn't understand. It hadn't been a conscious decision. It just came out that way.

At the sound of his voice, the low tones of Clive Darrow suddenly ceased and Martin heard a louder, inarticulate whine, the type of sound that someone might make if trying to scream through a pillow. This was followed by several thumps and then silence.

He waited.

To calm his exploding nerves, he began running through the ABCs in his head.

A, B, C, D, E, F ...

On *G*, Martin heard the door open. He stopped breathing entirely.

A second later, he saw a hand appear, moving into the frame of the bathroom door, carrying an object that Martin didn't recognize.

A gun? No, not a gun ... flashed through his mind.

A moment later the body of Clive Darrow filled the bathroom doorway, facing away from Martin, peering down the stairway, pointing whatever object he had into the darkness.

It was time.

Martin moved. Plunging forward as fast and hard as possible, he used four running strides to exit the bathroom and collide with Clive Darrow's body. Darrow must have realized that something was wrong a second before the log struck the back of his head. The intruder had begun to turn, perhaps realizing that the light he had seen was spilling out from behind him or perhaps hearing Martin's feet on the bathroom tile. But the intruder only made it far enough around to catch his right cheek and nose on the log as it came crashing into his head.

Before his attack, Martin had already decided that he would finish this job no matter the cost. Leave no room for error. He knew that the log might not be enough, so following the collision of wood on skull, Martin released the log from his grasp and leaped into the air, maintaining his forward progress and bringing his arms around the powerfully built man. Martin's forward momentum, combined with Clive Darrow's wobbling legs, thrust the two of them down the stairs and into darkness. The two men toppled over and down the steps like rag dolls, body parts colliding with the stairs, railing, banister, the log (which had become entangled between them), and each other. Martin's body ended up passing over Darrow's, turning Martin backward and upside down as he struggled to maintain his grip on the intruder. His forehead struck the railing violently and he felt his right knee come crashing down on the edge of a step, followed by the sickening sensation of something popping inside. A moment later, Martin's body connected with the floor below, just ahead of Darrow's body, and he felt at least one of his ribs crack. Still maintaining his hold on the man who was now falling toward him, Martin had the awareness to use the leverage of his now prone body to fling the intruder over him and into the wall opposite the stairs. He heard an awful smack and a squishing sound as the man's face was whipped into the wall with incredible force before coming to rest beside Martin's.

For a moment, everything was silent.

Martin lay still beside the motionless man, barely able to catch his breath.

Then Martin heard the whimper again, coming from the upstairs bedroom. It sounded as if Sophie Pearl had been gagged but was trying to communicate through the binding. Still on his back, with pain beginning to fill his head, knee, and chest, Martin called out, "It's all right, Mrs. Pearl. It's over. Your husband's unconscious but alive. And Darrow's . . ."

Martin realized he had no idea of Clive Darrow's condition. Pulling himself to a sitting position, he examined the man beside him, looking for signs of life. He was still breathing, but his respiration sounded wet and labored. A large gash stretched from the top of his forehead to the base of his nose, which was clearly broken. Blood was pooling in his eye sockets and spilling down his cheek. His left leg was contorted at a horrific angle, and his pants appeared to be moistening with blood in the area of the fracture. "Compound fracture, you evil son-of-a-bitch," Martin whispered to the man. "Not good. Just ask that stupid burglar in Jim's story." Lying beside his leg was the weapon that Clive Darrow had been carrying: a Taser, which Martin assumed had probably been used on Sherman Pearl.

Even if the man regained consciousness, Martin was sure that he would be immobile and harmless. "Darrow's down and out, Mrs. Pearl. Don't worry. Can you free yourself?" The pain in Martin's chest was increasing, making it more difficult for him to speak or even breathe without wincing.

Martin heard a muffled response that he took for a no.

"Okay," Martin gasped. "I don't think I can make it back up the stairs. I got banged up too." Despite the blossoming pain throughout his body, Martin suddenly realized that his anonymity was still intact. His DNA might be strewn about the house, with blood on the railing, the knife, and Lord knows where else, not to mention hair and skin, but Sophie Pearl had not yet seen him. Even though he had his doubts about being able to climb up the stairs with his knee on fire as it was, he realized that ascending them would be foolish anyway. The Pearls were safe. Best to call the police from the first floor and exit the house before they arrived.

"Mrs. Pearl, do you know where your phone is?" Martin asked, forgetting about her condition for the moment. He heard her attempt to respond through the gag and cut her off. "Sorry. That was stupid. My head isn't very clear. Listen. I'm going to see if I can find the phone down here. If not, I'm going to go to my car and use my cell phone. It's becoming difficult for me to speak, cracked ribs I think, so you might not hear me again until the police arrive. Okay?"

He heard a whimper of ascent from upstairs and then silence.

Martin managed to pull himself to his feet, though his right knee was now a raging ball of pain. Barely able to put any weight on it, he hopped over to the leather couch and scanned the room more thoroughly. A moment later he spotted the antenna of the cordless phone on the Steinway, poking out from behind a photograph of the Pearls standing on a beach on some tropic isle.

A far cry from their current state, Martin mused.

Martin picked up the phone and hopped into the kitchen. Almost any movement caused him to wince in tremendous pain, from both the bleeding gash on his head and the tenderness of his rib cage. But his knee was by far the worst, and it was becoming more painful by the second. Standing beside the back door, Martin called out one last time. "Mrs. Pearl, I've got the phone. I'm calling the police now!"

Martin dialed 911, waited for an operator to answer, and then placed the phone, with the line still open, on the counter. Regardless of what he might or might not say, he knew that the police would be on their way in minutes.

Exiting the house, Martin forced himself to put as much weight down on his knee as he could bear, ambling across the lawn and to the Subaru as quickly as possible. He wanted to be out of the parking lot and on the road before the police had time to respond. Throwing the car into drive and using his left leg to operate the gas and brake, Martin exited the parking lot just as the flashing blue lights of a police cruiser appeared in front of the Pearl's home.

Sophie and Sherman Pearl would be fine, and, with luck, Clive Darrow would spend the rest of his life in prison.

Martin had never felt better in his life.

Martin was diagnosed in the emergency room with a concussion, three broken ribs, and a broken patella.

"I've always been such a klutz," he said to the nurse as the doctor stapled the gash in his forehead closed. "No more midnight snacks for me."

Martin had told the hospital staff that he had tripped on a cat toy and fallen down the stairs head over heels, which in fact wasn't far from the truth. Including an exposed nail on the railing to explain the cut in his palm, his story seemed to be consistent with his injuries. No one had doubted his account.

In the past three hours, Martin's head, chest, and knee had been X-rayed several times. After examining the films and putting him through a physical examination, the doctor explained to Martin that he was fortunate in that his patella fracture was nondisplaced, meaning that he would not require surgery. Martin was shocked. As he hobbled into the emergency room, he had been sure that his entire leg would need to be amputated. By the time he had arrived at Hartford Hospital, the knee had swollen to three times its normal size and the pain was near blinding. Almost immediately following his arrival, doctors inserted needles into the knee to drain the building fluid, thus exponentially reducing the swelling and the amount of pain that it was transmitting to his brain. The doctor, a balding, seemingly disinterested man in his fifties, explained that Martin would be fitted for a knee immobilizer that he would need to wear for at least four weeks.

As for the broken ribs, these would heal on their own. "As long as you're not coughing up blood," the doctor explained, "there's not much that we can do for your ribs. Just be careful and have them rechecked in a few days."

The nurse had told Martin that, as a result of his concussion, he would not be allowed to drive home and would need to call someone for a ride. He was surprised when he found himself giving his father's phone number to the nurse.

Martin Railsback, Sr., arrived at the hospital just after 4:00 a.m. Having been a police officer, he was familiar with the workings of an emergency room and found his son rather quickly. The doctor was handing Martin prescriptions for pain medication and antibiotics, in order to ward off any potential infection from the open wounds on Martin's head and palm. The padded immobilizer was already strapped onto Martin's leg.

"Fell down some stairs, huh?" his father asked with a combination of suspicion and humor on his face.

"Yeah. Not very smart, huh?"

"Nope."

A minute later the doctor shook Martin's hand and left the two men alone.

"Thanks for coming," Martin said as he reached for the crutches that the doctor had left propped against the wall. "I'm sorry about this."

"No problem, son. I'm glad you called. Let's get out of here."

As they ambled down the hallway toward the exit, Martin found himself feeling more normal than he had in a long time. He was hurt, had been treated in the emergency room, and his father had come to pick him up. Just a week ago, Martin would've had to call his best friend, Jim, for a ride, and though Jim would have come without complaint, it wasn't your best friend whom you wanted in these moments. For the first time in what seemed like forever, Martin had a father when one was needed most. Despite his injuries, he couldn't help but feel great as he hobbled toward the automatic doors of the emergency room, side by side with his dad.

Ten minutes later, Martin was sitting in the front seat of his father's truck, crossing through the Frog Hollow section of Hartford and into West Hartford. Even with the medication that he had already been given, every bump in the road caused Martin's chest and knee to flare up in pain.

The two men had been silent for most of the ride, but as the truck crossed over the Hartford–West Hartford town line, Martin's father finally broke the silence.

"This has something to do with your friend, right? The one in trouble?"

"Yes," Martin answered, feeling like a little boy for the second time today.

"You didn't call the police, did you?"

"No. I planned on calling but things happened faster than I thought."

"They always do," his father said with a sigh. "Is your friend still in trouble?"

"No. I don't think so."

"You took care of it yourself?" his father asked, taking his eyes off the road to look his son in the eye.

Martin nodded.

"Do you foresee any problems for yourself? Legally, I mean."

"I don't think so."

"Okay," his father said. "Then that's that."

The two men drove the rest of the way to Martin's house in silence. Rather than parking in the empty driveway, Martin's father pulled along the curb in front of the house, leaving the engine running. "If you can get inside on your own, I'd rather drop you off here. It's been a long time since I've seen this place, and I'm not ready to go inside."

"Sure, Dad," Martin answered, feeling relieved. The tension between the two men had become more than he could bear. "I can manage."

"You need a ride to the hospital tomorrow? To pick up your car? To get your prescriptions?"

"I don't know," Martin answered, shrugging his shoulders. "Maybe."

"If you do, call me."

Martin gathered his crutches and the plastic bag containing enough pain medication to get him through the night, and gingerly climbed out of the truck. He didn't know what else to say to his father, so, without any pleasantries, he turned up the cobbled walk and began hobbling.

"Son!" Martin's father shouted through the descending passenger-side window.

Martin turned and waited. It seemed as if his father was debating whether or not to say anything at all. After a moment, he began. "Listen. I don't know exactly what happened tonight, but I've dealt with enough criminals to know you ain't one. At least not tonight. You got pretty banged up, but if your friend is out of danger, I'm guessing that you were some kind of a hero tonight. And there's probably some other guy out there looking worse than you. If that's the case, son, I'm proud of you."

Before Martin had a chance to reply, the passenger-side window had returned to its closed position and his father was gone.

The phone woke Martin at nine the following morning. As he rose to answer it, his knee and ribs flashed brutal reminders of their current condition, causing him to cry out in pain. Moving more gingerly, Martin reached out and plucked the phone off the receiver on the bedside table on the third ring despite his difficulty in getting to it.

"Hello?"

"It's me. Are you excited about tonight?"

It took a moment for Martin to process the voice and the question that had been asked. After a few seconds, he managed to respond. "Laura, how are you?"

In order to combat her tendency to launch herself into a conversation absent pleasantries, Martin had been using the strategy of answering Laura's questions with questions of his own, thus providing him with the time to formulate an answer to her original question in the event Laura returned to it, which she usually did.

"I'm fine," she answered, not missing a beat. "I'm excited about tonight. You?"

Martin had no idea what to say. Though he wanted to be excited about a party that he should have never planned on attending, he doubted that he could go in his current condition. "Can I call you back in a minute?"

"Is something wrong?"

"No," Martin lied. "Just let me call you back. Okay?"

"All right," Laura answered. "I'll be waiting."

Martin clicked off the phone and assessed his current condition. He had a headache that seemed to be awakening and gaining steam. His chest hurt like hell when he took a deep breath, and his knee was throbbing away underneath the sheets. His car was still in the hospital's parking garage. He had four more pain pills and would need to find a way to fill his prescription soon.

Hoping for a miracle, Martin shifted his legs to the edge of the bed, placed his feet on the floor, and tried to put weight on his injured knee.

It hurt like hell.

There was no way that he could attend Daniel Ashley's surprise party tonight. Even with crutches, the doctor had warned him that the first three days would be tough, and restricting his mobility would be best. Though he had never been pleased with the notion of attending a party for a client, the prospect of canceling on Laura pained him more than any of his physical ailments. Missing an opportunity to spend some time with her was bad, but the thought of disappointing her was almost too much to bear.

But he had no choice.

Martin spent the next ten minutes reviewing what he would say to her, and then dialed her number, which he knew by heart.

Laura picked up on the first ring. "Okay, what's going on?"

Martin had anticipated a question like this, and his response was well rehearsed. "I have some bad news."

"Let me guess. You don't know how to dance."

"No," Martin replied, though this too was true. "I had an accident last night. I fell down the stairs in my house and broke my leg."

"That's not funny."

"No, I'm serious. I broke my leg and a few ribs and I have a concussion. Or I had one. I don't know how long a concussion lasts."

There was a long pause before Laura finally spoke. "I'm not kidding around, Martin. Tell me. Are you serious?"

"I'm afraid so. It was an ugly fall," Martin said. He had originally planned on using the word "nasty" to describe the fall but felt that it might sound too cliché. "I'm so sorry, Laura. I know how excited you were about tonight."

"I'm coming over. Give me your address."

"You don't need to do that," Martin said, regretting it almost immediately. He would need help in getting through the day, and there was no one in the world he wanted by his side more than Laura.

"Shut up and give me the address."

"Really, it's not . . ."

"Martin, shut the hell up and give me your address. Now."

Martin did so and, before he could say another word, the line went dead.

Less than thirty minutes later, Laura burst through Martin's front door, shouting, "Where the hell are you?"

Expecting her arrival, Martin had managed to don a T-shirt and slide a pair of sweatpants over his leg immobilizer before descending the stairs, one at a time. In the downstairs bathroom, he swallowed the last of his pain pills and brushed his teeth before unlocking the front door and ambling over to the couch to wait for Laura's arrival. This would be her first visit to his home, and though it had been unexpected, Martin was relieved to see that the house, save the unmade bed upstairs, was in its usual order.

"In here," Martin answered, making no attempt to move. Though he had taken the pain medication almost fifteen minutes ago, it had yet to make its presence known. Even the brushing of his teeth had caused him considerable ache.

"Oh my God! You were serious," Laura said, rushing over and reaching out to embrace him.

"Careful," Martin warned, shying away. "My ribs are pretty sore." He could see from the look on Laura's face that she was genuinely concerned. "Don't worry. I'm fine. Or at least I will be."

"Tell me what happened."

Martin spent the next twenty minutes explaining to Laura how he had been on his way to the kitchen for a midnight snack when he missed a stair and fell. He told her about his visit to the emergency room, the diagnosis of his injuries, and his prognosis. For once, Laura listened intently with few interruptions, waiting until Martin seemed finished before speaking.

"How did you get home?"

"My father. I tried my sister but she didn't pick up the phone. It was late."

"You could've called me. You know that, right?"

Martin would've never thought of calling Laura, but her assurances sent his heart soaring. "Of course. Calling my dad just seemed like the right thing to do."

"Good. Does this mean you're not going to make it to your parents' anniversary party either?"

"I'm afraid so," Martin answered, trying to sound disappointed.

"Does your sister know?"

"Yeah. I called her about fifteen minutes ago. She wanted to come over and check on me, but I convinced her that I'm fine. She has a lot to do today, especially with me stuck here at home."

"I could drive you to the party," Laura offered. "Just to make an appearance."

"No," Martin answered, ready for the offer. "The doctor wants me as immobile as possible for the first seventy-two hours. It's best that I stay right here."

"Okay. So what are we going to do about you?"

"Me?" Martin asked. "I'm going to be stuck on this couch all day. But you've got a busy day ahead of you. Don't let me ruin it."

"Martin, don't be a moron. I'm going to spend the day with you."

"You can't . . ."

"Shut up. Okay? I can't just leave you on this couch all day. Alone. You have a broken leg, for Christ's sake. And broken ribs. Someone's got to take care of you, and I want the job."

"Honestly, Laura. I'll be fine. The pain medication is starting to kick in. And I know how much you've been looking forward to the party."

"Listen to me, you idiot. It wasn't the party. I was excited about spending the day with you. I don't care if we're at a party or stuck on this couch. I just wanted to be with you. Okay?"

Martin couldn't remember the last time he had been so happy.

When the knock on the door finally came, Martin was more surprised than he had ever been in his life. Though he had never seriously considered the possibility of being caught, he had envisioned the arrival of the police at his front door from time to time, and had even rehearsed his possible responses to their questions. Though he knew that his skill, planning, and precision protected him from the possibility of detection, there was no harm in mentally preparing for all possible circumstances, and though he would never admit it, the prospect of discovery was fun to imagine. Without the constant danger inherent in his occupation, Martin's skills and the pride that he took in them would be meaningless. It was exhilarating to remind himself about the risks of his profession. It kept him focused on and engaged in the work at hand. Nevertheless, when he opened his front door, sixteen memorable days after his encounter with Clive Darrow, he was speechless.

While the prospect of spending a month at home hadn't appealed to Martin, his careful planning and willingness to save had placed him in a secure financial position. Realistically, Martin could miss more than a year of work without much concern. He owned his home, free and clear, and he was judicious in his spending. And as long as he returned to his job at Starbucks (he was currently on medical leave), the health insurance that the company provided would pay for any future medical bills like the ones he faced after his fall down the stairs. Even though he genuinely missed his clients and his work, his temporary immobility left him with little in the way of financial concern.

In fact, the previous two weeks had proved to be especially satisfying to Martin. Laura had stopped by the house nearly every day since the accident, sometimes for an hour or two but more often for most of the evening. Though they had yet to be intimate, the two had become close, with their first real kiss taking place at 8:04 on the night following his accident. After picking up his prescriptions earlier in the day and cooking them an elaborate lobster dinner, Laura had sat down on the couch, toasted to Martin's health, leaned over, and kissed him. Though her embrace had caused his ribs to flare up in pain, Martin managed to ignore it long enough to enjoy the kiss and make note of the time.

Thankfully, it had been the first of many kisses that week, and after a few days, Martin had summoned the courage to initiate an occasional kiss himself.

Most of the time they had spent together had been filled with conversation, a process at which Martin was growing more adept by the day. Though he continued to plan and rehearse possible conversational elements prior to her arrival, much of his recent dialogue with Laura had been completely spontaneous. Martin had learned a great deal about Laura in the time they had spent together, and the more he learned, the more he liked this clever and quirky woman.

In order to fill the time, Martin had also spent many hours working on his novel, and after a week of pleading, he finally allowed Laura to read the first chapter. He couldn't help but stare at Laura as her eyes scanned the words that he had placed upon the page, watching as the sentences forced smiles, frowns, and looks of confusion from her. He marveled at how he had managed to create an entirely new world from his imagination, and how real his characters, and in particular his main character, had become. Though he couldn't be certain, he thought that she enjoyed the story a great deal, and he was proud of what he had accomplished so far. He had written more than thirty thousand words, filling more than a hundred pages, and his story had taken an interesting turn. His main character, Matthew Stock, had turned out to be a smash-and-grabber, an ordinary thief with a little more finesse than most of his kind. He was in his mid-twenties and living a bachelor's life, with a large number of friends and acquaintances and a constantly rotating stable of women in his life. His friends considered him the consummate frat boy, with a well-paying job in an IT department at a major insurance company, but in reality Matthew was a much more private person than anyone knew. As a smash-and-grabber, he specialized in jewelry but had recently found himself becoming more interested in the people from whom he stole than in the actual jewelry that he acquired. One of the women whom Matthew Stock planned to rob was suffering from leukemia, and in the midst of chemotherapy, her husband, a coward by the name of Paul, had moved out, unable or unwilling to deal with the stress of the situation. Matthew Stock suddenly found himself needing to take care of this woman in her greatest moment of need, but not knowing how to do so without being caught.

Remarkably, the novel seemed to be writing itself. What had begun as autobiography had quickly diverged into the story of a man whom Martin never would have imagined until his fingers began striking the keys, and this burst of unexplained and seemingly uncontrollable invention thrilled Martin and made the days pass by with ease. Though he had no idea where this story might lead, he had learned to stop worrying about plot and allow his imagination to take control.

He had pretended to be a writer for years, never knowing how easy writing could be.

After she finished reading the first chapter, Laura had grabbed Martin's face, kissing him and telling him how proud she was of his accomplishment. "You're so talented! What made you think of writing about a thief? And a thief who I kind of like."

"Honestly, I have no idea," Martin had lied. "Maybe I read something in the newspaper that day. I don't know. I came home after that night at the Elbow Room and just started writing. This is what came out."

"Well, I think it's brilliant. I can't wait to see what happens next. Can I read the next chapter?"

Martin had told Laura that the next chapter wasn't finished and that major revisions were needed, but in truth, his first three chapters were complete. He just wasn't ready to share them yet. As much as he wanted to hand the pages over to Laura immediately, he worried that the story might fizzle out at some point, leaving him with an interesting character and no place to go. By parceling out the chapters one at a time with days or weeks in between, Martin hoped to avoid disappointing Laura if things weren't going well.

He had been sitting at the dining room table, working on chapter five of the book, in which Matthew Stock confronts Paul at the hotel where he is staying, when the knock came. The sound startled Martin out of his fictional world, causing him to wonder who might be at the door. It was two-thirty in the afternoon and Laura was working. The two had spoken less than an hour ago by phone and had planned to dine out this evening, the first time (other than doctor appointments) that Martin would leave his house since the accident. His visit to the doctor yesterday had been good. His leg was healing nicely and his ribs were nearly pain-free. The two had decided that it was time to celebrate.

Martin rose from his chair, grabbed his crutches, and made his way over to the front door. As he reached for the knob, the person on the other side of the door knocked again.

"I'm here," he called, turning the knob and swinging open the door.

He should have recognized her immediately, but the possibility that she might one day be standing on his front stoop had never entered his mind. She looked different than Martin remembered, with purple and yellow bruising under one eye and a swollen, bruised jaw. She was wearing a sling over her left arm and looked as though she had been through hell, and yet she was smiling.

It was the smile that Martin finally recognized, for he had only seen this woman smiling. Had only seen her in photographs. Standing on tropical beaches and in exotic locales.

"It's you," Sophie Pearl whispered in a soft voice, her eyes moving from the immobilizer on his leg to the healing gash in his forehead. "I can't believe it. I found you."

"Me?" Martin stammered, feeling his entire body begin to shake. His instinct was to slam the door, turn and run, but he knew that it was too late for anything like that. Besides, he doubted that he could manage the maneuver. He was trapped in a state of frozen trembling.

"It's okay, Martin," she said, causing his terror to spike to new levels.

She knows my name, he thought. *Oh my God. She knows my name.*

"Listen," she said. "I'm not here to get you in any trouble. I'd like . . ."

"How? How did you know?" Martin interrupted, still trapped in place by a nervous system on overload.

"Can I come in?" she asked. "Please? It wasn't easy finding you, but I had to meet you."

"How?" Martin asked again, not because he wanted the answer anymore but because it was the only word he could manage to say.

Sophie Pearl sighed and reached into her jacket pocket with her unencumbered hand. A moment later her hand emerged from the pocket grasping a small, rectangular piece of plastic.

Martin recognized it immediately.

Attached to his keychain were several small plastic cards from the various businesses that he frequented. Grocery stores, pharmacies, retail outlets, and even gas stations distributed these cards to consumers in order to build customer loyalty. Whenever Martin made a purchase from one of these establishments, the cashier would scan the bar code on the back of the card and as a result, Martin would receive a discount, a coupon, or a sale price on items that he purchased. In between Sophie Pearl's thumb and forefinger was an orange card for the Stop & Shop supermarket, its top left corner broken off.

"How?" Martin stammered again, this time with genuine curiosity.

"I found it in my backyard," she explained. "Underneath one of the garage windows." She paused a moment, seeming to wait for Martin's response, but when none came, she leaned forward, closing the distance between them. "Please, Martin, can I come in? I won't be long. I promise."

Martin was still processing the idea that Sophie Pearl had found his Stop & Shop frequent-shopper card in her backyard. He understood how it had ended up there almost immediately. After spotting Clive Darrow's truck inside the Pearls' garage, he had fallen, landing in the grass below the window. Since his keys were stuffed in his pocket (a place they never would have been during a regular visit to a client's home), it was conceivable that the fall had caused the card to snap off his key ring, depositing it in the grass as he stood up. And since Laura had been doing his grocery shopping for the last two weeks, the loss of the card had gone undetected. He couldn't even remember seeing his keys at all over the last two weeks. But how had Sophie Pearl used that card to determine his identity? There was no name or address on it. Just a bar code. Martin's mind was stuck.

"Please, Martin. Just five minutes. Okay?"

"Okay," he managed, knowing that he had no choice. To send Sophie Pearl away at this point would be impossible. Martin turned and moved out of the doorway, making room for her to enter. Once she was inside the house, Martin motioned to the couches in the living room and began moving in that direction.

"I wish you'd stop shaking," she said as she moved aside a pillow and sat down beside Martin. "Honestly, you're not in any trouble." It wasn't her words that allowed him to begin to relax. It was her smile, followed by her hand as it reached out and gently grasped his own, that finally stilled his nerves a bit. "I came here to thank you, Martin. You saved my life. You saved my husband's life. You're a hero."

Martin's eyes filled with tears as Sophie Pearl spoke, a mixture of gratitude and guilt. Had he followed his father's advice and reported Clive Darrow to the police, Sophie Pearl's face would not be plastered with bruises. She would not be wearing a sling. Though he knew that his intervention had probably saved her life, Martin also knew that his initial inaction had placed her in danger in the first place. He opened his mouth to say as much but was unable to speak.

"I know that it was you who came to save us that night. I wasn't sure until I saw you, but once I saw your leg and your head, I knew. I'm so glad that I found you."

"But how?" Martin asked again, clinging to those words like a life preserver.

"The card," she explained. "I found it in the backyard about a week ago. I knew that it wasn't mine, and I knew about that evil son of a bitch parking his car in our garage. When I saw that the card was underneath the garage window, I thought I might have found my man. You."

"But my name isn't on the card," Martin stammered, still not in full control of his faculties. Sophie Pearl, client of more than nine years, was sitting in his living room, and this made parts of Martin's mind wonder if he was dreaming.

"No," Sophie admitted. "Your name isn't on the card, but your bar code is. And the supermarket has your information tied to the bar code. I hired a private investigator to find its owner. The police had told me that you probably wouldn't want to be found. Even though you saved us that night, they said you were probably in some kind of trouble with the law, and that's why you ran away like you did. 'Fled the scene,' one officer kept saying. But I didn't care what kind of trouble you might be in. I just had to know. So my private investigator found someone at the grocery store who was willing to scan the card and give her the information. Then she gave your name and address to me."

Martin was impressed. He wondered how long it would've taken him to think to use the bar code on the card to identify its owner. And even then, he would've had to find a way to convince a grocery store manager to scan the card and provide him with the information. Not an easy job. "So you found me," Martin said, finally regaining control of his speech. As Sophie Pearl had told her story, he'd begun to relax, realizing that this woman meant him no harm.

"So the police were right, huh? You're in some kind of trouble?"

"Not really," Martin answered truthfully. "But I guess I could be if I'm not careful. It's hard to explain."

As if sensing a chink in his defenses, Sophie pounced. "Martin, I need to know something. And it's not because I want you to get into trouble. Completely the opposite. I think you deserve a reward. A medal. You risked your life to save me, and I'll never forget that. I'll never forget seeing you throw yourself out of my bathroom that night, launching yourself down the stairs like you did. You know that he almost died, right? You could've died too."

"I was just doing . . ."

"Hush," Sophie interrupted. "Don't do that. Don't belittle what you did. You risked your life for me that night, and I'll never be able to thank you enough. But Martin, I need to know something. How did you know that I was in trouble? How did you know about the man in my house? And how did you know my name? And his name? When you called for us, you used our first names. *You knew who we were.* And you knew his name too. Darrow's name. And even though I've never seen you before, you recognized me when I was standing on your front stoop. How did you know so much?"

For more than a decade, Martin had wanted to share his life with someone, to tell another human being about the career that he had created for himself. He wanted someone else to know how careful and clever and precise he had been for all these years, and now, sitting across from him, was someone who wanted to listen, who wanted to know. Someone who was indebted to him, who referred to Martin as her hero, and who had reminded Martin moments ago about just how close he had come to death. In the end, it was this reminder about the fragility of life that compelled Martin to tell his story to Sophie Pearl. His willingness to speak, to share his most precious secret, was born from a fear that he might one day die without anyone ever knowing about who he really was and what he really did.

And so Martin Railsback, Jr., told Sophie Pearl the story of his life, beginning with the incident in his parents' driveway so many years ago. He explained the rules by which he operated his business, described a few of his more interesting clients, and explained how he was able to earn a living while remaining undetected. He told her about his friend Alfredo, and about how the incident in the Claytons' home had led to the letter to Alan Clayton, and how that letter might have saved the Claytons' marriage. He told her about Daniel Ashley's surprise birthday party and the means by which he had intervened to preserve the surprise. He related his encounter with Cujo and Blondie, and how his intervention in the Ashleys' affairs had led him to Laura. He told her about Laura, their blossoming relationship, and he admitted for the first time (even to himself) that he might be falling in love with her. Finally, he told her about the day that he saw Clive Darrow leaving her home, about how he followed the man to his house and ultimately identified him. He told her about how he had accurately deduced Darrow's plan, including his intent to use Noah Blake as a patsy for his crime, a fact which Sophie confirmed, though it had taken the police more than a week to figure that out. Though he wanted to leave it out, he also told her about how he had ignored his father's advice, and how this mistake had ultimately allowed Clive Darrow into Sophie's home. His eyes filled with tears as he apologized for this error in judgment, and they remained teary as he described his entry into the Pearls' house that night and his brief but decisive encounter with Darrow.

When he finished, almost an hour had passed, during which time Sophie Pearl had remained nearly silent, interrupting only when asking for details or clarifications. At first Martin had welcomed her silence. It had allowed him to narrate his story with rhythm and ease, but as it grew more protracted, Martin began to feel anxious, wondering if the absence of interruptions was an indicator of her growing anger or terror.

Nevertheless, he had pressed on.

Martin ended his story with a description of his injuries and a brief recounting of the past two weeks, including Laura's increased presence in his life. When he was at last finished, he said, "I guess that's about it" and breathed a sigh of relief. He had done it. He had shared his story with another human being, and regardless of her reaction, he felt as if an enormous weight had been lifted from his shoulders. In some odd way, he felt more real than he had ever felt before.

"Remarkable," Sophie finally said, after a long moment. "Absolutely remarkable. You're telling me that you've been stea . . . acquiring things from my house for more than nine years, and I've never noticed?"

"I don't know. Have you?"

"No," she said, still clearly astonished. "Not once. I remember noticing that the earring was missing, but that kind of thing happens from time to time. Once I couldn't find it, I put the other one out of my mind completely."

"I know."

"Absolutely remarkable," Sophie repeated, clearly attempting to wrap her mind around everything that Martin had said.

Martin gave her a moment to sort things out before asking the question that he was afraid to ask. "Okay, Mrs. Pearl. Can I ask you a question? I know it probably sounds stupid and presumptuous, but can you forgive me? I can't imagine how you must be feeling. Pretty disappointed to find out that your hero turned out to be a bad guy, huh?"

Sophie Pearl's face instantly transformed from a blend of confusion and astonishment to one of sympathy and surprise. "Martin, you are most certainly not a bad man. You saved my life. You saved my husband's life. And you risked your own life in the process. I honestly don't know what to think of your career choice, but in the end it was your . . . it was your job that saved me. I can't say that I'm happy to hear that you've been stealing from me for the past nine years, but I can't say that I've ever noticed either. In a way, I guess you've been like my guardian angel. I kept you fed and clothed, and when I needed you the most, you were there for me. You put your life on the line for me. How could I ever complain about that?"

Martin paused a moment to collect himself. Ever since that day in the driveway with his stepfather, Martin had wondered if the man had been right.

If he had turned out to be nothing more than a low-life criminal.

He never knew how much he had wanted that question answered, until now.

"I don't know what to say," Martin sighed, wishing he did. He had just shared more about his life than ever before, and now he felt as if there were no more words left inside him.

"Now listen, Martin, I'm not saying that everyone would feel the way I do. But that's how I feel. As my mother liked to say, you and I are square in my book."

"Thank you," Martin said, wishing he could say more. He wanted to let Sophie Pearl know how much it meant to him to be able to share his story with her, but he doubted that she or anyone else could ever understand.

"So where do you go from here?" Sophie asked, catching Martin by surprise.

"I don't know," Martin admitted. "But I promise that you're not on my client list anymore. Even before you showed up today, I had taken you off my list."

Sophie laughed. "That's not what I was talking about, Martin. I was thinking about you. Did you know that the police found your blood inside my house? On the railing. On the phone. All over. They didn't have your DNA on record, so they couldn't match the blood in my house to you, but you should know that there's a sample of you on record now. If they were ever to find your DNA somewhere else or get a sample from you, they could match you up to my house. And like I said, the police suspect that you don't want to be found. Most of them think that you're a hero, but that you're a hero with something to hide. You'll need to be very careful in the future, if you plan on continuing in your line of work."

"You wouldn't report me if I did?"

"Martin, you don't listen very well, do you? I can't say that I approve of your line of work, but in the end, I don't think you're hurting anyone. And Martin, you saved my life. There's no way that I'm going to send you to jail for stealing unused jewelry, forgotten dishes, and laundry detergent."

"Oh," Martin said with genuine surprise.

"But with that said, I really think you should reconsider your choice of career. You're a smart guy, Martin. Brilliant perhaps. You must be. You could be doing so much more."

"Maybe." Martin thought about his novel but doubted that he could make a living writing. Still, it was at least an alternative.

"And what about Laura?" Sophie asked. "You said that you might love her. Do you plan on lying to her forever?"

"I . . . I don't know," Martin answered, suddenly feeling defensive.

"Martin, from what you've told me, I think this woman might be falling in love with you, too. But you won't have any future together unless you tell her the truth."

"I can't tell Laura the truth," Martin protested, the mere suggestion sounding ridiculous to his ear. "She'd leave me in a second."

Sophie reached out and took Martin by the hand again. "If you don't tell her the truth, she's going to leave you anyway. Your lies are just holding back the inevitable. And in the end, they will hurt her more than you can imagine."

The thought of hurting Laura stung Martin more than he'd have thought possible.

"But you may still have time," Sophie continued. "You've

only been together for a few weeks. I'm not going to say that your odds of staying together are good, but if you don't come clean now, you'll have no odds. If you want a future with this woman, you need to tell her the truth today."

Martin knew that Sophie was right. He had known it from the moment that he and Laura first met. Sooner or later, Laura would demand to meet his imaginary parents or his fictitious sister, and when Martin couldn't produce them, she would know that he had deceived her, and she would leave him. He had known this for a long time but had been avoiding it until now.

"What should I say to her?"

"Tell her exactly what you told me today. Everything. Leave nothing out. She's going to be angry at first. She'll probably storm out of the house before you finish. But she may come back after she's had some time to think. I can't promise that she will, but she might. And if you need my support, I will be there for you. I can make a hell of a character witness, especially for a guy who saved my life."

"Thanks. I might need one," Martin said, realizing that, without any deliberation, he was going to follow Sophie's advice. In the end, he knew that it was his only chance to be with Laura.

"And you realize that if she decides to give you a second chance, you'll have to change careers. If she loves you, she can't let you continue on as you've been. It's going to mean a lot of changes in your life. Is she worth it?"

"I think she might be," Martin said. "I never thought that I'd meet anyone more important to me than my job, but Laura might just be the one."

"Then you're a lucky man, Martin. It may sound strange, but you've got it pretty easy. You don't have to worry about making the right decision. It sounds as if you only have one choice."

"I think so."

"Good," Sophie said, standing up and reaching for her purse. "Then I think it's time for me to go."

Martin stood as well, meeting her eye to eye and reaching out to shake her hand. Sophie swatted his hand away and hugged him instead with her one free arm.

"Thank you, Mrs. Pearl."

"No, Martin. Thank *you*. You saved my life. Never forget that. I certainly won't."

Martin nodded, unable, for the moment, to speak, distracted by the vaguely formed notion that Sophie Pearl may have just saved his.

Sophie turned and walked to the front door, leaving Martin standing beside the couch, overwhelmed with the knowledge of what lay ahead of him. At the door, she turned and said, "And Martin, just because I'm walking through this door doesn't mean I'm walking out of your life. Sherman doesn't know about you yet, and I'm not sure if I'm going to tell him. I can keep secrets too, you know. But I'll be here for you if you need me. You made a new friend today, and I'd like to think that I made one too."

"You did."

"Good," she said. "Then call me Sophie. And call me when you have some news about your lady friend, okay? I assume you still have my number?"

Martin smiled. "I do. And I will. I just hope it's good news."

"Me too, Martin," she said with a smile.

With that, Sophie turned and left. Martin remained standing in place for quite a while before deciding upon his next course of action. First, he would call Laura at her office.

"Change of plans. Dinner at my place," he would announce, without even saying hello. Give her a taste of her own medicine. "And I'm doing the cooking."

He would cook her favorite dish, chicken marsala, and he would order half a dozen black and white cookies from the Elmwood Pastry Shop in hopes that she might still be around for dessert. Over wine and dinner, Martin would tell Laura his story, and he would hope and pray for the best.

He wondered where he would begin.

Matthew Dicks grew up in the small town of Blackstone, Massachusetts. He was a Boy Scout, a pole-vaulter, a bassoonist, and a proud member of his school's drum corps, and he has the distinction of having died twice by the age of eighteen before being revived by paramedics on both occasions. He left home at eighteen and worked in a variety of dead-end jobs until being robbed at gunpoint at the age of twenty-two. This brush with death finally propelled him to college, where he worked his way through school as the manager of a McDonald's restaurant, graduating from Manchester Community College, Trinity College with an English degree, and Saint Joseph's College with a teaching degree. Following graduation, Matthew went to work as an elementary school teacher and has been teaching ever since. In 2005 he was named West Hartford's Teacher of the Year. He also owns and operates a DJ company that performs weddings throughout Connecticut. His writing has appeared in the *Hartford Courant*, the *Christian Science Monitor*, *Educational Leadership*, and the Los Angeles Times-Washington Post News Service.

Matthew lives in Newington, Connecticut, with his wife and colleague, Elysha, their newborn daughter, Clara, their Lhasa apso, Kaleigh, and their bulimic housecat, Owen.

While *Something Missing* is eerily well-researched, Matthew Dicks has confirmed he is not, himself, a thief.

Matthew Dicks grew up in the small town of Blackstone, Massachusetts. He was a Boy Scout, a pole-vaulter, a bassoonist, and a proud member of his school's drum corps, and he has the distinction of having died twice by the age of eighteen before being revived by paramedics on both occasions. He left home at eighteen and worked in a variety of dead-end jobs until being robbed at gunpoint at the age of twenty-two. This brush with death finally propelled him to college, where he worked his way through school as the manager of a McDonald's restaurant, graduating from Manchester Community College, Trinity College with an English degree, and Saint Joseph's College with a teaching degree. Following graduation, Matthew went to work as an elementary school teacher and has been teaching ever since. In 2005 he was named West Hartford's Teacher of the Year. He also owns and operates a DJ company that performs weddings throughout Connecticut. His writing has appeared in the *Hartford Courant*, the *Christian Science Monitor*, *Educational Leadership*, and the Los Angeles Times-Washington Post News Service.

Matthew lives in Newington, Connecticut, with his wife and colleague, Elysha, their newborn daughter, Clara, their Lhasa apso, Kaleigh, and their bulimic housecat, Owen.

While *Something Missing* is eerily well-researched, Matthew Dicks has confirmed he is not, himself, a thief.